THIRTY YEARS

THIRTY YEARS

John Fraser

'There is nothing to be done about anything.'

'After the war is over...' (song)

AESOP Modern Fiction
Oxford

AESOP Modern Fiction
An imprint of AESOP Publications
Martin Noble Editorial / AESOP
28 Abberbury Road, Oxford OX4 4ES, UK
www.aesopbooks.com

First paperback edition published by AESOP Publications
Copyright (c) 2016 John Fraser

www.johnfraserfiction.com

The right of John Fraser to be identified as the author of this
work has been asserted in accordance with sections 77 and 78
of the copyright designs and Patents Act 1988.

A catalogue record of this book is
available from the British Library.

First paperback edition 2016

ISBN: 978-1-910301-30-2

1

I might try my hand at metalwork. I need a white metal funnel to connect the gas, or the current, to the outlet. The winters are a scourge here. There's lots of workshops, but it's crude stuff done – mostly collecting scrap and trying to sell it on. There's some guy, Maurice – Australian, American, maybe, with curly yellow hair and brogues, who tries finer work.

'We know where the gas comes from,' he says. 'From tubes, they're planted in the ground. Gas is hottest. Where does electricity come from? No one knows. It costs more and doesn't warm.'

He gives me some food – it's mostly white, a plate of rice or mashed stuff – they call it manioc, or shredded radish, potato even. 'Eat it all,' he says: he presses his knee against mine. 'The stuff that goes with it is finished. I have a local woman, she brings it, but it's finished.'

It makes you gag. Maybe he has a flame. A cylinder.

'You need more than a tube,' he says: 'You need a rad. That's crude stuff. I can do mermaid's hair. I didn't come away from home to do crude stuff.'

'The anger guys have here – it's justified,' I say. 'But killing guys, and doing it for cash and jobs – it's puerile.'

'Well,' says the guy, Maurice, 'you're the one with cash. You get to hum the tune. There's always fighting here, on and off. You could turn it into poetry – lots try,' and we look across the road – a guy in dusty bib and brace stares back. 'All metals,' says the sign, but in the shed there's only dusty poles and tubes, all grey and aimless.

'There was a factory here,' Maurice the craftsman says. 'For furniture. But when they'd cut the trees, they saw they'd need to wait a generation for some more to grow.'

'I don't want a relation,' I say, and he says, 'But you like art.'

'If it isn't tarted up somewhat,' I say, 'it's like, well, mashed potato.'

He takes me into a shed out the back: it's full of tubes and globes. It's burials, all ritualised – skeletons: some tubes quietly gathered on their sides, others doubled up, legs on their chins, the globes dented in. 'You see,' he says, 'It could be a whole, or sold separately. Each item, or mass grave. For the garden.'

'Yes,' I say, 'I get it. All white metal, all ritualised. All naked. Made to last.'

'Look at those shepherds,' Maurice says, 'up on the mound. Bones all over, each a story, aunts and sucklings. Go far back, everything has a common source. Stars – must be made of the one thing, which becomes a mass of interlinking properties.'

'Yes,' I say, 'but once they separate, those things – they don't go back. The bones stick out.'

Maurice is quite cast down. 'All is one,' he says, playing for time.

'So – who'd want to bury metal skeletons on their patch of earth?' I ask, crudely, irritated.

'Projects. Creation – doesn't mean too much to you?' he asks.

'These primitives here,' I say, 'they do the hunting, the planting, vendettas too. But – they couldn't think the wheel. The push – it isn't here. Survival's taken up their time.'

'You need the shining light,' says Maurice. 'In a movement, you're all equal, and together – you are one.

Science, religion – it gives you everything: yourself – and all the other guys.'

Should I tell him, 'Maurice... that's just what you haven't got. The light. The thrust. You're in the pit. You'd never say – "no images, and screw the books, and burn the scholars too..." You want a patron you'll despise, but who provides meat sauce.'

Beside the dusty workshops there are dusty bars. We sit, he pours the liquor in, it first makes smoke, then alabaster, of our jars. I think, 'You can't get drunk on this, this white thick stuff you drank in infancy...' I'm wrong. I stand, quite bent. 'I'm through,' I say. 'Through the wall, into the clay.'

'I can't do conversation,' Maurice says. 'You owe for all this booze.'

He pulls me to a table in the back. His mates are there. 'No, I don't smoke, or other stuff,' I say. 'I'm here because I don't believe in it. I came from there, I was in everything...'

'This here's Curtis,' Maurice says: there's a guy nondescript, the bib and brace, a doglike animal at his knee. 'He's anglophile. At least, his father was. That Curtis, the original, he helped the natives, I believe. "Ladies don't move," he said.'

'That's milord Curzon said it, but no doubt he helped,' I say. 'A slight confusion. Curtis – an actor. Bisex.' It means I'm drunk, to comment.

'Screw the ladies anyway,' shouts Curtis, laughing round.

'Is that a dog or wolf?' I ask. I see it's wolf, but I am doing conversation. 'I don't know what you see in having either, Curtis – they say they're so intelligent, but you could find intelligent friends and walk with them, and they don't shit and pee along the track.'

He says, aggressive,

'The line from dog to wolf is like the line from you to me. That's how it is. I aspire to wolves, and you, it seems, are up for intelligence. A super guy. How come you're here, then, and quite silent?'

'Look, guys,' I say – they're all metalworkers, sitting round. There's a big pipe to smoke, and screws of dope – 'I know my head, right through and through. I know it when it goes to paste, or cloud, or tumbling, and you read unopened books, the pictures painted from sealed tubes. I must avoid the dope, the booze...' and I laugh, to show how close to them I feel.

'No, no, none of that stuff,' says Maurice. 'Sit here. With us. And smoke. Be one of us. And so your life will go. There is no mystery. Relax. Nothing revealed. Here, it's smoke and dust, and us.'

'Things are slow here. If everything took off,' I say, 'We'd be wage slaves, or worse – handing out leaflets, taking debts, dodging machines, and thinking of suicide. They'd paint the buildings. We're better off as is.' Inside, I'm not so sure.

'We can think of suicide right now,' says Maurice. 'At least we can handle the shepherds. They steal. Drills. Compressors.'

'Yes,' Curtis says. 'You may think we're trash, but you're one of us, against the goddam shepherds.' The dope goes round. I came here to get away from it, and to watch the shepherds stealing sheep.

'The tub!' shouts Curtis, and here, out the back, a steaming metal can, for giants. He strips off, making like a burlesque queen. 'The sex is optional,' he says. 'We're moderns – we're not shepherds,' and they all take up the chant, stripping off, and running out, into the rain. They're hopping in and out the cauldron, the grey steaming water ... leaping like ginseng roots, their lower halves – hairy as Pan's.

I make a sprinter's crouch, as if I'm taking off a shoe – then run. I hear the chant,

'He's one of us, for ever, one of us.'

Here's a shepherd – brown sheep, brown woolly socks up to the knee.

'You'll not be one of them, nor one of us,' he says. 'Besides, your place has neither water nor a plug – I'll sell you wood...'

'No, no,' I say. 'No wood, no dead trees. I came here for the energy. It's everywhere, just lying round. You guys, abandoned by the cart of history...' A cart: a tumbril. He doesn't recognise the word.

'You hesitate, the price goes up,' he says, and I finish – 'Up and up, you guys will rise...'

'Tourists,' he says. 'They come, no interest in wood. They go. Then comes the cold.'

It's poetry. I hate reactionary thoughts that creep into my head. I won't give in about the wood, the dark wild wood. The anger guys should feel – it's overlaid: commerce and the tub.

'The karst,' says the shepherd. 'That is our soul. That's what we are; our children stone, a vast plain of them. Sheep rootling above. We love it, it makes us eternal.'

*

From the outside, my house – it's a witch's haven. Those few panes of glass – opaque, like sheets of sugar mints, the door, – splattered with spyholes. The roof – permeable as gingerbread. Inside, waiting for me, there's this woman – a sharp smell comes off her, crushed nettles. A local sweat, no doubt. She says,

'You should have gotten in the tub. Without that, you won't be one of us. Or, you could buy the firewood – but you'd need to burn it in the road. Here...' she waves around. 'There's nothing like an oven...'

'That's fine,' I say. Maybe I rent the place from her, her folks...

'I deal with all the postwar stuff,' she says. 'When it's all over, when the battle's moved off somewhere else – that's when you begin to suffer. That's my qualification – I survived.'

'That's fine too,' I say. She heals, for sure. I don't have wounds. I make to shunt her out...

'I see you have a mind,' she says, 'that's quite exquisite.'

'Well, how's that?' I ask, flattered, preening...

'It's your material self,' she says. 'The face, the rest. I'd need to shut my eyes, if we got close enough to kiss, all that. So – there's always compensation. Yours must be spirit: body it is not.'

Later I ask Maurice, 'Who's the healer?' He says,

'Nina. She stayed. She says, "Things terrible, how awful – yours, just like mine," and hugs you. Takes some cash. She's reason – but not science. Sometimes she sells you dope.'

'Does she think she's special?' I ask, suspiciously.

'No,' says Maurice. 'Just different sizes of animal, all of us. Some big apes read books, is all.'

He's wary. I didn't bathe with him. 'It's the suffering,' I say. 'After the conflict, reflecting. I could sell some story. Go into politics. Nina – goes to the root.'

'Oh no,' says Maurice. 'It's just hugs. Good and bad's a waste of time. The past is not her business.'

'I guess,' I say, 'if we were cleverer, us animals, what we do to show it makes us – well, worse.'

He doesn't follow. He fits pipe into pipe, and lives by it.

'There's not many creatures round, that we could compare,' I say. It's clear why it's that way, why there's only sheep and goats around.

'The women – they're away. On the game, and such. It's better so,' he says.

'Consequences of the war. That's what I'm here to find,' I say. 'I guess you saw the tail of it, whisking away.'

'Oh no,' he says, 'I didn't fight. Though I was trained in useful things, for war.'

A mystery.

Intelligence? Resistance? Truth and justice? All useful trades in war.

A lawyer looks for the tiny rock of guilt in a sea of innocence. A lawyer looks for the tiny rock of innocence in a sea of guilt. That's their trade.

'Maurice,' I say, 'even if you came in late – you must have seen the people here....'

'Oh,' he says, 'it all just happens. You fit in. Things drop haphazard, too. Me? I stayed on – my trade...'

He flies his reticence up high, a kite, a twisting train. 'Those Arabs now,' he says, 'just fighting everyone,' and he laughs.

'Stories – those, I'm interested in,' I say.

'Any ones at all?' he asks. 'You from an agency? You weren't clean with us.'

'I've never told a lie,' I say. 'It's been a drawback. I'm in everything for myself, alone.'

What can he have done, Maurice, in the wars? He says, repeating me, 'Sometimes the tourists were English, leaving a name. Curtis is disappointed. Not the milord, it seems – some actor, American, bisex, they say.'

'In the war, and after, Maurice?' I insist.

'All about names, they are,' he says. 'The wars. Then, after, other tourists come, bringing trade. All the countries here are like all families, fruit on the branches: beliefs in spirits, things you never see ... the states have names – you call them out, as if you call to them. They send you off, you often don't come back.'

'Maybe you see the spirits at your death,' I say, to cheer him. 'In silver light, like the screen, brightest when the movie's done.'

'Oh no,' he says. 'I've seen mine. It's a wall. Your face goes up against. Grey, it tastes like tin that's just been scrubbed with acid.'

'Well, Maurice,' I say, as his grey eyes drift over me, not much involved. 'All trades are handy, war or peace.'

'I broke horses,' he says. 'Horses for the guns.'

We stand in silence. I'm eager to know everything, but not quite from him. Some perspective, but not borrowing what Curtis has – perspective quite too large. A guy who's name is wrong, from birth...

'It's all so simple,' Maurice says. 'Simpler than you'd think. One reaches the end of the road, turns, and looks back. It's difficult that there shouldn't be a moment of reproach. The worst thing has been, for those who follow on, not to give the right value to another life. The other person always knows it, even if that is what they want – being underprized. That means they have a secret worth. And then ... it goes. The value goes.'

'This humane stuff,' Maurice,' I say, 'it does you no credit.'

'Well,' he says, 'I guess we've all done something wrong – so what's the point in searching?'

The field is laid out, hummocky, a quilt, like it covers you in dreams. There's people bent, all over, picking the stones in silence, bags round their neck. All men, dressed like they're medieval.

Where the stones are harvested, below, it's a grey-green, not earth nor weeds.

'We do this,' Maurice says. 'Smiths and shepherds, gathering in the stones. Then, farmers will come. This is our future. Forget what obsesses you, the violence here. It's fear and anger. That's what monkeys feel. Then, they're curious about the bodies that result. We're brighter. We're not curious, we know. That's it.' He shouts, 'Go home! Even monkeys have them, homes.'

The stones are piled, worm casts. No singing, no calling out. The metalworkers make a circle, arms woven round the ring of shoulders.

Curtis is eating – can it be an aubergine? Dark, with a cheesy look inside.

It's half a sheep skull, cleft from the nostrils – 'The eye, and half the tongue, the brain part, what makes you climb, eat gorse, and veer to right and left,' he says, and offers me – 'Here's the other half, the better one, that looks for messengers and messages, the mystery that ... we know is not,' and he laughs. There's a basket full of half-brains.

'Forget it,' Maurice says. 'Come to the brew, we'll make electrum. All around there's gold and silver, dumped, abandoned, nicked. And after all, you are the golden man...'

'Yes,' Curtis says. 'Test your experience. We're bubbling up the gold and silver. Slip right in – you never know. Electrum-plated – you'd last centuries.'

'And what else?' Maurice asks. 'You want to know how we survived the war. And all those Arabs...' and he laughs, 'At each other, as though they'll never stop. You guys pretend to be aghast, as if it happened on another star, as though the truth was trivial. As though you didn't know... As though your sages hadn't said, "the truth is precious, without it, all the rest, the freedom, the justice – it's just rhetoric". What do you want – to start a clinic, a barracks for the cops, a ski slope, a tarts' hotel?'

I draw back. His breath is on me. 'No, you'd need a partner, cash... I'm like you, I want the truth,' I say.

'Then you would need to fight,' he says. 'The best thing is the war.'

'You made it sound like monkey stuff,' I say.

The tub is heaving with the molten loot. There's Nina, throwing in some drops.

'Into the tub!' shouts Curtis. 'The test, the assay, fusion, alloy... Let's all immerse ourselves,' and he pulls everyone towards the rim. No one jumps in.

'This electrum stuff,' I say to Maurice, feeling they're jostling me, urging me in once more – the metals fuse, it's milk and honey, it bubbles up and roars like hell. I guess the guys in hell – they like to sing in unison, making a joyful sound. What else can you do? 'Maurice – I bet you sneak electrum in your skeletons?'

'Oh no,' he says. 'Just one or two, it's hidden, they are buried. I don't raise the price. Of course, you can have one, in your garden, like a tuber, a truffle – your secret, and your guard. Or thousands, in a field ... as if there'd been a city there...'

He talks on, and Curtis pushes me towards the heaving crock, and shouts, 'Maurice – have you sold one yet, a single one, a head, a heel, a clinking set – a child, a nymphlet, some old sage – brittle and rusted, with golden teeth and bristles all of silver...?'

Maurice grasps Curtis, 'You broken shitstick, Curtis! My stuff is made to lie unseen, buried, anonymous. It's not for gawping, not for sale – its value is intrinsic...' and he shouts over and over at Curtis, 'Intrinsic!' and changes it to 'In! In, in, you smartass,' and he forces Curtis to the rim. The heat burns off the clothes, and Curtis bends, quite naked, back over the crucible, his sweat flares up like kerosene, and you can hear the guys down there in hell, maybe they try some harmony, and differentiate their registers – what else can they do? Music, they say, must start and end – it's quite anomalous in their eternity... Yet – it's worth a try, or else time with no end is just a flash, a bore that hollows out your bones, for what's for ever's gone at once, a rat into its hole, a falling star from long ago that slides across to futures you will not experience...

'Time, Maurice, time,' Curtis whispers at his end – 'We're in the midst of time. It's not eternity, it's passing, what we have right here, what we experience, and miss, and weep for what we've lost. You give me suffering, Maurice, the prime human gift... Eternity – it's wallpapers rolled up tight and sealed, designs unseen, maybe there are bluebirds, boar hunts, runes...'

'I spare you, Curtis,' Maurice says, relenting, pulling him into a hug. 'Poor Curtis – neither the ladies nor the earth have moved for you, and when you ruled in India – elephants in phalanxes parading, dumped their crap before your rostrum. Milord Curtis! Viceroy who couldn't recognise a vice, nor practise one...' and on he rants.

Nina pushes through. Curtis says to me, 'Nina's not soft. She's the one who comes into your house, and seeks your guilt. She pulls you close, traducer's hugs. She's vengeance. Some guy offed her man... I tell her, "Anger, fear. You never know how much you've got. Or doing what the others do – it could be anyone... Forget the deed – it has no ownership,"' and while he talks, Nina makes a fist, and thrusts it in the metal brew. A pale, pale Central Asian gold, panned from the steppe – her hand consumed, she has a new, a precious armoured paw, made up of pieces now anonymous – a chalice, lid of hanap, lamps and bracelets – now all hers, fused where the flesh has been.

The pain! It helps, I hear her chant '... the pain – it shall be mine.'

Revenge is always pleasant – the metalworkers watch as Nina waves her golden-silver arm aloft. Then Maurice says, 'We can't have Nina outplay us all,' and leaps, wavers on the rim – plunges, out comes his silvered foot, and then a hand, pale as a winter sun. He shouts through tears, 'See! At last, I'm up to it – the journey of a thousand miles starts with a silver foot – an idiot can fight for territory, family, or because they're told. We need the big idea instead...' and Curtis says to him, and sneers, 'Walking? An idea? You're crazy,' and he handstands on the edge – his head goes in – it's out a smoking helmet, last silver from exhausted mines, 'Come, you!' he shouts to me, through cool and rigid lips, 'Join us, show how we're brighter than the shepherds here,' and other guys are ladling out and falling in – the melt is cooling, but out come pairs of buttocks, nipple caps, a knee, a squidlike penis, an electrum nose...

I think, 'I've failed the test again, and thankful too.' The guys, survivors, perpetrators, victims – all of this and none ... erase the pain, and add a quintal more. The metals, gold and silver – never can belong to anyone, and so you try to fit them on you, to become them, make them becoming. Armour and fortune, a glistening parade.

'I've given up on you,' says Maurice. 'It's clear you are a spy. Our project – you want to steer it, give it therapy, and take a fee. You are dross, lees, you are tailings.'

'That must be the pyramid where past things are buried and the big guy waits to be washed clean and up into the sky,' I say. There's a huge mound, a scrapheap. It's not a metaphor.

'No,' says Maurice. 'To you it's junk. It's junk we'll smelt into the new. Look!' He pulls gold candlesticks, out from a maze of wire. 'See! And these are rubies, dumped carelessly,' he says, and makes to gulp some down.

'I need to find a rad – one not made of platinum...' I say, pulling at a jagged pile.

'No,' Maurice says, kicking at me with his precious foot. 'Leave it! Nothing here is standard. Nothing fits. That's why it's here. A lesson for you,' and he laughs.

'I'd leave old stuff here, and try to polish up the new,' I say, tugging at pipes. 'Find some youth, slip my brain into her head, and leave my skeleton to her – she will install her grey slop, its invention, its adventurousness...'

'No, no,' says Maurice. 'We have tried those easy ways. You must go in the tub, the crucible. Burn off the old, prepare...'

'To do it all again?' I ask.

'Oh yes!' shouts Maurice. 'We're a species. We can't leave everything to giraffes.'

I'm still looking for my rads. There's no way out – winter comes. They use explosives to turn the engines over and start them when it's really cold. The goat's udders go solid – it's a massacre.

Nina stirs a sauce with her gold and silver hand. 'This way, they'll eat gold, like the Chinese say,' she laughs. 'Suicide. A fortune, if you need it and can arrange it.'

To me, she says, 'If you want to watch the tribe, you have to eat the grubs and sew buttons on your foreskin. You – you don't join the circle, join the game. It's just to make a buck, I guess, that brings you here. Compassion or shock – not for here, but back in your nestly home, you make your name.'

'Nina,' I say, 'don't be banal. You guys are plated preciously. Your accessories – they're worth more than the old world they found them in.'

'We have a project,' Nina says, pouring rare dust in her stew.

There are the metal-workers, ranged on a knoll, their silvery appurtenances shining in and out, like birch leaves lifted and abandoned by a breeze, or festive lights, on, off. No one is metallised all over, they stand, half-protected, as though one suit of armour was distributed among them all. No one will gun them down, not for disbelief, mistaken identity, fun with adrenalin. Teutonic knights, the caliph's guard – they are

a sacred grove ... each shoulder shore's a comrade firm...
'Hey!' Nina shouts to me. 'There's not a shepherd nor a sheep
in sight! What a feast we had!'

It's true – I had in mind to make some bucks from helping
these sad guys. I've dropped all that. All I need is winter heat.
Nina says,

'Countries are done. Here, what a mess they've made. It's
vilayets. An empire with its squeaky heart quite far away and
– finite provinces, where little orders, the clan chiefs, keep the
peace. Guys here – they get no cash – and so, there's nothing
for them but to be a bridge. They will facilitate, and take a cut.
It works that way for subalterns.'

'This Godfearing stuff?' I ask.

'Oh,' she says, 'they're sure afraid of God, and much
much more, and worse.'

She stares at me. She doesn't think God sent me: she says,
'They're all exactly like you. Soldiers, saviours – maybe their
shoes are different.'

She pulls me to her, to her oily wool, a drape, a sail,
knitted with staves. She makes a droning sound – maybe a
song? I peer between the stitches, here must be her white skin,
her legendary breasts – no: more wool ... I weep.

'There!' she says. 'You weep. The suffering of others.
What'll you do when you've suffering of your own?' She
keens.

'Warmth,' I mutter, 'to show the cold's not infinite.'

'You idiot,' she shouts, throwing me from her lap. 'The
winters here can last two years. And if you die in them –
there's your infinity!'

'What happens now?' I ask. 'Now there's no shepherds,
and we ate the sheep?' The question's epic, but she says,

'My view's this – it's back to Ottomans. For us, the
choice is Turks, Chinese – or Russkies... Turks is best. Kurds
too, some Turks. They borrow. They deny their massacres.

All sensible. The vilayet, and mercenaries. A hierarchy like capitalism – those who believe are at the top, the rest content themselves with hopes of heavens, paradise exclusive, all five-star, the sex en suite...' She rambles on, a pilgrim through her politics; the Yanks are over there, Arabs dissatisfied with everything, the Africans should cut their roads so no one comes to make them toil...

'That's how the world will be,' she says. 'Now, take this pill. It takes away your memory, and when your brain is white and flat – you'll see the mystery of everything. What it's about – is time. Time's everywhere. The search we're all condemned to – is seeking something out of time. Time brings you happiness and misery. What's out of time – is peace. And then you'll want another pill, some more epiphany. But...' she says, as she leaves, 'you haven't paid the first one yet, and pills are bad for you, besides.'

Up on their mound, the metal workers, heating engineers, wait on. They need to cut a deal, be middlemen. And yet – they're armoured. They'll be the mercenaries. I weep – I suffer for them too.

I take the pill. Epiphany. Exactly as she said. The greatest disappointment – truth's the same all round, for everyone, like rocks.

*

I stare at Maurice: my lookalike, my brother. Fancy shoes. Inside, one fancy foot.

'Nina's told me everything,' I say.

'Ah yes,' he says. 'She's good on ends. Not on ethics, though. Willing the means, making universal laws, doing what the others should. Not getting caught, is one. Universally accepted. Like a broken boiler. I replace, it's economics. All are pleased.'

'That's old stuff, Maurice,' I tell him. 'And if you're the one who's broken it...'

'Well,' he laughs, 'not getting caught! That is the nub.'

'Nina says that here some did bad things, and others had bad things done to them...'

'And most did both,' he finishes, and laughs. 'It turns out much the same.'

'It doesn't seem at all the same,' I say.

'Then who will help you when the snow is here?' he asks.

'I'm not so sure about the doing and the having done,' I say. 'Besides, they said the weather would be hot.'

'Well, there you are,' says Maurice. 'It's all one. Hot and cold, doing and done. There's no intention, though there's lots of will.'

2

I leave them, knights on the hill, waiting for the Turks. Resist, be recruited; convert others, be converted...

Is that a battle I can hear, past the plain – or stones cracking in the cold? A flat sun from the steppe lights up a pale gold arm, a leg, an ear.

In the capital, I meet my sage. Without an elder, you're left ignorant. Guys in dull red coveralls unload a ship – they run and hop like imps, boxes of pipes and thermostats to carry on their heads, up into alleys where there's dusty workshops... 'And they never learned to steal!' the sage says. 'They don't know what it is.'

I await his wisdom, and our truth. 'Hmmm,' he says. 'That Maurice, and Curtis – they're exactly you. I don't want to hear about them. And the primal mum, Nina – what does she resolve? Nada. She's a Ninanada,' and he laughs at his *boutade*. 'The hinterland is all like that. They walk on karst, and fear the depths, all the profundity they spout. For if they fall, they fall for ever. There's no bottom to their thought. Their eyes are on a top – it's just the sky. It should be black. instead – it's blue. Those Italian painters made it so, and the illusion sticks.'

'Master,' I say, 'they've been through rubbish times. I thought to join them, or to help...'

'No, no,' he says, 'you're just a tart. Move on to other clients – that's enough. Joining, and helping – arrogance and bluff. For – in the end, you're here, to start again.'

We're exasperated: the other's pitiful. He rises, opens the door. 'Time for my hunt in bookstores – the books all gutted, secondhand and eaten, just the bones and skin remain.'

In his room, there are no books. He goes on, 'Nineteen's too young, and twenty-two's too old.'

He takes a cutthroat razor, dryshaves along his empty jaw. Pours amber potion in an armpit.

'That's where you hunt the women, then?' I ask.

'You're disappointed? I'm a carnivore. All sages are,' he says, chuckling.

'No, no,' I say. 'It's most encouraging. You open them, ease their spines, blow off the dust, rub at the gilding, then...?'

'I love them raw,' he says, sticking a grassy trilby on his skull. 'Out of the shell. You see – without a sage, you'd just be ignorant. Not know the world. You mustn't try to pal with nature – she will get you in the end. That's her purpose, after all. I don't collect fine thoughts or scrolls – rare moments, they're the best.'

We're amidst the traffic. 'Moments – the only things,' he says, 'you can be sure of.'

'But – you're still on the Left?' I ask, gulping down Turkish food from a stand. 'That seems to be for ever.'

We dodge some mule carts. 'There!' he says, patting the animals. 'Our new comrades. The beasts. Only us, the wobbly ones – we survive. We shook so much, they couldn't have aimed and hit us,' and he giggles. 'And you're eating! Before you hunt! What ignorance.'

This frequenting of the bookstores, picking up – I wonder – is this porno, then? 'No, no,' he says. 'There's no intention to excite. Nor to exploit. It's to impress.'

The books have lost their fullness, their youth, the coloured powder on their wings. I find an uncut one. I doubt that it will ever fly. He's mouthing away, across the stacks: I hear, '... smaller and smaller groups. Not friends, not family. Not production. Cells, like the bees. Too many to be squashed, too disparate to be connected. Like frogspawn, rather – with no common creed or purpose. A huge underground, stinging from all angles, sipping at power, draining the state, its coherence, its joining-up ideas. Tough nuts in the grass, too many for the rubber sledgehammer – the state, the economy, the country – to crack...'

He's made a little crowd. None of his favourite women. 'Anarcho-syndicalism!' I shout across, and he hushes me.

'Oh no,' he says. 'No general strike, no action. Only discipline. And rigorous talk.'

'I've just come from that,' I say, thinking of the shepherds and the smiths. 'There's not enough to eat. It's cold, the food's beneath the snow...'

'Ah yes,' he says. 'But it's conserved. It'll be frigid there, untouched, when you have died your hungry death.'

He's not bad. He doesn't go for making records – it's all for publics, all is danced and sweaty. It's all happened, and he knows it – what the Russians did, then everyone with camps all over everywhere – nations kept going in them, others put under. My Sage does his act well – then pays himself off in humans, their young flesh. Everything is in the eye of people. He deserves a woman to walk off with, if that's all he wants, the throwback...

I'm for the Russians – they know how to get things done. I'm for the Turks, though. I'm not sure about them, but they're few, and little countries are a farce, you need a patron, and they're a farce as well. Isfahan – remember, the best city in the world.

Aha! He's hooked one. His tale – subversion like a field of toadstools, riskless, indomitable – he's reeling in a beauty – long, or, rather, tall. 'Only in anarchy,' he says, 'can the principles of order make their glow.'

She looks like Nina – but then, everyone does, somewhat. It's a function of a country. Does she want a philosophy, or a mate? They come over: it seems I'm the body, he's the soul.

'Why'd I want order – and from an anarchist?' she asks.

'Order is all there is,' says the Sage. 'It may be a disappointment. That too's in all the orders. That's known as disenchantment. Of course, in the end, there's maybe some uncertainty – within the order.'

'I didn't ask for this,' she says.

'That's the point...' I begin, but the Sage says to me, 'Now, body! Let's see how you make out! Sex, maybe.'

'No, no,' I say, 'I don't perform in public, maybe not at all. You'd never know.'

'Not the mechanics,' says the Sage. 'Not repetition. Make something new. Flesh turning into flesh, brain into brain.'

'No,' I say. 'Look – she's *masculine*, made to be looked at. A courtier unattached, with no allegiance, and no sustenance. A page, a Pan, a Ganymede, mother, fucker – it's all there. It floats, distant. Every part, each role, is visible. There's no transgression, no room for trickery. It has all come together, beyond nature. A box of games.'

'Absolutely not,' she says. 'I'm no picture, no mirror, no blazoner. I'm different, I'm what nature's all about, exactly. Fusion, the complementary. Hiding the components. A whole.'

'Well, well,' says the Sage, bored, disappointed that his sexual quest has ended in a stall. 'Sort it out. Interest in that stuff is limited. You can read about sex for an hour – but in the world, I last some twenty seconds.'

She's no good looker, either, even if she's aiming at perfection – or something, some force, that does it for her. The pieces are all there, but soldered bad. I think of Maurice, and his bony pipes, unblowable, misjoined.

'Look, you kooks,' she says. 'It's maybe you're talking about sex and appearances – but in a way that doesn't at all attract me...'

'Oh no,' says the Sage, 'it's the usual, about nature and after the hunt – the metamorphosis in something else's digestion... That never attracted me at all.'

We go back to his room, his postbook room, he calls it. There's a big plate, 'Consultancy and diets', it says, 'Doctor Petar Cheikha'.

'I'm Petar too,' says the Sage. 'Petrović. So I didn't change it, but I don't do diets.'

'Well,' says his catch, 'in that case, my name's Magda, but on my plate it's really Sonia. I don't do diets either, and I want some eats! – heaped on my empty plate. I know some tricks to fill that square of brassy gold. "Investigations". I'm crime – and you,' she points her long arm at me, 'you're punishment.'

The old man's delighted, and they laugh wildly together, like drunken peasants in a frame. Sonia says, 'It's like we're a "dinner on the grass". We could take our clothes off, though none of us can paint.'

I say coldly, 'It wasn't dinner. It's lunch.'

'Well, there's nothing to eat here,' laughs Petar. 'And I've no money,' he lies.

'And I'm not hungry,' I say.

'Oh,' shouts Sonia. 'There must be Chinese hereabouts. They'll fix us up.'

'Hey,' says Petar, the old sage. 'I'll tell you my idea. It'll make us all as rich as anyone can be. Colombian tungsten! Everybody needs it – those rebels everywhere, the mafia, the states that use it for their arms – we'll be the agents over here. I'll ship it in, and you guys hand it out!"

Sonia's entranced, and Petar dances on the spot, flashing his bald head in and out a beam of sun.

'Oh yes,' she says, 'that's my crime, for sure. Tungsten! It's macho stuff. And if they catch us, our heads will go rolling like we were the queen of France!' and she joins the old guy's dance, the floor springs up and down, the dust comes up and dances in the beam.

'I have a friend,' says Sonia, tumbling in the chair. 'He sleeps with me. He's young, and he can steal for us, when we are travelling.'

'Oh no, Sonia,' I say, 'not on the road. Not that again. They beat you while you sleep, just like when we had the socialism...'

'That's crap,' says Sonia. 'He's too young to get caught. Besides, I need him in my sleeping bag.'

'That's the spirit,' shouts Petar, and he sings a few lines from a hit song. '"All I want's white chicken meat",' and he's delighted with Sonia.

She says, 'I'd take issue with that song. I want more!'

'I'm not in your scheme,' I say softly, but Sonia says to me, 'You know everything about the metals – Petar Petrović – a fine criminal name is that! – was telling me...' and Petar interrupts. 'Oh, I was pardoned, as it seems I was an innocent. And sure – this guy,' and he nips at me, 'knows all about the turning rocks into gold, and then the armour to defend it.'

'I'll get my little friend,' says Sonia, 'and we can party. I'm sure Petar here could win a prize. He needs the book to go with it.'

'Petar's a rat,' I say. 'He betrays. He goes to hook, and comes back hooked.'

'Oh no,' says Sonia. 'All of us – we're in it. It's a roast!'

I see she has a wrestler's thighs – Graeco-Roman is her style, not so much spectacle, as grunting. 'Hey!' she says, 'I can't wait – those Colombian piers! And why they call them piers? It's for the pierrots lounging on them!'

She lunges about, sparring and laughing: a tall youth peeks in through the door. It must be her sleeping- or her combat-mate. 'Come in! Go away!' she shouts. 'You spy! My fortune is my own – go find yourself some heavy metal' – and out, away, he goes. 'He's not a party guy,' she says.

That will have been her plan – to find another band, more profitable, with travel to Pacific shores. And dump the inconvenient.

Petar, Sonia – it seems it wasn't sex or wisdom brought them here, but contraband.

'I'm not in all this,' I say. 'Guys like you – you start off quite aggressive, but you end defending what you've lost.'

'I haven't lost my golden boy,' says Sonia. 'It was just a spit. A spat. Though – I wouldn't cut him in,' and Petar says, 'Quite so. We are a trinity. Four is another game. Four into one won't go.'

'I don't throw,' says Sonia, quite decidedly, 'I pin. They lie, defeated. Beneath me.'

Her boy, Jozo, pops his head in and out, grinning like an idiot at a fair, framed in a horse-collar.

'That lad,' says Petar, 'I don't think he has it in him, for an operation as sophisticated as ours... The old things certain, that we pinned in covers, fortified with spine and glue, are in the tip – now, we must hone our wits....'

'Petar,' I say, dejected, 'where's it gone? Your vision? The Left, resistance, then those little groups, starting from the hidden roots – talking till there's trees like radio masts, a forest of them? Your vision ... subversion, all the rest?'

'No!' he shouts. 'You haven't twigged. It's not the roots you start from – it's the axe! The steel! All the talk – it ends up in the mixing bowl, like all the rest. What matters – is your plan, your scam, your thing, your sting. It all flows in to Order, marries with it, shores it up. All the molten flux – solidifies. There is no overturn, fulfilment of desires that generate fresh fantasies, enjoyments that will have you rolling legless, joyful, on the grass! Forget it, all the stuff that used to fill this room, the tomes trucked off and shredded, mashed into paper masks... Those pads and liners – those are made of our dead thoughts, our forebears scribbling in their dingy caves. The word is one: remember it! It's tungsten. Wolfram, if you love the animals – the wolf that's nearly caught the sheep! Unpack the word! There, that is your destiny.'

'If I can't take Jozo, then I'll have another – but exactly like,' says Sonia, between tears and ultimatum.

'Take one exactly like,' says Petar. 'Leave this one. We won't tell the difference.'

'Petar,' I say, 'where does this idea about steel arise?'

'Oh,' he says, 'I just thought of it. I always thought of it. What's the difference? Everything has a push. The tree gets leaves, when it dies – it's burnt, and your blood sizzles, and the smoke goes up and down and in your throat and eyes. You choke on it, you're buried in a wooden box. The leaves sprout up from it... We need someone who knows about the steel...'

'Oh,' I say, 'I know lots of those.' Curtis, Maurice.

'And the axe?' asks Petar, 'like the giant in the opera forges, and brings love and catastrophe to all?'

'And consolation, after it's all gone down,' I say, thinking of Nina.

'No, none of that,' says Petar, 'even when it's all over.'

We brood on that. Then, Petar says,

'Let's see how skilled we are with metals,' and he's up the walls, pulling down the amber paper – no! It's sheets of brass. 'Now, my friends,' he says, 'show me what you make of this' – and Sonia starts to twist and bend the brass, makes cones and cylinders, and tubes so tight the water wouldn't pass, and horns for gramophones, and Jozo says, 'We'll spin it, do its arms and legs on a mandrel – I've some friends, they all have them,' and Sonia says, 'No, we must solder – lead or silver? And it will be a vehicle...'

'Ah yes,' shouts Petar. 'Transport for everything – for sacks or music, thoughts or waste...'

'No, no,' I say, 'that's out of date. Transport now – it needs no time, no effort, and no space. Your thought goes round the world, and back into your brain in zero time and space. Maybe it's not gone anywhere...'

We've made a brazen bull – a barrel for its thorax, a single blaring horn in front, a twiddly tail, and Jozo says, 'No solder – copper rivets, that's the thing,' then he puts away his shears, and screws on yellow testicles.

'Wait, guys!' I say. 'This yellow brass – it's like a field of daffodils. Let's melt it down, and put more copper in. Gold brass.'

And that we do. A bull, ruddy with sunset, we have made: fit for a labyrinth, a sacrifice, a massive impregnation – or a ride...

'Well,' says Petar, reluctantly, 'it is magnificent. But – it's not steel. Soon, you can pour the steel, and then we'll see if you are capable...'

'Goddam it!' Jozo says. 'This here's a masterpiece. Sonia's bent and twisted, I have stuck the parts together – we have shown we're fit to join the enterprise. This guy,' and he pretends to plant a line of rivets in my face, 'just shaded down the colour. That would have changed in any case.'

'You see!' says Petar, much enthused. 'Do, don't read. Without a word, you three produced the same design. That's what it means – "up from the roots", brains humming along in harmony.'

'So, Petar,' I say, 'it wasn't about sex at all?'

'Well, yes,' he says, quite eager. 'Yes, why not too?'

I say, 'You were recruiting. And you find these crazy guys. Hammering away, like it was the souk in Isfahan. Metalwork is dead, Petar. I didn't need all this. At most, I want to help the world. Be useful. Have an alibi for being live.'

Jozo jumps in – 'You could be pumping gas,' he says. 'It's useful. People may say "thanks".'

'I wanted more,' I whisper.

'You'll get more,' says Sonia, 'if they catch you. Then, just take it in the spirit of the game.'

'I had a vision, see,' says Petar. 'It was this park, like Eden, only lots of guys around – some decapitating homosexuals, some singing hymns and shaking out their piggy banks, some making atom bombs, some putting sarin in the gin... And then – there was the Lord God, standing there beside me: "Jesus Christ!" he says, "did I give these guys free will?" and He turns to me, and says, "Look, Petar, you know all the tropes, the culture and the languages – advise Me for a bit." And so I'm getting ready when he does a riff, his hopes – about the lion lying quietly with the jackal, and the wolf... And "Yes!" I cry. "The wolf lies with the lamb, the will-be ram – to make Colombian wolfram!" And that is how we got to here.'

It's virtuoso stuff. More ornamented than the other time he told, as if he was its prime inventor. We're not impressed.

'Well,' says Jozo. 'It's quite nondenominational. And where'd you get the brass?'

'It was protection for the walls, when they shipped the bookshelves off,' says Petar.

'Our bovine,' Sonia says, 'could win a prize. I see it in a show – you'd put a windup gramophone inside, and play a march. Lots of soldiers, up and down – they say the more there are, the more they can protect...'

'No,' says Jozo, 'they don't help. If there's a lot, they go and beat on someone else. Or maybe turn on you. Don't let these visions fool you, Sonia. We all have them, time to time.'

3

I fetch Maurice. 'I don't deal in ores,' he says. 'I'm into base metals, not the heavy ones. And I don't do class war.'

'It's contraband,' I say. 'Nothing transgressive, no ideas. It strengthens everything – the smugglers and the cops, the states, the lawyers, the makers and the fakers...'

'Yes,' Maurice says. 'That's the effect. But the aim's subversive. It just goes wrong, is all.'

'It'll pay you off,' I say. 'Those buried sculptures, the pipe skeletons – no one will buy...'

'Oh yes they do,' he says. 'Global positioning. You bury, and with the system, you know where they are. No headstones and no cemetery. There's millions who lose people, want to know where they have ended up, their graves, but not flagged up...'

'But you don't make bodies, Maurice,' I tell him. 'Yours is art. Bones. It's tubes.'

'It's better so,' he says. 'That lasts many times as long as flesh. It's memorials, and you can carve a name.'

Maurice distances himself from Petar and the plan, on principle. He'd like the money, though. I'm even further out – I'm not up to all the stress. And – there's no quest – it's just a job, ending bad, like they all do.

Sonia, or Jozo, puts out a meaty smell. Perhaps it's stress. It'll be the sport, heating them up, and you don't want spending time with that.

Petar too is backing off.

'He'd sooner keep the bull,' says Maurice, 'than bother with the smuggling.'

'Is that a twisted joke?' I ask.

'I know all about the golden calf,' he says. 'That was no joke. I stick to graving humans – that way no wrath's incurred, and they get buried deep.'

We hear Petar shouting. 'I don't advocate anarchy – I observe it, dressed in its uniform and forming fours and fives. Without anarchy, I've told you this before – there'd be no order. Work it out! You don't advocate the sunrise, and you know it brings the darkness. Grow up, Jozo. Don't paste meaning on the meaning. Nonsense on nonsense.'

'I bet Jozo's got a pistol,' Maurice says.

'Of course,' I say. 'Those Colombians don't fool around. And if we back out now – we're the weak link. They'll be after us.'

'You idiot bastard,' Maurice says.

'You can't say things like that,' I say.

'Go fuck yourself,' he says.

'You've got a precious hand,' I say, 'but I must hide you, and your useless hand. Find a catcher's mitt. They'll think you're wounded in the war.'

'You came and fetched me from my mates,' he says, beginning to cry. 'We were about to give a pardon to ourselves and all the others... It was only cash I wanted...'

Petar is shouting, 'Just my royalties! Ideas are worth just five per cent. And let me keep the brazen bull...'

We are in disarray.

'Your impotent friend,' says Petar, 'with all his talent in that rigid hand – unusable, save in farewell – let's go and hide with him. My wall's uncovered here, the cache of banknotes all exposed – see where invention leads us! Jozo and Sonia – they'll take all the risks, and all the cash. Life's just a spool of incident for them. They can't spend, they don't fear the end, torture will be just a fresh experience...'

'I told you I was crime,' says Sonia. 'Punishment has nothing to do with all that.'

'Nonsense!' shouts Petar. 'Trade, distribution – that is all.
No crime, no punishment. You're innocents! You may
eliminate some hopefuls – and that is punishment. No one
should hope. I've learnt that now...'

'Enjoy your animal, Petar,' says Sonia, kindly. 'It's Jozo
who'll make up the rules. It's just, that you should follow
them. Tungsten – who knows where it comes from, where it
finishes? It's a gift, just lying there and buried. It's right that
we should have a piece, and up its value.' and she lies back in
Petar's chair, and we see where the brass once was, there's
old yellow papers, Borba, Pravda – struggle, truth – we read.

'If Petar leaves,' says Sonia, 'we'll fix his room with
stainless steel.'

'He should have an orgy when he goes,' says Jozo. 'It's
the least thing anyone deserves.'

'Only a little one,' says Petar, preoccupied. 'I must stay
wide-awake.'

'That's your choice, of course,' says Sonia, 'though it has
its price. It's best to take things as they've been implanted in
your nature, like beans set in a pod.'

Petar, in a few hours, has lost much. His scheme, his new
friends – all gone. His walls too. Jozo, Sonia, they're moving
fast, into the big time. Sonia could have a book written about
her. She and Jozo could move higher. Corner, trade – rare
earths, currencies, people, weapons that can change the atlas:
– or end like turkeys – no heads, no hands or feet, their guts
removed, slipped back up their anuses. In those yellow stripy
envelopes for internal mail...

And in exchange – at most a sexual rocket, Jozo lighting
the fuse and taking off, the rest of us left to gape and burn
beneath his sparky tail...

How many of us, I wonder, may be heteros? Sonia could
take on the lot of us, no doubt, but she would triumph over
each with winning falls, in seconds. Not that any of us is

simpatico... you don't catch anyone's attention, no one puts you in their history book if you dig your burrow, eat the dirt you excavate, don't squeak or growl...

'Hey,' shouts Jozo, 'the animal. You should put wheels on it, otherwise how'll you trundle it?'

'It's poor work, that,' says Maurice. 'It labours under more than one crap idea. But you can't say it is conceptual. Anyway, I don't do wheels. They have to come out round, and that's industrial.'

'There's not much we can do with it,' I say, hoping it can be left behind.

'It's what we have,' says Petar. 'We must make of it what we can.'

'People are going to ask what the thing represents,' says Maurice. 'They don't have problems with my stuff...'

'Screw them,' says Petar. 'They should take things as they come. A thing's a consequence of just another thing. It's succession and reaction. That's all you need to know. And – that offer of the orgy – that was a fine suggestion. Those, you can take and leave.'

We pull the bull along. It's bigger than a metal dog.

Maurice whispers to me, 'These old guys – they have an idea to change the world. They need us guys to bring it off.'

'No, no,' I say. 'Petar has lost his walls. He's through.'

'He had the intuition, though. Metal lasts,' says Maurice. 'That's why I work it, carry it with me in my bones. I came to bring them freedom – guys like Curtis, bearing unserviceable names... I was their Byron, even though back home they paid me as a spy...'

'No, Maurice,' I say. 'Metal doesn't last, not like clay. And – you're not Byron – you're a Manfred, with stinging fairies round his head.'

We go into a bar, to spend some last few coins. Petar whispers, 'Maurice's fist, banged down, will bring the service running. Now, if only we could cut it off, his golden hand, and melt it down... We could live on it for a year, we three...'

'Jozo seems a flattened lad,' says Petar, making the best of his destitution. 'He'll run his race. He'll finish first or last – what is the difference? You've used up all your breath, your legs are shot.'

'Sometimes you carve a crooked tree,' says Maurice. 'And at the last – you find it is a totem. You start off as a bandit – then the cash is all dug up, the victims all pardoned and revived. And so – you're a benefactor, statesman. You carve your universe from nothing. Moses!'

'That's a myth,' says Petar. 'The bandit tries to conquer Africa and does a deal with Mister Big – and ends up in a turkey bag. It never happens like you say. Jozo's a cutpurse – promoted – he'll cut throats. Small crooks – they become the Duce, and they end as bigger crooks. Moses! What a con!'

They bring us sausages. If we can't pay, we'll pare off one of Maurice's nails. He'll not object. He's full. He pukes.

Petar's on the table, and he sings, he chants, he tries a dance. *'Ein Taifun!'* – a quaver, a bellow, then, 'This here's the still point!' he shouts. 'The eye of the typhoon. All is swirling round outside, the roots wave in the air, the continents float like plastic boats, the wind, the wind – blows Jack into Jill, all is changed, transmogrified, the destinies – they interweave like knitting left to cats...'

'It's all quite improper,' Maurice says. 'Let's leave the animal, and sidle out.'

'They'll take Petar on as cabaret,' I say.

The bull – it follows us – someone must hold the string.

'Nina's consoled almost everyone,' says Maurice. 'We're ready to defend ourselves again.'

'The bull,' I say. 'We could sit beside it, on the sidewalk, see if it attracts some charity.'

'No,' says Maurice. 'It's a cult. It could be made to sing. That's our idea – we plumbers... When you turn it on, the heat, the cold, it sings. This bull – you could put a fire inside. Roast chestnuts on it, put incense in its mouth.'

I think of Sonia. Nina's atoned, but Sonia's crimes are all to come, and – what if she ends up bad before she can conciliate?

'Look at that ticker on the palace over there,' says Petar, down from his ecstasy.

It's the quotes on the metals market. Lights and figures, jigging up and down

'Bears all over,' Petar shouts. 'Not a bull in sight! Jozo's fiddled all the strings. He's moving into something else. Booze or eats.'

Maurice and I can't follow him. We sit on the street corner. Our bull has no eyes. We try to poke some in. It's to look busy, innocent.

'It's all to do with mathematics,' Petar says. 'Sonia must be the force. Wrestling's all about stress and load. That's what drives the markets. She's the genius. Maths is the basis of all modern crime, you know...' He waits for us to disagree.

We go back to Petar's room. He says, 'Any idiot can solve a problem. The thing is – to start a new one.'

'That's so,' says Maurice. 'When I was in the Service, we made up *boutades* like that. These phrases, fashionable words, they're common coin, they don't mean anything... They plop like mortar shells, in everybody's soup. It's culture wars.'

I say, 'Maurice, I thought a guy is always in the Service,' and he says, 'Yes, that's another one, *boutade*. An invention – doesn't mean it isn't true. I went to free those people – then I was inducted. Converted. Into the tub. Now, I suffer with them,' and he waves his gold and silver hand. 'My treasure is my handicap. The struggle's loot and mutilation.'

He moulds another crude horn for the bull, fudged from its testicles, and Petar shouts, 'Fuck you! Trying to be a benefactor, worse, a realist! – that totem was a unicorn. Now, you've given it two horns. A *cornuto*. A fall guy. It's a sacrifice. Desecrated, junk. Impure.' He turns confidential, like old guys do – it is the fear of having nothing more to say, of death: 'I used to be a founder of a Society for the Pursuit of Everything. Then, we ran foul of another one – society for the Pursuit of Everyone,' and he laughs. A mild blow to the chest – it often does for guys like Petar – it's a thing he must be watching for.

I say, 'It's true, Maurice. You went to fight them, then you joined those guys. And now their wounds are closed – they'll start it all again... You changed sides – for what? Intelligence? Or folly?'

'No,' he says. 'We've had our war. It's your turn next. Guys say ours was a failure of intelligence, you can avoid the hurt. It isn't true. War's when intelligence shows its full strength...' and on he talks.

We sleep. We dream – each has his bull to chase. Mine's on a plinth, a mystery. Its copper rivets – they erode, their blue-green flowers spread in the square – a sea, a sky. The body pops wide open. It gives a birth...a shape, a form... I clamber on the plinth to see... what is this new-born? Monster, maiden, maybe another bull... an egg? containing monster, maiden, other eggs...

Petar is up and prancing: 'Bookshops!' he shouts. 'Time for them again. The rustle of nature, of sexual congress... We should take the bull along, poor *castrato*, he's art, but not so modern. No finesse, no quiddity.'

'A botch,' says Maurice. 'Like the past. A simulacrum, thing like some other thing. An idol – you can't cut off a steak...'

'No, no,' says Petar, draping himself in brocade and heaving on some spats. 'He's nothing like another thing. True – he is a thing, and not a threat of thunder in the sky. But he is shockproof. He doesn't hurt, he's quite indifferent. Pray to him, admire... he doesn't give a snort. The real sacrifice? Sonia and Jozo! They don't know it, but they'll run their enterprise – and suffer in the end, like king and queen, despoiled, buggered by the executioners, and hacked about... That's what they entered into, that's where they'll end: being bad, atoning. Seeking the punishment...'

'Regretting, when it comes,' I say.

'Everyone's a sacrifice,' says Petar. 'Being wealthy smoothes the end.'

He drags the bull down the stairs. Maurice and I stare at each other. 'Petar knows a lot of truths,' says Maurice. 'But there's an infinity of them. Justice too. It's inexhaustible. Show them – with a breath. Don't scrape and chisel every one. Don't celebrate. Don't struggle with environments. Lie back.' And as he talks, we scamper off, away from Petar, his strange beast. We're the first schism, so it seems.

'Petar's encapsulated in his questions,' Maurice says. 'These episodes, these women, books – any idiot can keep on asking questions. I've a workshop: I'm encysted in the answer. It's so big, I can't imagine it, and I am part of it, the gristly part that grows out of my hand, the solder, ingots, ores... My beautiful hand, the best alloy there is. Until it's off, and swirling in the crucible again...'

'Maurice!' I shout. 'We've dumped Petar. Now, I don't want to trek with you. I don't want Nina, consoling muse – and Curtis! The cretin, his wrong name...'

'Oh well,' says Maurice, not put out. 'As for Curtis and his name – if you're an emperor, or just carrying the name – foreign parts are much the same.'

'Maurice,' I say, 'I think you're on to something big. Your work... yes, it's everything our life's about, and all invisible. You could say – it's crass...' I mean to qualify that with more praise, but – Maurice himself is rather crass. And anyway – so what? Who cares? It's 'what you've all been waiting for' – and now it's come. You don't buy in. It's second hand before it's first.

'My work,' says Maurice, irritated, 'is graft and sales. And when it's done, it's memory.'

'A ditch,' I say, 'is just a line of nothing, but it bears the water to and fro.'

'That's casuistry,' says Maurice. I can't say he's wrong.

It's good to dump Petar. I'd like to break with Maurice. Then he says, 'Look – everyone knows the name of my place, my land. I've come from a drama. I want to be important now. It's due.'

'You have distinguishing marks, Maurice,' I say.

'Yes, but you don't,' he says.

He pauses, then, 'I admire Mercury,' he says. 'A ball of rock and steel. Like we made, forging a country – when we weren't the good guys, none of us. Homosex helps, of course – for sure, there's other planets far away, with life like ours, like mine. Exactly equal. With generals. All the armies, fighting, all the love and hate – the root is homosex, the consolation too. It's all desire, pursuit...'

'That's bleak, Maurice,' I say. 'And not exactly new. Those planets quite like ours – maybe they're bleak as well.'

'Those astronomers,' he says, 'they smile, they laugh – looking for life elsewhere. It's what we want, of course. A place where all's the same, but different. It isn't so. There's tented camps, and squaddies bedding down. That's the reward. Not mountain ranges, friend,' he says, holding out his precious hand for me to squeeze, 'it's tents.'

I wish he hadn't called me friend. The Greeks – they had a better word, 'O Stranger'. Easier to dump the guy you meet along the road.

'Our homosex kids,' Maurice goes on, 'plugged in and tough. You see, it's not about the money. It's about combat. That's what Jozo and Sonia have been set up to do. It's why your Petar chickened out. Their cash will go on banks and guards. And in the end – well, every crime will have its punishment, every Sonia her Jozo. That, we know. It's all been written down. They'll never spend their money – from the first, it's all in hock to keeping and protecting it. They buy the fear. The certainty that it will end...'

'That's obvious, and bleak,' I say. 'You never made my rad. That would have brought you spoonfuls...'

'Who cares, but you?' he asks.

'Something new, something different,' I say. 'Fiddle the harmonics, shuffle the deck.'

'You?' he asks. 'Just you? Experiment? Slip in a fifth suit, a second joker? Things will happen, that you can't invent, and can't foresee.'

'I know all that,' I say. 'Everybody does. They know it will all change. Everybody does.'

'Look at me, at us – not as guys unemployed – but as platoon,' he says. 'That makes a bigger sense. All the types are there. I'm the one surviving, the creator. See the beauty of what's been destroyed, blown up, and silent. And one day, that twist and crumble, girders like sugarsticks, that old story, will be the core of something entirely new – a plant, for making stuff that's part of other stuff.'

'But Maurice – you had another plan,' I say.

'Yes – there's other things in the future, naturally. Tattoos and fighting – that's what the working class does now. Making cheap stuff and living cheap. That's not for me. Out there – there's great deals that's legal too. I could do that. I bet they've never seen another one like this,' and he waves his heavy hand. 'It would be a start. Firm handshakes. You need that too, if you go pouring steel.'

'You've no idea...' I say, and he jumps in. 'That's your mistake. It's not ideas, it's single-mindedness. You can't believe how well I'd fit with guys like those. It's climbing up and cashing in, and hoping you will live for ever. I've got all that.'

They're all frozen, suspended, waiting – Nina, Maurice, Petar, Money, Crime and Punishment, Sonia and Jozo. It will come to everyone, and disappear.

'We should steal the bull,' I tell Maurice.

'It's true,' he says. 'It's mine. Everything is everybody's – but desire and usefulness – they have a part in it. They have an owner.'

'For me,' I say, 'it's desire. That makes things useful. I watch, I learn the tricks. Maybe one day, desire will come... It just needs, well – a tickle.'

'Do things the difficult way,' says Maurice, using his hand as a grappling iron to climb the wall, and in through Petar's window. He comes down with the bull.

'Petar's amorphous now,' Maurice says. 'A blob, a jelly. A mass, a flux. His highest point is never reached, it slips away. He reaches neither order nor its opposite ... nothing's resolved,' and I say,

'You didn't have to beat him?'

'If the spirit's lacking,' Maurice says. 'You must take it out on flesh. The second best.'

I don't enquire. 'What'll we do with the animal?' I ask.

'Oh,' he says, 'we'll park it in some building. On a plinth, so's it'll be admired, and not get touched. Or tickled, with darts and prods.'

So, there it is, all set up, on its plinth – a church, a funeral home – resignation, hope, both of these and more, a haven, until it's wheeled away.

'If you work with metals,' Maurice says, pushing me a distance away from him – 'It all comes from the earth, it's true, like terra cotta, flax or manioc. But fire's the medium that transforms what's friable or grit, and hardens it and in its time, twists it and weakens it, and back it goes, or if it's saved – it goes in the melting pot. And all the stuff you used to talk about – the countries and the lineages, the history, the character, the spooling out of circumstance and trying to maintain a self – those waves, the water running out, your comrades drawing lots and you the object ... all that stuff, the psyche, psychology, doctors and nurses, mothers, fathers – all that stuff is dead and ready to be stuffed, into cushions.'

'Maurice,' I ask, 'do you have the infant's tear? The one Dostoevsky wrote about.'

'I never heard of that,' he says. 'I don't expect I do, in any case. You saw us, gathered – the best, the worst, in prison. In prison once, and then for ever. There, in that land, and that imprisonment, you must forget. Invent new times, forget the old ones, good and bad. Me – I have no hope,' he says cheerfully. 'It's a relief.'

'Well, you ended up there, Maurice,' I say, 'That country; not yours, I think. Though it seems the ending there was only temporary. You were a foreigner, I guess… it wasn't home, your motives mixed at best...'

'Oh well,' he says, 'there is that hymn – "Coming Home" – it's in the New World. I went home, and then I left, I'm leaving.'

'I didn't see the prison,' I say. 'When I saw you all, standing on that mound, I thought "knights in a castle, someone's castle". No particular country.'

'Well,' he says, 'you can call it a castle, I suppose. When you've been held in one, you can do anything to anyone, only you mostly never get the chance.'

I know that's not true. The chance abounds. I say,

'Some advice, Maurice: never drive yourself – get a pro. Don't have a walk-up office, and remember – assassins hate the country. It's there to be hidden in. Killers only know the subway. And – stay clear of sex.'

'I know all that,' he says. 'And no giveaway, no benevolence. I've no intention of letting go of anything. People don't remember, anyway, if you were charitable.'

Maurice is off to make a life settled on gold and silver, so 'Farewell' I say.

He never did that job for me...

4

'They were new humans,' I say. 'New man, new Soviet man – that didn't work. I know new humans.'

'Forget them, your Balkan friends,' says Kaja. 'I'm here to tell you what you can, not what you want.'

'I want to eat trees and run faster than panthers,' I say.

'That's just it,' she says. 'Really. No pop. No r'n'r! Just *can*.'

'Really, that's what I want. And not just Balkan – now, everyone's quite wild to get in everywhere, in every country's history. When you say you want to be free, you really mean you want to leave wherever you may be.'

Kaja. I can tell the village that she runs from – innocent as everyone, she's always running back like us – who she pretends not to recognise.

I found some pincers, coming here – for cracking lobsters, but they've the shape of lobster claws. Fine old beasts, lobsters, not giving a damn for their crap death. I stole them. Kaja goes out. I try out my pincers on her desk. Then I crack her screen with them.

She comes in, fired high. 'You cracked my screen!' she shouts.

'What I've been experiencing,' I say, 'is a short decisive history of new humans, that cracks the world.'

They all want to buy and sell the world, or more – except for Petar who's to old to want anything at all.

'You see, Kaja,' I say, 'metalwork could be my thing.'

'You can't be unemployable,' she says. 'It's a new job, mine, to fit you in. Even into poverty, not sleeping, eating roots. No handouts!'

'I was quite bourgeois,' I tell her. 'When I was with the survivors.'

'You didn't join in, because you wanted to give orders,' Kaja says. 'Besides, the war was big for them – but we've all moved on, forgot.'

'Just give me some money,' I say, 'and I'll leave this country. No bother.'

'Oh,' she says, 'there's no money. There's just me – "Advice is worth a thousand ingots" – it's a proverb. Look, it's on my desk.' That's so: in gothic script. I wave my claws, salute the pokerwork, the sign. 'Fitting in, not cash,' she says. 'You see, I fit in here quite perfectly. This job is my success, my thing. I'm curious about you all,' and she waves towards a glass door, a sheet of faces pressed behind it, most looking upward, like they're done in coloured inks, hoping a falling angel will drift into their arms, reward them... 'And your illusions. I give your stories shape.'

'Your friends,' she goes on, 'made an error. There is no money now. The game has changed. They thought they wanted peace to make their cash. It's over, done, redone. No one will graft all day and night to make them rich. What you must do,' and she takes my pincers, snips a nip out my arm, 'is go be soldiers. Those guys behind the glass – they didn't want it any more than you... They love their lives. They are attached to them. Forget it. That is finished,' and she thrusts a tiny lead hussar into my palm, red, yellow, blue. 'See,' she says, 'you could be Romanian. Here in Germany, they've lost the taste, soldiering's another thing they're anxious to forget.'

'Oh well,' I say. 'I'm here by chance. I guess I could go back and steal my animal, though there's no market for brass bulls. It could be melted down, I guess, and be a culverin.'

'Be careful where you steal, and where you point your guns,' she says. 'The days of scattershot and blunderbuss are done. Be very very prudent...'

'The bull,' I say, improvising hard, 'was a sport, a creation. A unique, once-for-ever thing. To be admired, aspired to. "Beat that", it says.'

'Steal it!' Kaja says. 'Before it does some harm. Union with the cosmic forces! You rave about the modern humans – they're just following their destiny, the history all laid out – those cosmic forces... They're not benevolent, they're complementary: one is mathematics – your long gun, the pointing finger, like on the ceiling – winkles you out from every corner. Mathematicians, artillerymen – they made your world. Magic is the mother of science. Knowledge is always – to know God. The force behind it all. Then – there's the cosmic force that you can't see. What we know – is magic, gods and demons, algorithms. What we don't know, is what we reason out, our secret weapon: science, our purity. Hypothesis is stronger than the faith. It's the ladder that reaches to the stars, beyond. That is the quest. Not by boat, but with a spade. The eggs, the chocolate eggs by Fabergé, buried in the garden! The first force that made us modern – it's the design, the divinity we know, the rules self-evident. And what we look for ... well, we know in the long and short term – we shall find it. It must be there. Everything is.'

We pause. What Kaja says – is everything too, more or less. 'Of course,' she says, 'in the interstices, the joins, the faults, there's universal fighting.'

'I always thought it was the other way,' I say, shaken. 'I thought what we found out chased away the demons, and what we didn't know was a defence against still more of them. Instead, they copulate and breed like frogs and toads!'

'Maybe they do,' says Kaja, 'but you're quite wrong. We look for cosmic forces – in the book, the temple. In the laboratory, and in the gun sight. But then – there's all the rest: everything we shall discover. Everything there is to come – more cosmic force, our future and our quest.'

'Kaja, you know it all,' I say. 'What shall we discover? Our fine brains humming on...'

'No, my dear,' she says. 'What we discover – is short lives. Ours. There's no decisive battle. There's lots of them. There is just an end.'

'The cosmic force – it does for us,' I say. 'The quest is toxic. But anyway, the force would be our nemesis. Looking for it makes no odds at all.'

'Who knows?' she says cheerfully. 'A wise man bets against the favourite winning every time.'

'Fitting in?' I say. 'You can't fit into this, your picture...'

'Not "fitting in" *to* something. Just fitting. I love your stories,' Kaja says. 'All you drifting guys. And seeing your faces when I say there's no money, and you must put on uniforms.'

'Those eggs you talked about,' I say. 'Fabergé – he worked in metals. Now you say they're made of chocolate.'

'Oh well,' she says, 'I love the stuff. Chocolate. It's full of iron. He was an artist through and through.'

I try to think it out – first, magic and divinity, the guesses, the hypotheses. Then the certainty, the fission. The big bang in the future. Those big bombs – a trivial foretaste. The cosmic forces bringing our extinction ... helped along by our artillery. Petar was right – sex and metalwork – the best way to pass the shortening times... The money – smelt it in the cauldron, plunge into it, be strong. 'Kaja,' I say, 'you are the sagest of them all. You must have found in me a follower, one receptive to your truths...?'

'Oh no,' she says. 'I tell everyone. It doesn't change a thing. It's not the cosmic forces that do for you – it's seeking them. They exist, of course, they bury you in silt, they fry you, and they eat your food. But – you call on them, you needle them.'

Her screen is dead. She stares at me, shuts her misty eyes, weak eyes that won't let her join the hunt. She says, 'I don't give out cash. I tell you all: "You'd better join an army. If it doesn't suit, well, you don't fit in, not anywhere. That's why you came to me." Your new humans – well, remember the new Soviet man. He drank too much, and lounged around. That was good too – but you don't want to go that route.'

'Our destiny is suicide? Eating gold? That's the cosmic force, Kaja?' I ask, hoping for a cheering answer.

'Who knows what they are?' she says. 'The forces. Maybe they're up in the sky or in the ground. Our destiny is something else. Our eyes – at least our eyes are open, not like the dinosaurs,' she says. 'It happened to us, us people, all too quick. Big heads, big brains – promotion. That's the disappointing part – up and down, a twinkling. The brighter you are – the less you last. You fiddle with the machines – then they don't work.'

'That's too bad, Kaja,' I say. 'You, bringing in the dinosaurs – it shows it up – the banal, the trite.'

'Well,' she says, 'that is the way it goes. The truth is total triteness.'

'I don't see you doing metalwork, Kaja, so it must be sex for you,' I say.

'Of course,' she says, 'but not with you. I'm the pilot of a tug that has to pull you through the wave.'

'I couldn't bond with you,' I say. 'You aren't too bright. Those ideas – they've been around and round.'

'That's true,' she says. 'They're quite banal. But no one listens. Now – you'd best choose a regiment. A country too.'

Yes – it has its point. To join a little band, of murdering brothers. The big society – is tepid, those commandments no one heeds – the dry dust seeps right up your nose. You obey, you hide. Then comes the letter, sent to all.

I say, 'I don't see myself in uniform. They never fit.'

'Then – a militia. That way you dress casual,' she says. 'They're even better, for promotion and some cash.'

'I'm not sure I can believe in anything strategic, Kaja.'

'It's being, not believing. Do what the others do. You can't go wrong.'

'Yes, Kaja,' I say, 'but it's being with all the others who are being too. Not just doing. That's the pain.'

'You broke my screen,' she says. 'I've nothing to look into. No mirror. It's just me, all round. Absolutely natural, no rules, and no conventions.'

'That's when you need to start pouring steel,' I say. 'That snaps you out and into something else. Small amounts of it – spectacle frames, *chevaux de frise*, spurs, triggers, concealed blades. Necklaces that remind you of Alsace.'

'Oh,' she says, 'you're too deep for me. Bringing those trinkets in, then steelworks, and long guns that can reach to Paris. Or Berlin. My aim's to fit you in, into yourself – not into history. Not into dialectics – there's too many strands of time, and wheels revolving fast and slow, and systems of quite different kinds, that's all in place, each with life processes...'

'Small things, Kaja,' I say, 'those are the best. The larger ones – they won't go out through the window frames. You need things to fit...'

'That's it, exactly,' Kaja says. 'You're there at last. Back at the start!'

The guys behind the glass – 'All they have is their desire,' says Kaja. 'But even for sex, people are designed quite bad. You need to get it over quick – instead, the culture makes you linger on, try to enjoy, until you're bored. Now, there's another room, the victors of the age...' and she pulls aside a tapestry, and there they are, each drinks a different kind of wine, eats squabs on skewers, and they talk – their faces better wrought and finished off, clothes made to fit.

'You see,' says Kaja, 'these give you hope, or maybe despair. It's metaphysical. They sail the ship, they're voted in, paid off – the rest, the guys behind the glass, is ballast, cargoes of working stiffs. They pump the water out, they tend the goats, they row the boat when there's no wind...'

'Well,' I say, 'the thing's to be on deck, not in the hold.'

'You haven't understood,' says Kaja. 'This is a voyage. Who knows where it is going, or is supposed to end? Someone must know, have an idea. Who knows where it's best to be? And the cargo – is it just people? Or are there goods? These guys, who drink the wine and talk – aren't they the passengers? Not guys who know how ships work ... they watch the waves ... it's dreamland. Peak after peak, up and down, the everlasting swell – maybe it wakes libidos... They go from shore to shore, from port to port – always the same, eternally returned, but meanwhile – the towns decay, or prosper, each time unrecognisable... The same, identical – something never given: it's never so. It's always a transformation. The name remains – Bilbao, or Surabaya – back you go where you were born ... quite unrecognisable, the place and you, and yet it's yours, your nest, your refuge, history. The stories and the language – nearly what you left, what you remember, as you lurch along, dragging your feet in classy shoes. Up and down, the everlasting swell...'

'Maurice,' I start – I can't say 'Maurice my friend' – 'Maurice would have joined the working class. His foot was quite Byronic, like a claw, and – his stout hand could serve him in the battle. Struggle, he sought – but to have a chance to win. And so – he spat on that, and has another path ahead. Then there was – an old guy, who knew everything – an awful curse. He ended bad. And Crime and Punishment, Jozo and Sonia – starting off in contraband – and into heavy metal, all of them... Would you have put them all in fighting gear?'

'Oh yes,' she says, 'that is my job. And flag you up –
before my screen was cracked. Those sergeants – they would
come for you, down through the years. The boundaries are
flexible, the holy books as well. They catch you out, they set
you on the run, those soldiers do.'

'I'm looking for a hearth,' I say. 'Even a thatch where
sparrows come, dispute...'

'Oh,' says Kaja, 'I know your sort. It starts as cash you
want, then it's more complicated. You think – "you move
around, nothing will disturb, no church, no temple destroyed
or built, no new passport, no new oaths of allegiance or
denial". It isn't so. Tomorrow – maybe. Today, and all the
future you might invent ... even if you run away with me, we
have to speak a language. Have to peel the fruit as mother
taught. Besides – the sparrows went extinct.'

'That's too maximalist for me, Kaja,' I say.

'You're empty. That means you can do anything or
everything. So you think!' she says.

'Yes, that's so, Kaja,' I say. 'You're empty too, and look!
you've signed everyone. You've named the animals, the
plants, everyone who scrambles in your jungle.'

'But I have no illusions. That doesn't change a thing, all
that I do. It's frontiers, holy books and warriors – that is what
counts,' she says. 'You—' and she thumbs at me, 'you don't
own a piece of earth, or what walks on it – animal, human –
nor what lies beneath, on outcrops ... you won't fight for that,
what you don't own, what runs with that warm blood that you
don't have...'

'Well,' I say, 'those stone heads on spikes, out there in the
park. Thinkers. Did you put them there? Are they yours,
special to you, and their thoughts?'

'Yes,' she says, 'they're mine. I take the rap, I put them
there. They're heads, but not of stone, and not of thinkers, not
especially. No doubt they thought. But I shan't go to fight for

them. Their tongues don't warrant it: stone clappers on dumb bells.'

Someone's given her a protocol, that deals with everything she's paid to do... The jokiness is hers, I guess.

None of the people I have met has asked anything of me. That is a great good.

I leave Kaja's building, and I see the next shift's sitting at her table – she's not attractive, not like Kaja, and I don't feel like asking her to journey on with me.

I could have been any or all the people I'd been involved with: fear, aversion – these played a part in leaving them all to it. I had my judgement, my separate self: this gave me privilege. I felt I could survive, assimilate what happened to them, feel like them, and cast it off ... do better; be more true to the future I had planned.

Kaja inspired me to join up psychology, emotion and morality – probably the brain too, and national soils – in my reflections, as I left the park, its severed heads once full of thought, upon their columns, and their plinths.

A guy called Chester follows me and says, 'Look, when we're in Moscow, the rents of decent places are too high. We can steal military stuff – when it's been inventoried – and sell it on the street. It's all good jackets, boots, guns, all that.'

It's a comedown, after Maurice and Petar, but he would solve the problem of the rent. I'd learn to fear no man. That's a great good.

'No, no,' I say, 'the market's saturated with the military. You should have followed Kaja, her advice. You have no animals, no garden. The army is the place for you. You're boots and belts. In Moscow the people flow like rivers, embanked, and when there's ice, the water is not still beneath, it rushes on, up to a frozen sea.'

Kaja's laughter – shakes you up. 'Laughter is the key to hell', they say. I didn't know they locked those gates. It is a place of punishment, where all, I guess, is transparent, and you come out clean and good. Or not. The bad – it seems so full of life, or maybe giving life, and when that's taken out – those soldiers swirling round – down into hell – or up – you go; and you are washed in blood, and come out good and clean.

Well! Here's Kaja, in the bar! She jumps right in: 'You've got nothing. Except the big words you bring out – knowledge, truth, faith. It's pitiful! Even if you had a frame to put them in, they're not worth...'

'Kaja, you use them all the time,' I say.

'I know they float, like lilies on a pond, like those paintings, "ephemeras on the lake". It's my authority empowers. That's what makes the big words stick together, like daisies in a chain. You've just collected them, and laid them out against the wall. In wreaths. They're all you've got, you think because you found them you can bolt them all together, make a career.'

'It's "nymphets", Kaja, those white blobs,' I say.

'Yes, that's it,' she says, 'but don't try to weasel out. You have all the big words, but even if they made a manifesto from them, it would be one in thousands. But they don't. I – I could be a supermodel. Or a supervolcano. Freeze the seas, kill the fish. They'll be killed anyway, every last one. But – I assign. I dispose. I put in place, in order. No payoffs, just decisions, and a position waiting.'

'I have a trade, Kaja,' I say. 'It's just I haven't started it. It's the first stroke – I'm unsure.'

'Well,' she says, 'we'll fit you in. That's the lesson – everybody's fitted in. There's nowhere else. You're in, we're in. Now, surely, you don't want to reach some top? Those leaders – rapists, drunks and lunatics: white, black, yellow – all supremacists, their pig wars, buffalo campaigns, their bean wars, land wars, sea wars... All incompetent at office work –

the men of destiny, the man of steel – floundering in
paperwork, mourned only by the guys who did their
executions and now fear they'll have to take the rap... The
trouble is, you guys love to see some other guys that fight.
Give you a sheet of brass – out comes a bull. Why not a duck,
a lamb?'

'Oh well,' I say, 'it's only there for worshipping.'

'That's Jesuitry,' Kaja shouts: we're both quite drunk.
'The guys upstairs – they're just the same or worse: name
those dread names – that Loki says it all. Murderers,
pranksters, sadists every one: flighty friends, insatiable for
love – and cross them! they will cast you down, they'll judge
you, put that massive finger in your eye, your ear, your
everywhere! They'll eat their kids, or yours, or pin them up,
or tax the infidels – nothing's too outré ... you're damned if
you believe, and in eternal darkness if you don't...'

'Kaja,' I shout. 'Can it! The waiter'll cut us off.'

'Listen,' she says: her tongue is brown and sticky with
manhattans, and she slips it in my mouth: it's hard to hear her
pregnant words... 'I could fast track you, my dear friend,' I
think she says, 'I've a procedure that will shoot you up, give
you a topmost job. That must be why you came to Germany to
seek – a leader's post that's quite insipid now. No massacres,
no forming threes or fours...'

'No, Kaja, none of that,' I say. 'It was the German music
drew me. Threes and fours – that was the trick. The beat, the
rhythm they had here...'

'You can't con me,' says Kaja: 'you're like all the rest –
the Rheingeld! That's what draws you. Forget the tunes – you
are a metals man. You've got some trick to fool the guards,
the saints beneath the flux... You seek the ring! Find it, make
a new one – that's your game!'

'No, Kaja, absolutely not,' I say. 'I see myself with tongs
and hammer, beating a rod to make a shoe...'

'Of course!' she laughs. 'Apocalypse. Another one! Those horses mustn't cast a shoe – the guys upstairs, the gods, are keen on blacksmiths, since they don't use automobiles...'

'Don't make a joke of it,' I say, but she is off in laughterland, I join her, and it's loud – they cut us off. We find another bar.

We settle down, quite intimate. She puts a leg over my two. I feel quite confidential. 'Kaja,' I say, 'your trouble is, you're an employee. You've no autonomy. Now, me – I'm like that sheet of brass. I have all forms within me – on that expanse of nothing, everything swirls round, invisible, but – take the tools, the lathes, the *poinçons* – a marvellous shape will come, be me until it's time...'

She takes offence, 'Yes, it's time – to beat you flat. To throw you in the pot, to add fresh metals, change your colour and your density ... to spin you into tubes of ever-reaching length, so tight the water cannot pass, or into wires and hang you from the roof, and juice you up and make you glow white-hot...'

'Peace, Kaja,' I shout – her leg takes up a Graeco-Roman hold on both of mine and cuts the blood off so I cannot stand...

'Oh no,' she says, 'you passed the mark. There is no peace. I like to see the guys who fight, I'm just like the other powerful ones.'

'No insult meant,' I say, 'I've taken drink.' She is as strong as Nina was. I fall, I try to crawl, but don't know where to go.

'Your sort,' shouts Kaja, 'they always tell the truth. That's their downfall. It means there is nothing to be done, not about anything. It's all laid out and bare.'

The bar staff gather round, some nod, and some make execution signs.

'I could love you, Kaja, notwithstanding...' I say, quite desperate.

'Being nice – that is no remedy,' she says. 'Not for anything. There is no remedy. No, you kill a bunch of guys – no remedy, you're in the book. The past is an atrocity – you can only turn the page...' The waiters start to argue, and Kaja shouts again to me,

'I'll shoot you up, you crass ass...! You tinsmith! See – you're absolutely hammered now! Shoot you up – like they put guys into rockets, off they go! The shooting up ends all the same... Into the void. Into the bank. Into the army – what'll you be? Cook, sniper, payclerk? Teller, trader, thief? Remember – I don't benefit from what you do, your destiny. I do my job. If you come back from space, from robbery, from targeting – that's your affair, not mine. I'm not your luck – try gathering fortune from where you end – in space, in vaults ... or in the mess!'

Her audience applauds, the waiters load more rounds. I'm down among the shoes and boots.

'Lady, you're a reductionist,' a waiter says.

'Oh no,' says Kaja. 'There is all the rest! I see it all, my picture of the real includes the lot, even a snatch of recent past and future too... This guy here,' and she stirs me with her foot, 'could be a plumber. Once, they worked in metals too. But he is wedded to the stars, to lilting air beyond the winds, where only he will lift and twirl, in emptiness that's stuffed with every form...' And on she shouts.

She forks me with her legs back on the bench. 'Friends!' she says, and here's that viscous tongue again, filling my mouth, her raptor's limbs are one long breath, one muscle, trained for decisive joustings on the sand. 'I could place you on the track,' she says, 'that leads right to the top. But – no fanciful ideas. No exterminations. Just keep it quiet. Nothing done that's underage, or scaly. I had one guy – he feared that heaven was already filled with dinosaurs and aliens...'

'Oh no,' I say. 'I'm not obsessive. I'd be cool. But power – I'm not sure it's worth the while. Especially if it doesn't last.'

'Well, that's the sort we have,' she says, disappointed. 'If it's the Genghiz type you want – wrong place and time! Keep the pot a-simmer for a spell. Threaten, don't drop explosives, skim off, don't expropriate.'

'Maybe a forge and hammer's best for me,' I say again.

There's belly dancing on the stage – jelly-rolling, karaoke style. I remember Curtis-Curzon's snippet – 'ladies don't move' ... Kaja is dancing as she sits, twisting her long body like a hose.

'I'm not sure you're ready for a relation with a woman,' she says to me. 'It's a primordial thing. You have to touch your prehistoric root.'

'I know,' I say. 'Ladies don't move – women are quite different. Maybe you should choose my path for me. Dominion over mankind – or graving images. Bronze giants atop a building, maybe.'

Or – remembering that salt-cellar, gilt, with Neptune sat upon the rim ... I'd put some African on mine, an escapee, a-scrambling from the brine...

'No, no,' says Kaja, climbing on the stage and stripping off. 'No salt. No tall buildings either, nor with giants. They attract the wrongest sort. And no arty stuff for you. It's factory work awaits.'

She's not sincere. Those factories – dead like disco, all ephemeral. If power is in her gift, for sure it's all the same. If not – who'd want it? No qualities are needed – it's a primordial thing. There are no types of it. You need to grasp your prehistoric root.

Kaja dances on, heating the room.

5

'Oh yes!' says Maurice, 'How they're suffering, Sonia and Jozo. How well they're doing! The stress, the fear, the riches, all the retainers, the debts, the payoffs and the thefts they undergo. And yet – they can handle it all, for now.'

'Maybe it's the physical thing they have?' I say. He rolls right over that.

'I don't know how they carry on,' he says. 'Though there's no way that they can stop. It's like all of us, I guess – except you,' he looks at me as if I'm hope and revelation. 'You have your loneliness. It's unalloyed, it's no luxury, and no relief. It's everything. Poor us, poor me. Thronged around by every sort.'

'You're struggling somewhere near the top,' I say. 'When you've made it, then you can come down. And – I'm not lonely, it's I have illusions about the life I used to live. I might go into…' I can't say 'politics', though I guess that is the tool. 'Something. Or I might be unemployed.'

'Your trouble was,' says Maurice, pushing on, 'you only thought of comfort in your shack. We – we'd all been shut up, inside. So, after, we stood upon the open hills, in the back lots. No walls, no roofs, no floors.'

'Some of you must have been the guardians,' I say. 'Not all shut in, though all perhaps inside.'

'Oh well,' says Maurice, 'most did the killing for their families. I didn't have the joy of one.'

'I don't know what is right,' I say, 'so, I couldn't kill.'

'Someone will tell you,' Maurice says. 'That is usually how it's done. Or else some guy runs at you – that lets you know – he seeks his death. He risks. He makes you risk. Did you decide? Or is it just his plan, his ploy? But there's no odds to calculate, the outcome's chance: it isn't reasonable for you to dice your personal bones. And so – it's jousting to the death. Nothing is right or wrong. All that, comes after. Someone's kept the score. That's when right and wrong come in – not that it matters then...'

'I left this fixer, Kaja, belly-dancing,' I say. 'She can give me fame. At least – position.'

'Oh,' says Maurice, 'stay clear of that. I own the copper of the world. But the details – I leave those alone. I've been everywhere. It doesn't make a difference – but, I must be somewhere. Here we are in Stuttgart, where most people end. I watched people suffer...'

'We all do, Maurice,' I say, trying to avoid philosophy.

'Yes,' he says, 'but it was my mates causing it, and I was in the room.'

'It often seems to happen so, that you were there and innocent,' I say. 'Why do you think I should know all that?'

'You don't believe me, then?' he shouts.

'It seems that distance is a factor here,' I say, trying to pass him by. 'I'm not sure why. So close, and yet so innocent. But – all of this was on the field of battle, so it seems.'

'That's so,' he says, much cheered. 'We're all involved, and all concerned. The battle, yes. It's always going on. The truth. It's everywhere, like family and self-defence. The question's always pertinent.' We've nothing new to say.

'Still burying your skeletons?' I ask.

'Oh,' he says, 'there's other people make them now – I own the idea, that's all.'

'I've trekked the world,' I say, 'with various types. This Kaja – how she loves to party! Maybe a whirl with her...'

The idea starts to pall at once.

'I'm a benefactor now,' says Maurice. 'I could build a house back where we were. Of course, I couldn't live there, couldn't visit. But – a mansion, all white metal, with loggias, those chimneys screwed like barley-sugars...'

'Bronze giants on the roof?' I add.

'In copper, maybe,' he says. 'Me and Curtis – all the guys that frolicked in the tub...'

'I could design that,' I say. 'A cube. Not to be pretentious. Empty, but with a safe room for Jozo and Sonia. Matt. Brass cladding on the walls. Out of the brass can come wrought animals.'

'I was in the States,' he says. 'They don't have such a metal house. The people there say they have sex much more than us. It must be something in the tea. The coffee. It perks up your energy. They're powdering up their subsoil. Into their automobiles it goes. No one wanted sex with me – they thought my splendent hand and foot were store-bought. Fuck them all,' he says, boldly. 'I owned all they had, and I still do. They all belong to me, though they don't care.'

I say, 'You used to be quite bolshie, Maurice.'

'We had something precious, back there,' he says, 'in the foundries. Revolution, the molten flux. We threw it all away. Dross. Or maybe it was thrown already, and we had the whiff, the smoke ... and then we seized the tail, the grin, like it was that phantom cat ... And off it went!'

'I think the house should shine,' I say. 'Enamels, even.'

'Oh no, no poetry!' he says. 'It must be clear that it's a cube. And – a constant festival around – like California, where you can be happy, sad, all the day long. Each house a shrine; mine – a casino, tempting chance. My festival should express just everything; and everywhere. Especially as I shan't be there... I think of it, evolving, full of people I don't want to meet.'

'Love? Money?' I ask. 'A cube is not expressive of those things.'

'How'd you know?' asks Maurice. 'Not that I care. You think those "things" are crests, that you can surf. It isn't so. They cast you on the beach. Metals, though – they last you out. Even if – all wastes, corrodes. Nothing to be done.'

He grasps me by the shirt. 'There is another way to include it all. Happy and sad – a festival that gives you everything – heavy metal, nickel slot machines... And the beauty is – I shan't be there. The creator, ideator – absent. No one knowing what is mine, his – and what is yours, the *fabbro*.'

It's simple to design the house. I'd cast it in one piece – that's the hard part.

An immense foundry... You'd need a state to set it up that big: an appanage... a monarch, president, supreme leader, a caliphate, a Californiate. All the same. All executing, each a hanging on someone's word.

'Oh, Sonia and Jozo – if you could find them, they'd set you up a workshop somewhere,' Maurice says. 'Or that Kaja – she fixes everything. Have her fix you that.'

'It would stand out,' I say. 'Be evident.'

'You'd be surprised how much is. You want to hide the obvious. It isn't possible. You think a lot, but you're not thoughtful,' Maurice says.

'I see a sequence, Maurice; that is true. I don't study themes, like loyalty, remembering, regret. Besides, I see you passing through all that. There is a drama, then there's not.'

'I'm loyal,' says Maurice, 'but I don't hang around those guys. I remember everything, I don't put it into words. I don't regret – that's what everybody does. Once – it was fascists, that crew, who raved about the end of things. Now it's the scientists. I don't believe. I came through much worse than the end. I'd even run that Curtis for some office – he could represent our land! After all, the smallest tree's still part of the forest. And – I'll lay down copper sheets – I'll have the patina make the world green, for ever.' He tucks his gold and silver hand beneath my arm. 'You see,' he says. 'The metal house – it must be made in one. It's hard. People like Kaja will insist – it should be little bits all stuck together. No! That Greek was wrong – the half is never greater than the whole. It's like Jozo, Sonia: crime and punishment – they can't be divided. Seek one, you find the other. And crime is never done by halves, and punishment is always total. Have them remember that. Do you think it would have satisfied – to own some bits of copper? Or of tin?'

'Petar backed off,' I say. 'He had the thought. He couldn't do the deed.'

'That's why I had to bludgeon him,' says Maurice, comforting. 'You can't believe in things in bits. You do, or else you don't. You can't protect the bull! You have to throw it down and out, or else I'll do it for you. Cornering the market, living eternally – there are no halves! As for Curtis – he's the maker's mark. I made him. He's part of my design.'

He looks hard at me. Maybe he tries to find a grin on me. 'Remember too,' he says. 'What happens to Petar happens to everyone who isn't serious about their destiny. The sage – remember – said, "If you should raise a laugh – maybe there's a character you've inked hurriedly and made ambiguous... Perhaps your call for victory ends in farts. Well – the ignorant will laugh ... and that's the end of them. It's the curse of double vision. If nothing's as it seems, as it's intended – everything is ... just bull!" And that's what Petar said – "Your bull's all bull." He hadn't found the clarity. Every meaning could be doubled. So – that did for him.'

Petar's levity – floated him away, into the sky we see as blue that's really black, the void that's really full of massive stuff, the death for him eternal but for us a penstroke on a moving scroll of infinite length. Petar, left without his walls.

*

Kaja's exhausted. She's jelly-rolled till dawn. After all, she doesn't say the metal house should be cast in bits. 'So!' she says. 'It's metalwork for you. And this guy Curtis – a candidate! Someone thrusts him up the slope, to see him go careening down. They all do that – down comes after up. There is no upward, on for ever; not even for a lifetime.'

'The house must be one piece, then?' I ask. 'I'm not sure I want to build for him, Kaja.'

'He'll never live in it,' she says. 'It's like the copper – he won't shape it. He'll just lay down swards. And he's right – the bull is not a symbol, nor a double sense – it's the original. There's no reality that it's subordinated to, a copy of. That's why it's on a plinth.'

'You're no doubt right,' I say, 'but you are losing me. And – I've no money: that's why I came to you.'

'Ask Maurice,' Kaja says.

'He never did that job for me,' I say. 'And – he's right. I have the world. No country, and no faith, just guys with clubs from here and there, round about me ... if they spare me, it's that I don't count. If they hit me – I can't tell you why they do.'

'Oh my!' laughs Kaja. 'Everything is tarnished, even you! The left, the right, this faith and that, and Maurice sucks the money in, and you – you have your shining house to build, a ruin on a ruined plain before you start...'

'Just a string of cash, Kaja,' I wheedle.

'Don't whine,' she says. 'I'm not Nina. And I told you – it's not war that is the problem – it's fighting. In the army, you're quite safe. The peril's living next door to someone. That's to be avoided. When the money's gone – it's frustration, you, they, go molten: hating those familiar faces, their chants and their routines ... their rancid thoughts.

Although—' and she maybe has epiphany '—a metal house! That could be the answer. Without a door and windows. No chimneys – you use gas. And a safe room... Yes, Maurice has the best ideas.'

'He never did that simple job for me,' I say.

'That is his genius,' she says. 'Absence. An armoured house that you don't live in. Proof against bombs and neighbours ... those peoples of the book, the manifesto. Enlightened and less so.'

'Come on, Kaja,' I say, 'don't be reductionist.'

She's tired.

We seek fulfilment – the traditional way. Just as our forefathers did. Sex: an interlude.

I – we – find happiness. It is an idyll, it's a happy end. It's the compromise that's absolute, and joins the cat back on the grin.

'Well,' says Kaja, 'sex. Now that's done. Back to life mundane. You have a massive task, you must perform it, or duck.'

'A few coppers, then,' I say. 'Tin.'

'You want cash for sex?' she asks. 'For that? And your past adventures? Who you think I am? Or you are? – Doctor Zhivago?'

'I'm following the trail. The tradition. Life's oiled along by proximities. The brush of lips and hips. Otherwise it would jam,' I say.

'Don't think of that,' she says. 'Watch what your neighbours read, I told you. Go through their trash, and buy a gun.'

'Their traditions. No books – it'll all be hidden on their screens,' I say. 'The sons, the punks – they'll go back to origins. Purification, the dirty dogs! Thinking they're in charge. Guys like Maurice, looking for some fun and glory –

they'll cheer them on. Then – smashed, dispossessed.' It reminds her, with my claw I smashed her screen.

'On the road!' she shouts. 'Off with you!

6

The house: I sell the design. They pay me with a note, a percentage of some other thing. I'm free, at least, not to construct. I'm like Maurice, we're a success.

The road. Far away, there must be toilers. Here, there's pipes – containers full of stuff you need. Guys like me, who're waiting to be fitted in. As I'm like them, I don't need to sympathise, or fight their fight. Maurice left – he said, 'That bull – it resembled nothing much. That saves it from destruction, maybe it'll be admired – the metal shines, then it acquires its patina. A change of seasons.' Then – 'We've lost a lot, you know,' and waited for me to ask. He said, 'It's character.'

'Is that it? All?' I asked.

'We're not interesting, like we were,' he said. 'We're waiting for catastrophe, or a change of flag. The guys you know – they come, they go...'

'Curtis,' I asked. 'You pushed him to the top.'

'Not yet,' said Maurice. 'He came in last. He had no character. He couldn't spend the cash I gave. The young guys now – the kids – they have character all right. They're incomprehensible. I don't mix with them, although I'm young myself.'

I said, 'Try being younger, Maurice.'

'You never did that job for me,' he said. 'The house.'

I said, 'That bull was too full of nature. Maybe it didn't look too much like, but it was unmistakable. The cube, instead – it's a place where anything, all kinds of things, can happen that I don't want. Nor do you.'

'Of course not,' he said. 'I don't want to live there, nor work there. It protects you, though.'

'It's a target,' I said. 'It attracts what you don't want.'

'Jozo made a mistake,' said Maurice. 'They make a fortune, he gambles it away. They must make another. Sonia's frantic – this wasn't at all the punishment she was waiting for.'

'Maybe Jozo feels it is *his* punishment,' I said. 'And quite enjoyable.'

'Oh no,' said Maurice. 'Jozo doesn't enjoy. Not anything. Gambling makes you impotent. It's the probability, and the waiting till next time. Power – it's what I have. If I pull the copper out – no trains or planes. No current. Let there be no light. Full stop.'

'Come, Maurice,' I said. 'I know all about reality. A destiny must be real. I'm not alone in thinking that.'

'It's worth a try,' he said. 'I've no particular end. I don't know what occurs, without the copper. All stops completely. Or it just ploughs on. I've no stake.'

'Will it be better if it stops?' I asked.

'I can't think what you mean,' he said. 'It's like that Frenchman wrote: 'What've you got to lose. Think big, believe. If it makes no odds – you had the flutter.' There's guys all over – starting armies, executing, punishing the executioners, keeping guys quiet, paying them to talk. Just remove the copper. That's all I'm doing. It's a new theme. It's not like turning off the water.'

'It makes everything flow,' I said, 'so it's quite the same.'

'You think sloppy,' Maurice said. 'You do a big thing, then you see. Arguing from analogy – that's for youths.'

'It's a cartoon trick,' I said. 'It's like those old comic books, the movies before there was science you could play with. Some superhero in a lycra suit'll stop you.'

'So be it, then,' he said, quite satisfied. 'That way we'll see.'

After all, he bought up all the copper, past and future. That should buy a spinning of the wheel.

'Are those your guys, that steal the stuff?' I asked.

'Oh no,' he said. 'They use it as a currency. What you think? They wind it up again on coils by lamplight in their shacks?'

'Your income will crash,' I said.

'If it does, my value will rise enormously,' he said. 'Besides – how much d'you think it costs to keep me? Less than a shaving from a toe, a whitlow from a golden thumb.'

'It's like Jozo and Sonia,' I said. 'Looking for an easy trip, then nemesis in the grit.'

'Oh no,' he said. 'Those two are criminals. They're up against the rules, they want to beat the probabilities, and their own frivolity. Sonia likes sex, not tungsten. Jozo likes winning. And that's it. I – I don't like anything so much. I'm curious, is all.'

*

When Kaja's told, she says – 'How's he going to collect the metal?'

'I've no idea,' I say. 'He's far above me now. First, he didn't do a job for me. Then, I didn't do one for him. But first I was above him, then it was reversed. I don't know how he operates.'

'Is it sex?' asks Kaja. 'It often seems to be, or prison. That's what shapes the character. Me, I only know about the people I have sex with, all the rest are quite unknown.'

'You don't know much about me,' I say, defensive, but not interested.

'You've not fitted in,' she says. 'When you do, the design will be quite clear.'

Kaja whirls you: she says, 'Your Turks – they haven't come. Anyway, they're too neat and clean. I like to pig it, myself. Then – your bull – it's not quite an image. It's in between something and nothing. I don't see how there's room for it. It's no challenge to divinity.'

She's full of life, of verve, it spills out, so you know it must be finite. 'Die before you die,' they say. We've all seen it, how it's done, death – in movies, conferences, on the street. Seeing pushes it away, it's no nearer. You want more and more not to have it happen. Every day, the map is fuller of it – you don't have to look, and the toilers – they're still there, still toiling, like the good guys, the bad ones, the patriots, the rest.

*

'Where's the house?' Sonia asks. 'It needs to have a secret room. That might revive my interest in Jozo – though I know it's not that sexy kind of room, nor where you have that sexy kind of punishment.'

'I don't know about all that,' I say. 'The safe room was for hiding in. Not orgies *à deux*.'

'Oh, this is so faded,' Kaja says. 'Exposing and deflowering. It smells of Petar and the fishy glue you use to keep old books together. Why, look out, over the fields. Everyone there is doing things to everyone...'

'There are no fields, Kaja,' I say. 'There's only plains and suburbs. Fighting and hiding – that's what's left to us – all the rest is fantasy, inventing characters. Having sex and making riots – there's no traction in all that now.'

'If I understand,' says Sonia, 'you didn't make the house – not of white metal, nor of osiers.'

'Do your crime out in the street,' I say. 'And be anonymous.'

'Oh, you don't understand,' says Jozo. 'Crime ought to be a gas. Instead – it's paying off a chain of guys, and meeting punks and paying for their drinks. And quarrelling ... percentages and times and tickets.'

'Yes,' Sonia says. 'Punishment will be relief – except the intricate things we do is scarcely crime. It's just committee work, and Jozo gambles it away – the profit. You have to deal with inefficient guys...' And she sighs.

'It all sounds tame to me,' says Kaja. 'Not paying tax, shipping dust...'

'Oh,' says Sonia, laughing. 'It's not all routine. You know ... these things attract the gangs, the severed heads, crisis of institutions, buff envelopes and slavery.'

'And we don't even own the mines,' says Jozo.

Jozo's filling out. I notice he wears lifts – Sonia's a tall girl. It seems Jozo has position – he doesn't touch the failing guys – other guys are hired for that.

He asks me – and I turn away from Kaja, though I share her room, if not her secrets – 'How'd you get your cash?'

'I go to Kaja's bag. Sometimes I steal,' I say.

'That loses you respect,' says Jozo.

'Oh no,' I say, 'it's Kaja. She doesn't respect religion. Nor being lay, profane. And the cash: is money for the work you've done – reward? Or paid for what's to come – a blackmail? Respect's not part of it.'

'Then the stealing isn't stealing. It's work,' says Jozo.

'I've not done any work for her,' I say. 'It's all a penance anyway, and how you see it.'

You should look more deep,' says Jozo, sternly. 'If I pay before you work, and the rest when it's done – none of that's for past work. You're paid for your next job. It's a classic deal: the pay's to keep you working for me. The past: if you don't do the job, you don't get paid, instead, you're punished. It's simple, but it's the theory that matters.'

'We punish each other,' Sonia says. It's an easy say.

Then, the lights go out.

'It's Maurice,' Kaja says. 'We should complain, although we know the reasons.'

'Who'd you call?' asks Jozo. 'You can't use the telephone – not to call the cops. That's why the English call them coppers – they're at the end of someone's wire. Americans – they didn't see the joke.'

'The wire's like the one they put in your head, Jozo,' Kaja shouts, looking for money in her bag. 'You're a stereotype. Trying to beat the market like the rest. Besides – who'd call the cops because the lights go out? They'd go out in your safe room too, you creep.'

'Nothing safe's been built,' I say.

Does Kaja fit anyone in – or do they do it all themselves?

'Fitting?' Sonia shouts. 'If it all fits, there's no crime, and punishment's irrelevant.'

'No one gave you smugglers a ticket to ride anywhere,' Kaja says. 'When the lights come back, we'll hand you in.'

'We'll be gone by then,' says Jozo, shuffling a deck of cards. 'Five card stud. In the dark, maybe you can hear the pips squeak. Put your cash and watches on the table.'

'That's fine,' says Kaja. 'We can't see the table.' She must be used to showdowns with invisible cards.

The lights flick on and off. 'Maybe we didn't pay some other country,' Sonia says.

Jozo says, 'He can't take all the wires at once – even if he owns them all. And then there's all the other stuff – the copperheels and copperheads, that I don't know what they signify. If you don't recognise an animal, you remove its name – is it then extinct?'

'I don't know how we'd take our tungsten out those
girders, those machines, although,' says Sonia. 'It's great
publicity. All those buildings falling down. And battlefields –
the guys without our steel – they'd need to do it with bare
hands.'

'We trade enough to bring the prices down,' says Jozo
wisely. 'We're at the cheap end. Maurice, though – he has it
all – even the frying pans, bed warmers too.'

The lights all round are out. The cars are dark – maybe
they've stopped. We soon grow used to it.

'I know all about you,' Kaja says, waving at them, Sonia,
Jozo, as if it would make them disappear, like the lights. 'I
buttress it all up, because the people want me to, to make
them happy. London with its grit and dust, Rome sprawled out
ragged – I make them all go on. But once you've understood –
you want to go a little further.'

'It wouldn't all go on if we were exceptional,' I say. 'As it
is, you replace the heads on sticks with other heads – from a
distance, they look just the same. More realistic, maybe.'

'I can't think what you mean,' says Kaja. 'I'm not talking
about change and going on – I'm talking about *my* change. In
my bag.'

'I've no problems with you, Kaja, nor Sonia. If anything
sounds portentous, it's that I haven't figured out how to build
it, cast it, yet,' I say.

'Of course it matters what you do,' says Sonia. 'So long
as you're an artisan, and make us see it, and be proud.
Something for a sanctuary, a *takht*, a plinth.'

'Do you have some of that?' asks Kaja. 'The pride?'
making clear she's lots herself.

'No,' says Sonia.

'Here we are,' says Jozo, 'sorting out the world. Can we?'

'Why not?' asks Kaja. 'Who knows the others who think they can? We know what we want. We're equal to them any time.'

'Cut the hunting and fishing,' I say. 'I'll be a critical critic and make iron palaces.'

'Those get too hot,' says Sonia. 'But for sure, on principle, we don't want neighbours cutting our throats.'

'Maurice is a problem, if he's cornered all the copper,' Jozo says. 'But control – he'll find it's a bore. What'll you do with it? It's like Genghiz Khan – you simplify the admin – but there's your sons, wanting a piece of everything.'

'Oh yes,' says Kaja. 'That's the old road – the fable. Everything ending like it used to be, and you doing worse than the best. That's not me. I listen to no moral tales, no Aesop, no foxes and no crows.'

'Are we representative?' I ask. 'And clean enough, of the species?'

'They bombed my city,' Jozo says. 'That puts me in the clear.'

'I wear gloves,' says Kaja. 'Touching people makes me itch.'

'Maurice is a benefactor now,' I say. 'And for sure he's forgotten the unpleasant stuff – all give and take and self-defence.'

'When you get to a certain rank,' says Sonia, 'you have to do a deal. You're public – friend or enemy. It's like it happens everywhere – you hire some guys to do what you shouldn't do.'

'I've not done anything at all,' I say. 'I am the future. All promise.' We all laugh.

It's dawn again. We don't need copper now. We eat from cans – no copper, and no steel.

'Maurice is a kind of terrorist,' says Kaja, offering a theme.

'Oh no,' says Jozo. 'He's a Tory. All that empire stuff. That old-fashioned army talk – it makes you jump all right. The message is what granddad said – "Do as your granddad did." Down on your knees!'

'It's indiscriminate,' says Sonia. 'And there's no message in the indiscriminate.'

'It's wires,' I say. 'Don't interpret him so much. It's to control the power.'

'He's a benefactor,' Kaja says. 'He wants to show us in advance, what it's like when the lights go out.'

'He'll push up the copper price,' says Jozo.

'I could build the metal house,' I say. 'But I sold the rights.' No one is listening.

'We should be exempt from Maurice's outages,' Kaja says. 'After all, we are his friends. And we know all about the end of things – the wires, the light. Energy. The metals that keep it all connected. The earth.'

'Oh,' says Sonia, 'it's all a legend. I'm sure it's not Maurice. You can't remove what you've bought just because it's yours.'

'It isn't that,' says Jozo, quite angry. 'It's just the metal. Maurice isn't representative. These power stations – they're always going down. It's to do with grids.'

'I should be exempt,' I say. 'He missed a job of mine. He owes me.'

'It's true,' says Kaja. 'That ending is a relief, of sorts. The quest is better, so they say. It's healthier, species-wise – to travel, on your boat, on the wind. Back to your *pute*,' and she laughs. 'It's the hope of finding, not the losing, that gives the kick.'

What an idiot! How banal she is – her face is symmetrical. A prerequisite for being beautiful, but it doesn't work with her, though it may be how she got her job. She's ordinary. Should we waste time, describing faces, gestures, landscapes, when we've seen – not all, not everything, but enough to have a stock of types. What does it add, sticking the birds on trees, the pampas stands with their blonde wigs ... a zest? a tang?

Kata's still inside her bag: she shouts at me, 'You little fucker! you stole from me.'

Here, that doesn't make a stir. 'Without the lights, of course, there is no quest,' says Sonia. 'We can't see what we're looking for.'

'Cretin!' says Jozo – there's the daylight still. As for the meaning – it's the end of certain things – in this case, the illumination. And – will we find the something new?'

Jozo has one red eye, a little drooped. 'A Croat hit me with a branch,' he says. It hasn't spoiled him much, maybe the red warns people off, the Croats too. 'Of course,' he says, 'Maurice was in the same war, but in another sector. That makes it another war.'

'Cutting off the light – is that a wrong thing?' Sonia asks. 'Or is it a way to show us what comes next? A trailer. Crime is the punishment, always has been, and today we say the punishment's the crime...'

'You needn't keep on saying it,' says Jozo. 'Of course we're one and indivisible, Sonia. Or our story, anyway – like Layla and Majnun, though Majnun has the better part – the wilderness, the animals. And Layla visiting. Not staying on.'

He and Sonia whisper together. Does he hit her? Or she him? Kaja says to me, 'It's a terrible business, this Maurice.'

'Oh,' I say, 'the way the bull ended up, on high, being an object, of a cult. That was quite terrible.' Instead? Or also?

'Shall I take my sweater off?' she asks. 'That pleases you.'

'Well,' I say, 'only if you've nothing on beneath. I'm not interested in the underwear.'

It's a strange thing she asks, in the middle of a copper crisis. Many people are only interested in the underwear, knowing they'll never reach the naked symmetry. I can.

*

'Your life's a string quartet,' says Kaja. 'When it's over, you remember how it's moved – the good begins, then comes the jokey part, the uncertain maundering – inconclusive – till at the end, the memory, the tension – waiting for oblivion, the resolution – some hint of meaning. You'd remember it, that design, if it ever came back again, and you were part of it.'

'I don't need that,' I say. 'You're cheap stuff, Kaja, scoops of sugar, sentiment that rots. Think – the bull! Without copper – there is no more brass. My bull – unique from the beginning – now has beauty, cash value too, shining out, as if there was a light that came when you were polishing...'

'Right, my friend,' says Kaja, 'we'll take a break, and steal the bull. Compensation for what you've took from me. No one appreciated it when it was a lump – too bad for them.'

In string quartets, there is no brass, no copper, no metal – the strings can be sheep gut. Kaja's poetic sentiment, though ... unbearable.

*

Maurice says – 'The lights are always going out. Use candles, early to bed. I'm not responsible for anything.'

His friends are coming – seeking a refuge, tossed by sea, in rubber boats, like they were sailing back from Troy. The cops are greeting them – that's all too bad. 'No friends of mine,' says Maurice, 'Nothing to be done.'

*

Sonia turns on me – 'For us, withdrawing all the steel – it's harder than for Maurice. He owns the copper, all of it – and us – we only have the vital part, the core. And you, vestigial limb! – you pretend to drive the story. The choice is ours. Just think – if we stole rice! The toilers desperate.' She sneers, 'You're nothing: we decide.'

'Oh no,' I say. 'The orders come from me. I don't need travail about my powers – they're there. The heat, the energy, the house, concealing you and Jozo...'

'That's an illusion,' Jozo says. 'The energy's from us. You have no heat, there is no house. Petar, your friend – a mummy in his empty room. The bull – quite unappreciated...'

'It goes that way, Jozo,' I say. 'It doesn't change a thing.'

7

Here's the building where we parked the bull. My – how fine the structure is – a buff colour, no windows, could be marzipan, or from the Niebelungen set... Could be a cube, though in the dark ... all shapes, or none.

'There could be peasants here,' says Kaja, worried, 'Dancing in the dark, worshipping and boozing. I can stand it, when they're in the fields and doubled up. But the animals! Auschwitz! The livestock was the model: the cows and pigs are full of love. Unrequited. Off they go! Not a name, not one, to be remembered by. Farming. It's the key to every awfulness. Metals, now – you give them form, they last a while, don't bleat or grunt. Fire. Makes a man of you, a woman too. We come from it, and there we end.'

'They'll be like us,' I say. 'The guys carousing there.'

'Oh no!' she shouts. 'Like us? Like our lost twins, singing songs that we forgot? Tweed pants and sackcloth hats. Prostrate before your bull. The light turned into rite. Eyes set deep – lumps of chalcedony.'

'Nothing grew, where Maurice lived,' I say. 'That, you'd have liked.'

'Yes,' she says. 'He's a good man. The catastrophes – they're natural. He's innocent.'

'The guys that brought the peace,' I say. 'Maurice, his buddies – they ran sex rings, sold dope, and settled scores...'

'Oh, you're obsessed,' says Kaja, laughing. 'You think things can run out, or be withdrawn. There's always substitutes. Wormburgers, ersatz heat, babies grown from spawn. Watch more TV! Everybody wants to rule the world and lounge about. It doesn't happen, or not much. Here – I'll show you – a new game!'

She runs up the building, a merry gecko, I hear her feet go 'plop' and 'smack' – I'm on her back. I could have gone in for graphics: this is a cult scene, for sure – who'd be in my movie? Maurice for sure. A hero of our time. He soldiered, and he stayed. He was supposed to bring the peace. A victory at least. 'Why did he stay?' I ask.

'Oh, he was in love, I guess, or on a charge,' says Kaja. 'He had his craft. It's something you don't question – not like guys question deities – are they there, what do they think, what can they give? Or concepts – those are worse... What do they mean, to me, to someone else... On every dime – equality, my brothers, freedom too. Your bull – meant for dumb worship? Or do you polish it?

And – wow! – this must be Köln cathedral – 'no, how could it be?' she shouts. We're on a spire, it seems, she hugs me, spreads a flying carpet – and she shouts – 'Don't think of sex! It isn't that. Kick, kick – these spires are conical, we mustn't hit...' And off we leap.

We go down – the cloud she's brought supports us – I'm the monkey on her back. We go down slow – inside the marzipan there's roistering...

'We don't have a relationship,' I say: and, 'My! how the ground's banal!' Green, grey, some daring person sports a toque: a car, red.

'It's the best relationship I've had,' says Kaja, paying out some cords. 'I picked you out. If this was a cathedral – we could have been two goths. It's ours – at least the outside. I bet you thought you'd die, going up or coming down,' she laughs.

'Oh no,' I say. 'I've seen the scene on film. It must go on, on to the next.'

'There's no door, no window. Maybe the bull's inside,' she says. 'We had to scale the block – no stair, so from the top – we glide. It's all encompassed. Those peasants roistering – can't let them out, or speculate on how they got inside.'

'Up and down, Kaja,' I say. 'That's the sport? Everything small, down there, then a crap in your pants and it's real life and pinned by gravity?'

'Well,' she says, 'if you want the horizontal, you must put some effort in. The guys inside the marzipan – there's some big massacres and wars that resonate, that make so many different musics. Most get forgot. When you've had your history, when Maurice comes, hawkeye across the plains, the blackbirds busy with those open sockets – you're lucky to be left over. Nothing to be done. Best to roister than to seek revenge.'

'That bull,' I say. 'Don't place much upon it, Kaja. It doesn't stand for anything, it doesn't do, or sing, or wag its tail, or any goddam thing. If it is never found – it doesn't change a life. It was our whim, an idea that came to fruit. Like ours, that we can rule the world...'

'Oh, you poor thing!' says Kaja. 'It's our destiny to seek the missing beauties, uglies too. And – yes, we rule the world as well as anyone. In the past, guys have used other guys to do their will, inspiring them with tales of gold and rape, sending them letters with a time and place, the muster: "Kiss your beloved, fortune has smiled on you, new boots await. She'll screw her cousin and forget..." We're different. We have the resource. The light, the strength: the copper and the tungsten.'

'Come on, Kaja,' I say. 'Sentimental again! Here we are in Germany – think of the disaster here... Sixty million, they say, buried under those huge mounds. While they waited – they sang in the cathedrals, hugged under the gargoyles, dressed for the opera... *Capriccio, Intermezzo*... Then they were all hustled off, everything they'd ever known, packed in a parcel, the parcel thrown down, then them too... A number, a civilisation, unimaginable. What is our venture, Kaja? A threat? A warning?'

'Oh no,' she says, 'If it came about, much more. Doing things our way. Our will, our conviction. Now – no chicken squawks from you! Toughen up. Be an eagle. That was why – I bore you up – and we came safely down, to where they lie, those sixty million, expunged entirely, subject of song and speculation. Gone like mist.'

High or low, you're still in the same place. Even your eyes are the same.

'Besides,' says Kaja, 'there's no gargoyles here in Germany. You need to go to France for those. Here – all the people under the mounds – they left silence, of course – but there are recordings. It's all quite natural anyway. New people come, the language changes. There's groups shut up here and there in towers. We jump off them. It's bravado, inside and out. They roister, and for a while you have to let them – they can't get out! They've nowhere else to go. They have a peasant heaven too – some old tatty book with pictures, martyrs maybe, all copied from some lost original.'

We tell Sonia about our jump, that didn't get us anywhere. 'Americans?' she says. 'Oh, I'm sure it'll come to them. They cover up, but there's always guys who dig. They see a mound, and out they pop, the thin and bony ones, each ready with a tale.'

'And will they end up under the rubble, like they are here?' asks Kaja, though she must know Sonia has no idea.

'How the fuck should I know,' says Sonia. 'I'm a smuggler! It happens to most everyone, the docile and the loud alike. It's all quite natural.'

'It's all digging,' Jozo says. 'The copper mines, the tungsten. And everywhere – the stories. The only ones we have, and they go on, they're all we recognise. It's why you learn to read and sing. Epics, fables – dig up the fathers and the mothers, excavate the trailer parks, and then – open up the mounds built over. Looking for the thrones, the clay gods – and the bones. Looking for the massacred – always the past, always the responsibility for yesterday.'

'Oh, pickypick,' says Kaja. 'You're in the business. Stuck in the ground. I'm a bird, a survivor – I transform – from scales to feathers. Up up I go. Dance till I'm still and everything revolves around me.'

'Jozo,' shouts Sonia, 'don't play around. You dig! There's no third side. You dig or not. There's no alternative. If you don't dig, you die, and – Maurice will cut your power. No light. That isn't up to us.'

'It's shocking,' Kaja says, 'but nothing's our responsibility! We've had the shocks, it's all gone in, digested. It's just publicity, to show us awful things again. We've seen them all.'

'Yes,' says Sonia, 'and sure – they all repeat. Faster, and on a larger scale. Maurice says – they found a Chinese site, full of bronze stuff, so large and fine... We couldn't reproduce it. The knack – went to the knackers...'

'What happened then?' asks Jozo, who has heard it all. 'And human sacrifice in saucepans and retorts...?'

'Oh well,' says Sonia, 'naturally – they covered it all up. You can't admit, with all the boasting – that you've gone downhill. Down from the trees, into the foundries – one generation, and you learn the tricks. Empires and graves, your eating irons in bronze... What's come along since then – it's copying or doing worse. Faster, cruder – doing approximations, even on a larger scale – that isn't good enough. Nor is sparing your servants from the pot. Being nice – that is no remedy.'

'There's always characters like Nina,' Jozo laughs, who's never cuddled up to her, 'who make survival seem worth while. And guys like Curtis – so inoffensive, you'd not think that he could run a camp or tweak your intimacy, wheedling your vote...'

'Oh well,' says Sonia, 'I'd heard that Nina's doing politics, and Curtis has a studio with parchments by his head that let him into doing therapy.'

'And did they find a house,' I ask. 'A bronze house, a cube, an oblong?'

'They wouldn't dig it out,' says Jozo, 'if they were standing on the roof. You wouldn't know.'

'Suppose I did stuff as good as theirs,' I say, 'or better. That would tilt evolution, beauty, even goodness – quite the other way.'

They ignore me. I never did that job.

'Guys in the mines,' says Kaja, 'they'll be pleased, if Maurice blocks the stuff.'

'Yes,' Jozo says, 'the price will go right up. Their pay will zero down.'

Kaja hadn't thought of that: she says, 'Yes, but I could fit them somewhere else. Zinc, tin, nickel, even.'

'Those guys,' I say, 'the Chinese guys. They'd nothing to copy from.'

'Everybody does,' says Sonia. 'Everything is always there.'

'Anyway,' I say, 'Maurice is safe. He knows I can't do it – neither imitate, nor invent. It's a huge job, and I don't have the skills.'

'You have to learn,' says Jozo. 'I know! It's not easy! Maurice isn't that safe – keep him dangling.'

'He told me,' Sonia says. 'You commit atrocities when you feel safe. I never feel like that.'

'It's not about atrocities,' Kaja says.

'The figures in the bronzes – deities, kings – what strikes, is their cosmological eyes,' I say. 'They stick out, from looking at the sun, the sun – the one of many in the sky – that counts.'

'It's true,' says Sonia. 'We lost sight of that.' Maybe she's joking – I'd not thought she had the sense ... but being into trade, I guess she needs intelligence.

'I know,' says Kaja. 'Every group of friends thinks they can rule the world. It makes you feel a tenderness towards them.'

'Ah well,' says Jozo. 'Is it friends we are?' He has an edge, Jozo. Owning a resource – you have to grow some intelligence. All these guys, who've been near a war – they've been barons, or they know how barons work. Maybe they've been guard-dogs – but for sure, owning a resource is nothing to them. It's hard work... It is ever so – remember, "the war of steel and gold". Without us, you don't fight – except ... sometimes it's philosophers. One at a time, beneath the figtree, that's just fine. But – a platoon, marching up the street, or in their helis – no!

'Maurice doesn't care – if we can't repeat those bronzes – have we merely forgotten how? Is it decline, or gyring ... no, he doesn't give a fig for eyes protruding, staring at the sun ... he wants to dig more deeply...' Jozo says, 'Make something entirely new... A house, without an exit, or an entry, where you're safe, and there is booze and music going on for ever. I don't want to end in there.'

'Don't be a scaredy-cat, Jozo,' says Sonia. 'We all end up in something like. You know – we're trash. If guys get wasted over there hustling our stuff – they're trash, and we're everybody's benefactors. But over here, we're trash if we don't pay our bills, don't have the stuff keep coming in. You're trash, Jozo – and it was ever so, there's monuments to you and me in every park, just covered up with boughs and flowers, just waiting till we're dead. Then – you wait. The judgement's always mixed. It's always best to wait and see.'

'It's not enough!' shouts Kaja. 'I know how to handle guys like you, Sonia and Jozo. But it's not just finding bad guys. We need a villain. Those point up the sequence, the plot. Otherwise it's war and peace – not the libretto that we started with!'

I think – God save us from philosophers, as philosophers saved us from God – and ... oh no, here they come again, in linkstep.

Here, we're in jail, and you're free to do anything at all you like. Except leave. But you can scream –

'Go ahead,' says Jozo, 'we've heard it all, at every pitch. The world's your Met.'

'Kaja,' I say, 'we could travel. We've been everywhere, it's all different, but I'm always the same.'

'And all my clients are like you,' she says. 'Only the remedy is the same, just like the people. And it's not being nice.'

'Metalwork,' I say.

'That's right,' she says. 'No grief, no cry. No woman – but, buy a pill off me. I have them here, somewhere ... in my bag.' And there she goes again, digging.

We could fly together. See the world. Seek promotion. Read books, write books about the books we read. Children come – we know things children can learn to do, and learn our songs, and bury us.

'Jozo,' I say. 'Is there some job you need a guy to do – maybe not in Colombia, not on the circuit that includes the punishment. Filing, maybe, well paid?'

'Ah yes,' he says. 'Filing those white metal lugs, when you have broke the moulds. It's a job for kids. Petar would laugh – but he had style.'

'Oh, I have style,' I say. 'I dealt with Maurice – then he took off, became invisible.'

'Well,' says Jozo, easing off a running shoe – the foot is blue with leaking veins, 'there's Serbia. Ukraine. They make the arms. You kind of speak the tongues. It's easier than filing. You don't write it down.'

'Oh yes,' I say. 'I'm understood. What do I say there? – that you supply, or don't? They're all strong guys in weak places. Unsafe.'

'All business is just that,' he says. 'You supply, or not. You "take stuff off the market". Like you run a stall. You explain – in every circumstance, it's difficult. It isn't up to you. You'd love to have their cash.'

Sonia laughs. 'He's not cut out. He should just age himself, like wine, and think of elegies. Of love, of longing and of loss. Like those old French guys do, and write it down.'

'Oh no,' I say, 'I've known those guys – die of old age. Or Petar. The wrong pickup, the wrong shopping trip... Left like a stockfish on the floor, dripping red.'

Jozo can't work it out – if I'm remembering Petar's end, or if mine's an elegy, in general... He says, 'Wolfram. Those Eastern guys ... the word is in their fables. Further East – it's stronger still. Don't use the word. Just talk of steel, and how it's going out of use. They'll think of houses falling down, of pipes that curl like entrails. Whet their appetites... Have them think, "what if you don't buy, if at least don't order... What will happen then?"'

Sonia says, 'The house, instead. Find people that'll do it for you.'

'No,' I say, 'I wasn't educated to take on hands.'

'Well, we won't sub you anyway,' says Jozo. 'It was for us, the house – but I guess we'll do our penance kneeling on the grit.' He's bubbling out. His feet are full of blood, of grease in runoff, the hair creeps back, the skull rises to a point, eyes bulge like cabuchons. Success has eaten out his body. Sonia, instead, has grown her *nichons* – once, delicate courgettes, then albino aubergines, now great *cocomeri* ribbed and stippled. To each their taste. Further towards dear Nina, and her generous hearth. Except – Sonia cracks her tongue, whiplike. Her forehead has a black downline, slashed on for the stage. She's grown a repertoire of jerks and tics ... she's punished by the slur of time, then she'll hand some out, some pain...

'You guys,' I say. 'This work has ground you down.'

'You're older and older,' Kaja says, waving towards me. The others nod: 'I've given him my love, all that. It does no good – hastens the decline.'

'Of course,' says Sonia. 'The windowless house – that's what he should make. But off he'll go and work for us. In the long term, the house would be more useful.'

'No, no,' says Jozo. 'We must reflect. We need to see the enterprise as one. 'Let there be light' they said. Now Maurice says – 'let there be dark'. You can't just plough ahead, switching on, over and over, more and more. There's hot and cold. So – let there be light and dark. A pact of steel and copper – Jozo and Maurice.'

'This making stuff,' says Kaja, 'It's all a dirty business, hawking it around, and talking to dull guys. Money and power – I guess that turns you on, and fretting when you lose. This innocent,' and she waves at me again. 'He isn't made for that...'

'Oh no!' laughs Sonia, 'No! He's not, and nor are we. This rolling out the sheets of it, the dust that eats you from within, those chunky branch-like lengths – there's others that get off on that. Much satisfaction may it give – to them, and all the guys that toil for them. We're on a different angle, a more polished slant.'

My job has disappeared before I could decide it was beneath me.

'You guys,' says Jozo, tugging at me. 'You start as benefactors, helping people for a buck or two. We're into something else, as we come to our maturity.'

'Purity,' says Sonia, as if she's rhyming out a chant: 'This metal stuff – it's cumbersome and slow. We're into finance now – promoting good and bad indifferently, and let the shavings fall. Maurice is into purest power – we're into money – together...'

'That's not it at all,' says Jozo, irritated. 'With power or money, even both – you don't need run, or fear. Or want the safe house this guy here ... can't build.'

'So,' I say. 'You think it's you – the outages, the buildings that collapse...?'

'There's a first cause, of course,' says Kaja. 'We learned that at school.'

'Stop staring at my abundance,' Sonia says to me. 'I've had my fun. You never took yours out of its box.'

8

Selling is easy. 'Cheaper than anything, and better too.' That's what you have to say. I don't feel like doing it... discoursing with those guys who think they're clever... I go back to where I met with Maurice. A makeshift bed... Sleep in the stable, over the animals – they central heat you.

There's no light here to go out. In the dark, though – I can tell sheep from the goats. I don't know why there's ever been a problem.

Kaja's an office person, they sleep in chairs, on stools, no need for sleeping rough. All the people I knew here have gone – some becoming rich, some dead.

That house – it's not a metaphor – it's an old joke. You make the most enormous thing that's nearly possible – then you can't get in or out.

...They say nice things about shepherds, though most are not especially nice. Bored, certainly; and a metaphor.

Someone gives me a plate of sheep's ganglia, a grey web, sheepish thoughts stuck along the threads like flies. There's no fooling food. It's real, and it's embued with realism – painted on, enflavoured, sight and sound – must be absolutely realist to the eye, the tongue, so's to pass muster with the gut ... and yet – it was artists, they invented realism, then passed on to something else. Realism was *'oh, so vieux chapeau'*. Yet – your food is stuck forever in that style.

Nina stays on: 'There!' she says. 'You've quite recovered. Ready for the next adventure.'

'Oh no,' I say. 'I wasn't in your war...'

'Oh well,' she says, 'you can't have too much therapy.'

'The workshops?' I ask.

'No, it's modern food now,' she says. 'You get a plate of stuff, like the *plat républicain*. Then if you want a drink, you go next door. They kept the pipes and rads – it's history.'

There's guys in pie-crust hats and aprons, in a row. A storefront says – 'here cheese', another, 'chicken bits'.

'Curtis has an office now,' says Nina. 'It's no good for sex.'

'I'm selling metals, Nina,' I say. 'But they're coming to an end. The light, the structures...'

'You were never into those,' she says, pulling me against her cardigan. 'Terra cotta and prayer. That's what lasts.' I say,

'Maurice and Jozo – they want to withdraw their metals, leave Sonia drawing morals.'

'The simple life,' says Nina, drawing me into her warm wool.

'No,' I say, 'They want it much more complicated. So do I,' I say. 'Besides, that's how it is.'

'People want it better for their kids. Maybe they feel hugger-mugger with the planet,' Nina says.

'Not me!' I say. 'Most males eat their rivals, those cutey cubs. As for planets – there are millions – subzero or incandescent, most of them.'

'Well, then,' says Nina, more interested in a cuddle than cosmology. 'It's not about the innocents again? If there weren't innocents to take the fall – the guilty ones would always suffer: what would be the point? The guilty ones would turn to being innocents, I guess. You'd need to tweak the moral code a bit – it's often done.'

I can't go into this. I say, 'I hear there's squads around, seeking reprisals. And little armies, waiting for the postcard, for the muster... It's why Maurice went invisible...'

'Oh yes,' she says. 'It's all as it should be. It's wise to change your skin. And you – you should be going East and selling steel. Avoid the refugees – vengeance will come, so slow...'

Each animal has its own noise. The sheep – they wait for Easter; the goats – for Eid. The cycle wheels... I think of Maurice, and his buried bones. Maybe we should have made the brass bull on an industrial scale. Stamped, like the Athenian owl. A currency! A virtual trade! I'd have a herd of virtual bulls, maybe a cow for company.

'No, no!' says Nina, shaking me off. 'No sleep! This is a rocky place. There's no peace here. The guys with the electrum attributes – they're all sought out, for melting down, being recast...'

'But – Nina,' I say, 'I never went into the melting pot...'

'Enough that you were there,' she says, 'and made a note of every one...'

*

'I can't stay with you here, Nina,' I say. 'All you have is poor eats.'

'You chum with the powerful,' Nina says, pushing me down the ladder. 'You know all about them. You can buy or sell. The greatest things go on about you – like flies: you wag your head. This indifference – yes, it's a strategy. Your friends – they may rule the world, they won't rule you. And yet, and yes – there's nothing for you here.'

'It's all inside me,' I say. 'It's like the universe – you trek around and pick up dust ... the history is there, right from the start. Inside, we're male and female, live and dying, master and slave.'

'Yes, yes,' she says, impatiently. 'If you go East – they say the devil lives in the Ukraine. Give Him my wishes. He's always welcome – as a guest.'

'Oh Nina,' I say, 'I've supped with devils bigger and more wild. I don't believe that stuff. You must take responsibility yourself, not stick it on some buzzing glob with legs...'

'He puts on uniform...' says Nina, vague, and anxious to be rid of me. 'He's all legs, an infinity of legs... If Maurice pulls the copper out of everything – that bull of yours ... will just be zinc.'

'Oh no,' I say, 'the bull's in a protected place. It'll be worth a fortune, that's for sure. It's all our pensions, and our hidey-hole, our wooden horse ... we'll hunker up in there like acorns – then burst forth, armed cap-à-pié, and all in bronze...'

'You can laugh,' says Nina, scuttling away. 'Laughter is what you do when you don't know, don't understand...'

'You're cowardly,' I say. 'Think politics, instead. Think of the forces, the revenge, those who were driven out, now back with knouts – vendettas against who knows who, neighbours confined, their rivers dammed...' She nods.

'Come on, Nina,' I say. 'What's the meaning of it all. I mean – the meaning of the meaning. Not the consolation, the religious stuff. When those guys came and shot those guys, and then it was normal again, with experts and little feuds...'

'It means what it says,' says Nina. 'Don't be greedy. Sometimes the sound is nice, like singing from the bushes.'

'I insist,' I say. 'Being nice – that doesn't seem to be the remedy. It's an illusion. You need lots of other behaviours – and if you're sitting on a rift ... it doesn't matter what you do ... gravity, magma ... inevitable.'

'Why fret?' asks Nina. 'You're well sorted out. Kaja has a bag of cash. No man is your brother. You don't wear a metal suit, you sleep in the dark, you use a wooden ladder.'

'We're not on the same channel, Nina,' I say.

'It doesn't matter,' she seems to shout, far away and faint. 'It's to do with the sun, I think. That's where all the messages originate. I guess lots aren't sent. There's no one checking them. Look up, look in the sky, look at the sun. Be wise, be wise...'

'Maybe the Turks will come,' I say, trying to sound hopeful. She waves, there is no cry.

'Withdrawing the metals, Nina,' I say. 'Maurice, Jozo – it's not to do with fashion, nor with therapy ... It's iconoclasm. You lose the battles, you think some big poppy has it in for you... And so you feel you should atone. You must've put your toe in someone's pie. Off with the image – cover up those angel faces, have feathers foaming from the squinch down to the pavement. The metals – they offend? Your body's made of them – but suicide is not required... Just cover up, take out the copper, and the wolfram. You've been too familiar, made too free with what has been provided, left lying round...'

'Nonsense...' I hear her, perhaps. She's far away, too far for argument.

We are an evil species – along with scorpions. Later, I tell Kaja, 'The shepherds – they've come back. The metalworkers – they've gone into those kebabs. Nina – she's the only good person that I know – there's no sign of Turks, but when they come, I'd bet on her...'

Kaja says, 'Oh yes! I know your sort! You tell the story, so's nothing happens to you. You see us all crack up, make a design – while yours is the voice that swirls up from the rift, quite unattached, pretending you're an oracle, in at the start, and at the end. It isn't so! Your cash – it's ended, radically cut! You have to join the battle!...' she shouts on, she threatens... I say,

'Come, Kaja! Someone must survive to tell the tale and chisel it upon the wall...'

'No, no!' she says. 'Remember Petar's walls. No fancy scripts, and then no brazen cladding. All ripped out!'

She swings at me – her Pandora's body bag, the devil's sack. 'Join them!' she screams. 'The lines of sobbing people waiting for their gruel, the guys awaiting execution, staring at the quicklimed trenches, thinking their last thoughts – each one identical and unrecorded; join the toilers of the East and West – sewing the torn-out jeans, the Harvard t-shirts...'

'OK, Kaja,' I say. 'But you were to fit us in...'

'Oh, you'll fit in,' she says, the bronze clasps on her bag about my ears. 'I shall beat you flat...' then out drops a hatch of roundels – coppers overweight, some pierced like cash, bouncing, running, making for corners like a host of brilliant beetles –

'You cretin,' Kaja shouts. 'Maurice's coinage! Maybe my head on them, a turreted crown – a tasteful reverse, me with a cornucopia, being taken off by satyrs...'

Then, we see Sonia, Jozo – drawing out the steel. 'You take out everything,' says Jozo. 'All the steel. The wolfram can't be separated...' And there we see the buildings, sagging like empty kneeboots, or tall kebabs collapsed – their centre cannot hold, the steels leak out, down fold the tungsten heels...

'A catastrophe,' says Kaja, laughing with delight. 'Quite unexpected. All the rest – foretold, inevitable – the remedies available, ignored. But now – Sonia and Jozo – take back the pins from thighbones, plates from skulls... A challenge unpredicted, no remedy at all, the being nice irrelevant...'

The lights dim down. I say, 'Kaja, the coins – they're not pure copper...' and she says,

'Don't think of money – it's like the dinosaurs, the sun goes coppery and the heat ... dissolves the hard edge of the rocks...'

'Calm down,' I say. 'It's maybe only politics.'

She holds her bag close – there's even possibly a key involved. She settles down. 'This myth – the drawing out the metals. Your friends may rule the world – but they can't remove what's there. The buildings don't fall down. The lights – they don't go brown, don't flicker, don't come on and off at will... You're gullible,' she ruffles at my hair. 'It's sweet, but immature. Not politics, not the economy: the laws of physics – they're indifferent to all this catastrophic stuff. We saw it all in movies long ago – the little signs, the wise guy, sensitive but gullible like you – and then the *maquettes*, up in flames, the race to reach locked doors, salvation! – then survivors, wiser still, relaxed upon the grass... Up come the titles, everyone's long gone.

'The metals – stay just where they were. The selling and the contraband go on – the lights, though – they don't dim. The buildings stand until the wrecking ball, the dynamite, bring death and resurrection.'

'Kaja,' I say, 'being gullible is good. The lights, the girders – whatever happens to them, sure – it's not catastrophe... But when it comes, I'll bet it's unexpected, just like this...'

I'm not convinced by Kaja. If Maurice doesn't own the copper he has bought – what use is his survival? Where's the crime, the punishment, if Sonia can't suck out the steel...? Besides – the buildings fall, the lights – they *do* go out. We're the commanding species for the while – it's up to us to call the shots...

'You need diversion,' Kaja says. 'Maybe a racehorse? Or a greyhound?'

'Wow! Yes, absolutely, Kaja. But the greyhound – mustn't be a biter. And – no greys, hard going only – I hate watching losers in the rain,' I say.

'Greys and biters – that's what was in the store,' says Kaja, putting out my spark.

'It's the classic Chinese theme,' I say. 'Power versus talent. That's the insight that they lost, when Europeans came to China, painted in the shadows, perspective that stands beyond a pencil and your thumb. Realism! It will kill us all, first blinding us... I warn. I shall succumb.'

'Go then!' shouts Kaja. 'Eat while you can, while the stolen money lasts. Your food lies shadowless on your plate. There's no perspective, so your nose falls in the rice...'

9

Of course, there's serious goings-on. We're not a Romeo, not a Juliet, no Layla and Majnun. Each makes their road, each finds it barred in different ways. Kaja and me – there's no affection there. The buildings fall, guys are shocked and tortured, prizes and promotions handed out.

'Sonia and Jozo make the buildings fall. It's the punishment that renews. Maurice can pay to build them up again,' says Kaja.

'Oh no!' says Jozo. 'Maurice says – those tall buildings – on their roofs nothing can grow. He's into terra cotta bungalows, cows grazing on the thatch.'

Cities are gone. The earth is flat again, tessellated with the two-room huts. Equal living space, green stuff above our heads. The world is covered with the green, the brown, of sprouting thatch, the black and white of Friesians – mantras of blank and print – the roofs, the cows! – the peppers like full stops amid the prose of life extended infinitely.

'Maurice says – living like that, you can't muster guys,' says Sonia. 'No steel, no copper. No brigades. It's back to flints and clubs.'

'Sonia, that way you'll lose your cash,' says Kaja, enjoying this. 'Your cover, your protection.'

'No,' says Jozo. 'This can't be the punishment. This happens to everyone. There is no crime – buy cheap, sell cheap. So – bankruptcy. It's nothing. And those lovely roofs! – the marrows, like commas in the prose; all our species living hugger-mugger, all in the same lair, like voles or stagbeetles. No one to complain to, no ear pitched for the scream...'

'There's a flaw,' says Kaja, irritated, that now there'd be no empty space left for people to fit in.

'Oh no!' says Sonia, enchanted by the bungalows. 'Where it's too hot, you fix the roofs with goats.'

'So,' says Jozo, 'Maurice is the benefactor after all. It's all that gold and silver on his person – like the Greeks said, some guys were made entirely of them, one or other. The rest were crap. Those warriors – each guilty of some warcrime, killing the unarmed, rape in some animal guise – but if they're made of gold – it doesn't count.'

'Benefactor?' Kaja asks. 'The intelligence old Petar lacked? How'd you water that extent? You'd need kilometres, everywhere, of copper pipe. The price, my dears! The wealth!'

'Oh no,' says Sonia, 'that way, it'd start to rain again. Everybody would be just. And catch the rain in barrels. And as for Petar – that dreadful name: Petrović. The murderer. Who gets to stay in jail while all the innocent go forth. Petar squandered that fine brain on putting metals on the wall and chasing skirt.'

'Yes, Sonia, Petar was no benefactor,' I say. 'But remember – he was murdered, not the murderer. His aesthetic was at fault, is all.'

'We'd find a niche,' says Jozo. 'All that tungsten. Scythes, to mow the thatch. Buckets, for the milk.'

'Forget Petar,' I say. 'The eagle – the innocent – flies away, leaving the other prisoners... But – my house. The refuge, my masterpiece.'

'Stuff the house!' shouts Kaja, 'forget about the eagle. Maurice's plan – that is your mission now.'

*

Maurice says, 'No talking groups. None of Petar's syndicalism. How I hate that gobble-gabble!'

'Well, Maurice,' I say, 'you'll have a scheme for peace, bringing back the natural man. That's something.'

'Oh no!' he says, banging his gloved, expensive hand on some common wood. 'It's not that. It's the scope, the extent. Transform the world. Everyone the same, all not knowing why they're there.'

'Well,' I say, 'I'm your missionary. Give me the Word, and put it into words.'

'It'll take more than one guy to bring it all about,' he says. 'Not just you. The idea came when I left metals, went into futures. Then came the one idea, the revelation – that you spread quite thin, but spread around the world.'

'You don't think it'll guarantee us – the planet – long life and winning bets? Our futures?' I ask.

'Oh,' he says, 'I shouldn't think so. My futures isn't yours, not your kind at all. Besides, there's always guys want to dig up ores, keep slaves, sacrifice the animals – the fatty smoke blots out the sun...'

Yes. That's it. The sun – that's what Maurice venerates. The cows on the roofs, thinking of cheese. The sun tickling up the clover. A universal prayer to Sol.

'Survival, like socialism, is for poor people,' says Maurice, heavily. 'It won't cost me. If it doesn't suit – try something else. Back to the start. To make it work – stop eating beef – that way, there's cows all over.'

'It seems,' I say, 'the simplicity of it – irks.'

'Well, yes,' says Maurice, 'It's all exasperating – jobs promised, never done. Bloody people! In every sense. In no sense. I'm not a benefactor, of course. I formulate, I steer.'

'Your scheme, Maurice,' I say, 'it appeals. It's realist. It has consequences, you see what it means, start to finish.' I don't see. No one planned the bull.

'Get your money quick,' says Maurice. 'Those guys, in their terracotta pots, cow shit foaming through the roof when the rains arrive – they'll cook, boil, roast and broil... I shan't be around. I'll move on to something else – some real crap capitalism and everyone enrolled in something – but not me! People with no ideas, no talk, nothing to think about except getting cows up ladders – then, the maelstrom. Everybody walking into someone else's home, talking in tongues. And then – metals again.'

'The tub, Maurice?' I ask.

'Maybe,' he says, 'but next time ... you should try it.'

*

'It's work,' I say to Kaja.

'I see flaws,' she says. 'But since you broke my screen, it's hard to see them clear.'

'Maurice has another plan for when this all goes wrong,' I say. 'That is the novelty. Besides, he's given up his sculpturing – the people's skeletons go straight in the garden, no one needs Maurice and his shiny bones.'

'Have you thought,' asks Kaja. 'If this isn't all about that goddam bull? I love the cow, the mother on the roof, of course. But all these useful practices – become a funerary ritual, and then the guys are marching down the road again.'

'Love life, love death – that's what he says,' I say.

I don't believe it. Maybe Kaja's right. Don't trust a golden person, even if the metal's mixed with silver...

'Maurice is unpredictable,' says Kaja. 'He has lots of plans – none of them he carries out. Usually, a guy with power is stuck into a place. A tooth stuck in a jaw. He bites and bites and then he rots. He keeps the other teeth upright till he falls. The stomach – doesn't give a shit, so long as stuff comes down ground up... Maurice – doesn't live in a place.

His money freely floats. Alas – I'm in a structure – like the
lady in the tower. I let my hair down out the window – bugs
and snakes climb up. Who'd be a princess?'

'I can't think who your father was,' I say. I don't care.

'Oh,' she says, keen on this trip. 'There's fathers
everywhere. And mothers. Childhood – all you remember – is
five minutes in the llama cart, a beating, an Easter, an Eid ...
the chants. All the rest – forgotten. Like it was the bones you
take for granted, slipped by night, into your arms and legs,
prising open toes and fingers...'

'Well,' I say, 'I'm in no place either.'

'And so,' she says, 'you have no bones. And you'll
pretend to do what Maurice wants.'

'He never did that job for me,' I say.

'Faddle!' she says. 'Most things are never done. And no
one counts the hours. You're all parasites, you, Maurice, Jozo:
Sonia. All except me. And – if I'm one too, I do good things.
What there is, is not because of nature, or fatalism. When
things go good or bad – it's because the scheme has made
them so. Maurice has his scheme – and you must trek the
world to stock it up with cows and goats. His reasoning –
reduce the use of copper. The planet's saved. Forget what
happens to the price – think of the miners, liberated. All over
– everyone is self-contained. Milk and peppers – I can't wait!'

'It seems there is a flaw,' I say. 'It's like those guys –
wanted the big change, got capitalism for ever. I see industrial
cow farms – the rich eat T-bones, and the poor will shovel
shit...'

'Well,' Kaja says, 'that's not so bad: there's worse.'

*

Most places in the world already have what seems like cows
and goats.

I'm Maurice's ambassador. I go back to where I'm known – the stony plain. What they call religious wars, fought out with scythes and clubs...

I explain the scheme to Nina: 'I think there is a flaw,' she says. 'Cows fall – but goats – they jump. They mingle, too. We're close here to where the vision tends – but the beasts aren't into all that stuff...'

'I don't suppose that had occurred,' I say. 'Maurice doesn't draw the outlines in.'

'Maurice is a criminal,' says Nina. 'But then, we mostly are.'

'Oh Nina – there's a flaw in that thought too,' I say. 'There's gold and silver people here. The faith, the territory, the states, the heat, the cold – there's a solution to all that. The crucible, the cauldron, melting pot – when you have been through that – securing a goat upon your roof, forswearing copper, surely those are problems set, and now resolved?'

'Stay here awhile upon my lap,' she says. 'Before you travel East. And West. Empty your echoing mind. Away the blackbirds' songs! Don't pray – construct...'

'Ah yes!' I say. 'The safe house. Where the good and evil hide, and there's no way in for evil or for good. Where crime is punishment, and cancels out, where slates are clean...'

'Yes, yes,' she says. 'Hush now. One day you'll build the metal house, a refuge for us all...'

'Those guys in the East,' I say. 'They're tough. Give me some time. They have heart and soul – those are tough accoutrements too.'

'I know,' says Nina. 'We control everything. Our species – in the catbird seat. Don't be stoical. But don't forget that house.'

I go deeper and deeper. Into the Donbass. The Russians here ... how far they see! Viktor says,

'Yours is a rare vision. The houses, with their turf roofs ... bottling, drying. Fermenting. Each with their little piece of peace, a country retreat... Rubbish! It wouldn't do for me ... we have to get things right, sort out the past. No cities and no mines. No future. That's all.'

I tell him what Kaja says, about finding your place, guys above you and below, and lining it up with nature, slotting yourself in and knowing it's the right spot. It's Shinto, she says. And – reactionary. Besides – just goats, the cows – that's not much of nature to be fitted into.

'I'd come along your road, Viktor,' I say. 'But I'm selling quite another thing.'

'Oh yes,' he says, 'I'm talking to quite another set of dead men. I'm not even sure your crowd are dead... Remember – "Gold-work-gold-death": that's not for me, just to survive, for little whiles. A world of dachas – yes, it's plausible. If you want to live away from everything that much...'

I shiver, when he says 'gold' – it's the mention of a metal. Maybe it just means 'money', which is neutral. 'Geld'. Like 'gelding', growing the guelder-rose ... doing something intimate with cows, morning and night. Something sexual, in your rubber boots – something like childbirth.

'Hey!' says Viktor. 'Don't be sad. Your scheme will never come to anything. You won't need take responsibility for anything at all.'

'Lots of guys are already into it,' I say. 'The suburb. Growing stuff, drinking milk to stop the rot that's rooting in your skeleton. Think of the Midwest. If you're like your neighbour, he won't bother spying on you. And that's something.'

'It's like Africa,' he says. 'They have a good time there, I bet.'

There's broken plastic everywhere – that's where their war has ended up. 'You need more steel,' I say. 'You won't bother with the cows. They're a hard sell here...'

'History is full of steel,' says Viktor. 'It comes flying in. With luck, you don't feel a twinge – straight from your groundsheet to the war memorial. The next guy – he's a target too, he's not a shield. That's why he's comradeship – he's like you, he's bet his everything. The pack is full of twos and threes, that's how life is, you don't design the game. There aren't fair deals and honest cuts.'

'The guys I know – I guess they can finance you guys,' I say.

'We can make do with clubs and flints,' he says. 'The design's the thing. We have one of those. The other crowd – they're into cloth and coin. We truck – they trade. We drive the sixteen-wheelers. We seek the whole.'

The desire and pursuit of it – sometimes called love. Viktor says, 'Tell your friend – we already thought of the plan, to save the world, all that. And – thanks. We've got here what we need.'

'Maybe while I'm here, we could go see the Devil, who lives hereabouts,' I say.

'You'll see Him with his sack,' says Viktor. 'He is one of us. That is, He's on our side. That means we're good. He doesn't hang around with criminals.'

'I'd thought He'd have a pigskin twenty-four-hour case,' I say. 'Or plastic in a folder.'

'He dresses so's to suit,' says Viktor. 'There's nothing much to see. He does the things He's always done. He doesn't keep a count. In truth, He doesn't need to do a lot, things fall quite naturally.'

'Well,' I say, 'best be with Him than against Him.'

'That is so true,' says Viktor. 'That's right on. If the cause is just.'

10

Later, I tell Kaja, 'Their cause is just. I see it in their eyes. They have a powerful friend for sure, that lets them do what they must do.'

'You were a failure. You couldn't sell them modesty, a self-sufficiency: the cow above. Nor yet a revolution,' she says.

'Everybody needs their devil,' I say. 'All sides have one. The smarter, the better, even several: – one of those knapsacks on their back. The kind a trucker wouldn't wear.'

'Nonsense!' Kaja says. 'They are all yours, those devils, inside you. The revolution – done and gone. There won't be more. You saw it metamorphose ... quite like you. You started off so well – wanting to administer the damaged ones. Then faster and faster – down the path that seems so easy – till you reach its end. The others – have made history. You know, what you lack ... it's metal. The bull, the wolfram.'

'Those are just metaphors,' I say.

'Rubbish some more!' she says.

*

I tell Maurice I got nowhere with his scheme. 'That's OK,' he says. 'No one wants to save the world that much – looking poor and smelling of cowshit – who wants that? Not me, for sure.'

'I met all the big names,' I say. 'The usurpers gave more time. The legits had better offices.'

'Well,' says Maurice. 'You met the names, and now you have a name. I'll find a task for you. Maybe with Jozo,

Sonia... that Kaja – she's always sitting down. No work gets done like that. Though it's true – you've never finished anything. What can you promise me?'

*

'Oh,' I say, 'I'll promise anything, and set my name to it. Not the tub, though, not paddling in the molten gold.'

'It's clear,' he says, 'the higher work – is not for you.'

With that, I'm happy. Sonia and Jozo – they have trusted guys who do the violence, though it's seldom needed. That's not for me – I'm unreliable. Maybe there's more interesting things...

'Metals,' says Maurice. 'They change everything. Wood and stone – that was quite casual. But then – the copper, into bronze, the iron, and then the gold. We're stuck in the golden age. That is where our order sits, for the time being; therein lies our meaning. Don't look further – what meaning exists, is there. Copper – the toil, expense, the ingenuity ... up sprang the individual, the nobles – that started it all off. Any idiot can throw a stone or wave a stick – it took guys like me to make a helmet and a sword. Then the factories, machines, the iron: old Karl, at that old sewing machine, making mailbags for his correspondence. Then me.'

It's true. That's all you need to know. Maurice and I – we gaze at Kaja. We're asexual, of course. If you stare long enough, you see she's like those in the video, no makeup, a war victim. Some countries – full of beautiful people.

'Go away,' she says.

'The sentiments,' says Maurice, 'see how ephemeral they are.'

'That doesn't affect their value,' Kaja says. 'No that I'm into pricing them. I'm looking for the right guys to come along and spark me off. You two – just ditch-crawlers.'

Maurice laughs, thumps his electrum hand against the window. 'You never invented anything,' she says.

'Oh yes!' says Maurice. 'I did! Copper into gold. Then – all into air. To faith! Trust, confidence!'

She waves him away. 'Maurice, you've always been into ugly things,' she says.

'Maybe,' he says, 'but I wasn't responsible. No one punished me. All turned out well.'

She looks blank. 'Then it wasn't you? Can it have been Sonia, Jozo?'

I've no idea what this is all about. Those two – Sonia, Jozo – they can't be bothered with people, let alone with Kaja, her drab work, her lively spirit, her ordinary symmetrical face, all that.

'You had me lose my work, Maurice,' she says. 'That was me, my work.'

'No, Kaja,' he says, calm. 'I gave you freedom. I cut off the weight. Float up, Kaja, to the surface. Look around. Feel the abundance of the air.'

'Why, Maurice?' I ask. 'Why take it out on Kaja? It's irrelevant.'

'I told her bosses she was loyal to me,' he says. 'And now she is. Or even not.'

'You gain nothing, Maurice,' I say.

'Yes,' he says. 'It's loyalty. To me. Not about profit.'

'How far would you go with this, with me?' asks Kaja.

'Oh,' says Maurice, 'as far as I'm interested. It's not to humiliate you, Kaja, it's to have respect, recognition.'

'Kaja,' I say, 'now, you can be anything. Or nothing. Moral philosopher, for example. Your line's been about the fitting in...'

'That's a Scottish thing, isn't it?' asks Kaja, starting to cry. 'I could dance – that's nothing. But I don't have the feet. Hitting the ground. Fearing God. No, that's not for me.'

'Well, there's other things,' I say.

'You've tried them all,' she says to me. 'There's not much left.'

We walk down the street together. The power goes out sometimes, automobiles lose parts. I'd put my money on Sonia and Jozo – Maurice too, as who's behind it. Someone must be doing it. Lowering the power. 'Sonia went before a judge,' I say. 'But there was no rule big enough to cover her.'

'Look at these boys and girls, walking along,' says Kaja. 'You've no idea at all about anything they may have in their heads. That's why politics was no good.' We stare at them, they stare back, not kindly.

'Don't say we're scientists,' I tell her. 'It wouldn't signify.'

'Your friend Petar,' she says. 'He knew it all connected, what you eat, what you read, who you'd like to screw you. Do you see a join, a seam? Is it all made in a mould? It all sticks together, like your metal house – the ditties you first learned, those rough patting games in a circle with your spiteful peers – and – lo! there they'll be, in at the end, dressed in white peignoirs, a silly chanting in your head, above the tinnitus ... your little vision of the world. Soon to expire, along with you. Individually created, just for you, by you – a picture of whatever swam into your view – like you had a periscope, circling it round... A universe. A scrubby beach, some huts, hotels with vacant rooms – and waves, waves everywhere, the blue, the black, the grey...'

She howls. She turns to Greek. 'He knew, did Petar – nothing and nothing make up one...'

'No, no, Kaja,' I say, hugging her. 'Don't give up! You have to find a job. Fill your bag with cash again. You have responsibilities...' I'm terrified. Poverty ahead, a zero...

We're both in tears: I drag her into the arcade; the slot machines, that imperial one – the thumping march of coppers, coming near the precipice: thrum thrum goes the machine, brigades, battalions of murky coins – a fortune now, on the edge. We put a hundred dollars in, to buy a penny weight.

We win! The platform tips. A swarm, a hatch! A fortune, a copper trove. Metal shines for us, we rub up every coin to shine like gold. The copper isn't pure, of course.

'It's Maurice!' I shout. 'He *is* our benefactor.'

We play some other games – the fruits slide up and down, and framing them, the fruity lights whizz round like acid bonbons. We lose ... not everything. The power slumps, and outs. She pulls me, back in the street. Her bag's replete again. We're safe. I say,

'We'll work for Maurice, and for Jozo, Sonia too. After all, they made the bull. A motor for the world, a power. Things hammered out, they have significance, a connection with everything that's ever been or will be, encysted in our time. You make a thing, it testifies to all the rest, you put your seal – so! On everything. It all exists. It's not a word, a light – it is the bull...' and Kaja interrupts, 'Don't get exalted, idiot! We lost our fight – now, we'll need to fit in to all the world, without a prejudice. Work for those guys... One soul – is worth one *sou* – that's what your Russians calculated. A copper kopek. What seemed happenstance for Ulysses – was Homer's plan. What do our misfortunes signify? Not happy ends. Just ends. We each have them, whether we seek them, or they come... Zinc, copper, tin – hard metal, made to look like gold. That's what it means right now.'

I don't grasp what she says. It's enough – her bag is full of cash. We coast along a bit.

*

'Go down that nickel mine,' Maurice tells me. 'What do you see?'

There's galleries and vaults. No one digs – there's big machines that crawl about ... there's guys in crannies making little beasts of nickel, lapis for the eyes...'

'There's not much you can do with nickel,' Maurice says. 'Except make nickels. Plate those little pistols ladies use. But lapis – yes, you can smuggle that. "... and lapis were his eyes..." All that. It has niche appeal.'

'You need to see the sky, Maurice,' I say. 'Even if it's over-smoked, the rain will burn your face, the tailings turn the lakes a green and orange...'

'Yes, yes,' he says. 'Use your mind! It's like that on Saturn's moons. It's all experience. And – they'll never make a bull, nor something like...'

'A faulty charge blocked up a chimney, Maurice,' I say. 'An exalted guy – went up to free the rock, and down it came on him...'

'We need exalted guys,' he says. 'To say what this stuff is useful for.'

'And then?' I ask.

'We make it scarce,' he says. 'We take it off the shelf. The guys, the miners – they can hunt and fish. Even – they can criticise, when they get tired of slaughter.'

'The guys love their animals,' I say. 'Each has his totem.'

Maurice sheds a tear. 'I know,' he says. 'Let's be clear – I don't own the mine. I finance it. I don't own the deaths. Asks Jozo – he's the expert. And Sonia – she comes along behind, cleans it all up. Keeps the scores, settles them. Settles me too.'

'Maurice,' I say, anxious to be in the right, 'you've not done anything, not on the bad side.'

'I guess it's hot down there,' he says.

'Oh yes,' I say, 'but think how cold it gets outside. And in the smelter – that's real hot.'

'Well, my friend,' says Maurice, dismissing me. 'It all adds up. Remember – the essence of Confucius – "If you don't know the answer, don't pose the question." "Looking too hard for what suits you leads you up the garden" ... "Pleasing yourself sets everyone against you..." Store them safe, these truths... That doesn't leave much room for you, I know. But – see what a lot of rooms I have!'

'I didn't know you had a house, Maurice,' I say at the door.

'Oh, I meant room, not rooms. Forget that house you're going to build for me! I'm not in the hotel business,' he laughs. 'One room is always enough, unless you're into bilocation! Or –' and he's mischievous, 'unless you're Jozo and Sonia. How they hate each other. No one wants crime and punishment to be so hugger-mugger. What's the point?'

When I next see her, I ask Kaja, 'What have Sonia and Jozo got you doing.'

'Oh,' she says, 'just counselling. Not reconciling to fate, I'm pleased to say, but admitting guilt. Lots and lots, and evermore. I guess it's atonement. All the frighteners, the hitmen – thought since they took a risk, what they did was just a job. Sonia wants them to feel guilt. Makes them more obedient, she says... But – this crime, the punishment – I don't grasp how they fit. Jozo is good at both – even great. Sonia seem to find a disconnect... first you have the punishment, and so you do the crime. Jozo doesn't suffer, not one bit: the crime, the punishment, cancel out. Off you go again.'

'So you've said,' I say. 'We know all that. It's a puzzle. Jozo keeps at it – crimes, punishments, some he takes himself, others he shunts to someone else. He's on all sides... Before it makes some sense – you have to think there's law. Maybe – an order. But if you don't, it's all downhill for you.'

'Oh well,' says Kaja. 'I'm with Sonia. Repentance is the punishment. Going on to do good things – that's quite enough to settle bills. Enough you say the words – maybe you believe, but doubt's a necessary part of it, or else I have no job! My *incipit*'s the wobble... Doubt's a value, maybe the greatest thing our civilisation's made. That, and certainty. Doubt and certainty – justify, condemn, most everything... It's our high point.'

'Come on, Kaja,' I say. 'Don't be reactionary. If you don't go forward – fascism's all that's left. Surely they told you...? That march – the coppers, pennies – thrum, thrum, like guys in armour.'

'It's my rights,' she says. 'Losing my job. You've never had one – you're just scared of everything. It's my private self is violated...'

'It isn't fear,' I say. 'Though that could be required. No, it's talent versus power. That's what afflicts me. I'm not violated – rather, suffocated. But now – we both work for Sonia and Jozo. All our selves do. We're in their ring.'

'These dangerous guys,' says Kaja, 'I have them confess. I pardon them. Do I do right? They ask me out – so, do I bed with them?'

'Do what is right for you,' I say.

'That's not the answer that I want,' she says. 'Besides, what these guys do – it isn't printed on their cards, stuck on their desks. Instead, they've titles – just like kings and emperors.'

'Maybe I could go with them,' I say. 'See how they work. Although I'll bet they've no clue about metalwork or mines, but – it'd be part of toughening one up. They say that's how you get authority.'

'That's how I reason too,' says Kaja. 'Empathy. And – they pay for everything.'

11

Jozo says, 'I'll do what I want. If I succeed, that's good – if not, is it my fault? There's not much to be done, not much guidance, you know. Maybe I'll be punished – does it mean I've failed, done the wrong thing, made the wrong move?'

'I feel often – I'll chuck it in, all of it,' Sonia says. 'Punish and forgive. And then – withdraw all the proceeds of crime, and dangerous work – do the toilers have a side, I wonder, that I should take? And – there's always some belief that has a get-out clause. Do bad things – in the name of this or that. Often, you have respect because of it, how convincing you can sound, and have a magus speak for you.'

I sympathise. It needs courage to take a side... The metals, though – they are our life – they come to us unformed, a gift. We shape them – so, passed on and circulated, they become our gift. It's all calculated. It's like water in La Paz. You see the glacier's sick – the water, life – you leave it tranquil, in peace. Maybe it recovers, gives you life abundantly. So it is with Maurice and his copper – feeling the earth is sick, in torment ... slowly, slowly, you back off ... start pulling out the wires, the entrails... Sonia takes the girders, slides them out, like playing spillikins... See if the buildings hold.

'We may need a rite,' I say. 'Processions, drums. A ceremony. Make it obvious for the stupid.'

A march – like the thrumming march of coppers, but with humans, bent beetling up the slag, under their copper wingcases, some with anvils on their backs...

'Oh no!' says Jozo. 'That we don't need – nature anthropomorphic, priests and flags. Dig and smelt. That is the mission! It seems there's always supply, a reserve somewhere.'

Later, Kaja says, to me, 'You have only broken thoughts. There's nothing for it, for us: they're broke, our thoughts. The answer is – there has to be some kind of humanism... It's the only thing that helps us, that coheres.'

'I'm not so sure,' I say, 'I'm with the animals – at least, the ones large and slow enough that you can see. I guess we all live in bits of old philosophy – you can never join the pieces, but you're in them all.'

'I'm tidy!' Kaja says. 'I live a logical life.'

I don't bother to answer that: I say,

'Well, there's Maurice – must have killed people for their religion – now, doesn't have a faith, lives nowhere, all over the known world. How's that for metamorphosis? He'll be surprised when they come to get him – he sits, sucking out the copper wire as though it's macaroni...'

'There!' says Kaja. 'See – you've got the image wrong. There's nothing in macaroni, nothing at all. You see, you can't do anything about all this, nor even make a refuge. We're employees.'

'There's two things, Kaja,' I say. 'If you can't do anything, how could you make a refuge?'

'Make the house!' she says. 'Take on an outline, stop shimmering. You have to finish in one go – no doubt, no certainty. You do it, and it maybe slumps into a lump. Too bad!'

'You don't understand, Kaja,' I say. 'Making a structure like that – it needs something still larger, to give it birth and stand it upright.'

'That, now, sounds fun,' she says. 'I could get involved in it.'

'Those books of Petar's – those were refuges. Projections, futures, predications – though you couldn't live in them, they could get you killed. He got rid of them – metal cladding seemed the sounder thing,' I say.

'Yes,' says Kaja. 'Forget about all that. And don't think you can fingerpaint – you have to live in somewhere, not put up a graphic. You have to do it properly, in your skin, the suit they sent you in.'

'I'm not convinced,' I say. 'Safe things attract the vandals.'

'The alternative,' she says, 'is love story. Majnun and Layla. We could try that, though we don't like each other much. All the same, it is an epic. Deserts, fighting, monsters, loyalty... You need to use your fantasy – there's not much sex, so that should suit, and no religion.'

'It's just another thing that's impossible, or very difficult,' I say. 'Think of Jozo, Maurice – fiddling the metals, drawing in or puffing out... Deserts, fighting, monsters – it's the same thing as love stories – sending guys underground, life or death and mind your head – the shamanic twist; skimming off the gold, whittling brass animals. Setting little guys to strip the cables in the garbage... It isn't easy for them, the bosses – and think of all the broken guys they send for you to mend... Silver solder for the sliced-up soldiers...'

'Maurice thinks a lot about what he does – withdraw, commit. It could end bad, of course – but he's there to win. So's Jozo. King Copper versus Hero Wolfram,' says Kaja.

'Of course, they don't go in to lose. But they're not competitors,' I say. 'Surely – not with each other? That would be absurd. Both coming out well – that's all that matters.'

'So, if there's only one survivor, it'd better had be you,' says Kaja. 'But co-existence – well, anyone can live with that. The aim is – not to lose. But – if it wasn't there, the possibility of loss – you wouldn't be there, doing what you do. That's why being boss is different from pretending to be epic lovers

– that makes sense only if you both live on to have fun times. Or – both die. Or one survives, but spiritual.'

'I see you've thought about this stuff,' I say. 'While you were sitting at your desk and sticking limbs back on. But – there's nothing to be done, you say – hearts, metals – you spin the wheel, and wait.'

'Oh no!' says Kaja. 'You've got it wrong again. Some other guy is there and paid to spin the wheel. You've made your bet. You don't do fuck all. The same with metals – you may go underground, or strip the plastic – that is all. That's what "nothing to be done" entails – it isn't flying kites, throwing the switch...'

'Replacing bronze with steel,' I say, remembering the history. 'That's a big piece of doing.'

'If you're a Kurd in that camp at Kawergosk,' says Kaja, 'there's nothing to be done indeed, and so you sing "If I didn't cry and laugh I'd die." But things do get done, also if you're born a Kurd. That's not the point – it's the truth in existence, which means: you can mould and twist, transform: and there is still, always, nothing to be done. What you do, and what is done – those are two quite different things.'

'I understand perfectly,' I say. 'General, prostitute, senator, hetero – you can't do anything about it.' What brains we each have!' I say. 'Each of us grasps the subject precisely, but we don't understand each other, nor what each says.'

*

Maurice and Jozo split.

Collapsing buildings, power outages – they've seemed quite uncoordinated – yet, there is a logic. Price, warnings, geopolitics, apocalypse – it comes to much the same. They have been distant friends – now, they're opposed. It comes to much the same.

I've given up on Turks – too few to make designs for all the world. Maybe they'll make a war, each against all...

Now, Maurice and Jozo can't agree: what does each want, coordination or autonomy? Is there a destination that they have in mind?

Here comes a surge of power – the earth lights up, a firefly ... then steel's stacked up on continents ... the weight! The buildings gorge with metal, bulge and lean ... they're indestructible, unstable...

'Kaja,' I shout. 'Which side are we on?'

'Oh,' she says, 'it must be all connected. Does that help?'

Nina will know. She always understands what helps.

'Aha. It's you. On my tits again, I suppose, wanting it for free,' she says.

'I guess Curtis charges too?' I say. Her office has a birthing couch, for the monsters she draws out of us.

'He charges when you elect him, and he's paid you to get in,' says Nina. 'His ladies move for him, you bet.'

I tell her about Maurice and Jozo. She says, 'That Petar Petrović – don't start making him a metaphor. He took a murderer's name – the most famous in the book. He wrote his end. Nothing to do with stories – it was a rival who he killed, then a whole bunch. Books don't come in, when he's concerned. You guys cut off his last sentence, I expect. So what? Anyway, I don't do plots.'

'And if the copper and the wolfram disappear?' I ask.

'And if those fucking Turks don't?' she asks. 'Cement and gas fires – that's the answer to Jozo, and to Maurice. It all gets sorted out. I'm an infinity of consolation. I think I lost my civilisation – but there's other ways of making livings...'

'Oh, I agree,' I say. 'Some things Jozo would have me do, but I won't.'

'Losing the light, living in huts – it doesn't seem to me too bad a life,' says Nina. 'I'm sure there's worse to come.'

'I'm sure you're right,' I say. 'Perhaps Maurice and Jozo aren't so strong and in control.'

'Who cares?' asks Nina, pushing me outside to the rain. 'Sonia's the one who decides, if somebody's done wrong.'

Who cares? I think – crimes are defined and punishments bestowed. And there's an end.

'Petrović was the innocent – or so we're told. Petar took his name for that,' I say. 'His crime was politics – we're meant to sympathise.'

'That's not how I recall,' says Nina. 'Anyway, those crimes are the worst. They're what the guys round here all suffer for. The names don't enter in. It was a mistake to let that guy, that Petrović, go free. That Petar – he got his. I'm glad.'

*

'This is so different,' says Kaja. 'It's not at all like you read in newspapers, or see in maps. There's no map for what Jozo does, or Maurice... It's really dancing with your clothes off!'

'No,' I say. 'You need be very careful. Remember the tub... Think of Jozo and Sonia – sitting around all day – they don't dance, but often you find them naked, sitting in their armchairs, exercising the power you don't read about, that's not a metaphor, not an allegory. How I hate all that – the story underneath the stories. All false, or in another dimension... Nina – she's so vulnerable. We all need consolation, or being told we have our own reality, and stick to it – but I expect she'll end up bad. Someone'll get annoyed. Or tell her something they regret, then hire a guy to shut her up for good.'

'Nina doesn't sound vulnerable to me,' says Kaja. 'All that religion she has to excuse – really, it's all sex, I guess.

Skins, materials, bonding, families, binding. Who you can, who you can't. Generating and oxidising.'

'You need to make an effort,' I say. 'To see what it's really all about.'

'Oh well,' she says. 'I'm sure there's more to it than you can put into a phrase. Design, strength, expansion and malleability – you could go on.'

'That bull,' I say. 'We made him gold, not yellow: he's like the sun close up. If you get it right, he shouldn't pinhole or rot. He'll last, but he's not something you'd admire.'

'I'm sure he wasn't made to be admired,' says Kaja.

'No,' I say. 'He just got made, quick.'

'We're tight on Maurice's and Jozo's back,' she says. 'Like little monkeys holding on. Those two, they are a farce – no doubt for good. Even if they're enemies. It's points of view...'

Really,' I say. 'I've not played any part in this at all.'

*

I go from mine to mine – Africa all over, some dug, some sucked right out; some supine underneath the scrub – they wait. Our children, if we have them, when they ask for bread – with luck, they'll get a stone. Some maybe not.

America – full of them – the cobalt, platinum, the emeralds, nickel for those ladies' pistols ... Russia, Poland – scattered about, deposits of that and this, the brown, the black, the grey ... just heat it up, and out come tubes like veins and bones, quite indiscriminate, 'hang those green stones around your neck, my love, and step into your tungsten car'... And drive it off that copper bridge.

'*Es ist genug!*' I say to Kaja. 'Enough! We've done our task. Finished! It's all explored, there's holes all over, nothing to fill them with. Recycle everything, draw out the wires and start it off again, it won't avail. The mission is complete!'

'Oh,' she says, 'that's so dull! Waiting for the next species, "what'll they drink, make their nests of?" Crime is much more interesting. The things you might be punished for.'

'Of course,' I say. 'The future's dull, once you get used to it. You surely don't advise those guys, what they should do?'

'It's inevitable,' Kaja says. 'And interesting. The competition. Shoring up the roof. Paying guys off, paying their lawyers – all that stuff.' I say.

'You tell them what's a crime, and if they might get off? If someone else might take the blame? You're right, it's fascinating...'

She looks sulky. 'Put like that, it's quite banal. I do the psychological side.'

'Do guys feel bad when they come? Or when they leave?' I ask.

'Not bad. Curious. They feel different,' she says. 'Different all the time. That's Jozo's people. Maurice doesn't have guys. He has information. That way, he calculates. He has ups and downs – those don't sit down to lunch.'

'You send Jozo's people into battle. Some must desert, I guess. What about Maurice? His guys?'

'Spirits,' says Kaja. 'Out of my reach. The others – they get hooked on good and bad. It's a passion.'

'Who'll win, between Maurice and Jozo?' I ask. 'Jozo has the warriors...'

'Oh, Maurice will win,' says Kaja. 'He's got a line in mercury. He runs between the floorboards.'

That was the metal in the tub. That's what makes the bond. 'Truth and being nice, they don't come in...' I say.

'Oh absolutely not,' Kaja says. 'But you don't miss them.'

'Maurice won't settle down,' I say. 'Won't decide, whether to pull things out or leave them in.'

'You haven't understood,' says Kaja. 'That's power. Reality, the material kind that you can touch and fall down on – how long does it last? It's immeasurably short – and then it's past or future – untouchable, unreal, immaterial. The power – is there, for always.'

*

'I don't pay you much,' says Maurice. 'Because you don't do decisions. That way, you're really not involved, you just travel for me. No, I don't think you're rubbish, a parasite.'

I don't have a million-dollar hand. 'I could handle some more cash,' I say.

'You have this idea about the Turks, about the world cut up into vilayets,' he says. 'It's crap. It doesn't change a thing – not the thing that interests you, and me. You should be like Kaja – nothing happened to her. She fits the people in. It happened to her mother, though – things it's worth running from.'

Of course, things happened to her, they happen to everyone, they've happened before you're born and again and again after you die.

'When you thought you were the boss,' Maurice insists, holding my arm with his claw as if he wants to crack it, out the white flesh. 'You talked and talked. Now, you just scurry from hole to hole,' and he laughs, as if it's the funniest thing. 'Peering down, reporting back. You good, so very good at it!'

Maurice has trained to be beyond a law: beyond crime, beyond Sonia.

12

What a war! Jozo's steel – blows off your head. Maurice's cash reserves – chew off your feet... You sit outside your hut and whittle sticks. As they say, war's not the worst thing: far from it. Brings peace, cash, and Nina. Jozo has faith, the flag. Maurice has the hope – that it will all calm down, that you will walk again, and even run.

Maurice – the brotherhood. Jozo – the law. Sonia – the judgement.

Kaja and me – we don't much care. I didn't enter the tub, and Kaja doesn't recognise a law. Our indifference to those we serve won't spare us any suffering. It's a shame, I guess, that we don't like each other more. We don't make up some compromise, nor try to take the best bits, from ourselves – nor from Jozo and Maurice somehow purified...

*

'Well,' says Maurice, 'it's over! That was some war! The right side won. When I first went into metals, it was all more physical. This time, it's the ideas that swirled around. Jozo's are quite into second place.'

*

'It's like the movies say – "No humans were harmed in the fighting of this war,"' Kaja says. 'The territory's untouched, the nations are just as they were. Nina will listen to the tales, and hug. Everyone survived. Some found strength and love.

Some found loot, some – adventurous sex. We'll talk about it all.'

'After the battles I was in before,' says Maurice, 'I didn't venture into this. It was tough, but everything I wanted – I maintained.'

Sonia says, 'Bad things were done – there's fewer being cogitated now. Does that mean fewer punishments, or just milder ones?'

Jozo's face is crevassed, like someone's being digging in a turnip with a nail: 'It's ageing,' Sonia says, and he reacts, 'You cretin, Sonia! The punishment is done by the same guys that do the crime...' and he hits her, maybe he has an ashtray in his hand – alabaster, malachite; or a marshal's baton or an artillery spotter's theodolite... From here, I can't quite see: her jaw goes far away, you hear the sinews whistle, it won't quite go back in place, she lisps, 'You lost, Jozo. Everywhere there'll rise up shiny refuges, not a trace of steel, proud above the plain...' We remember the Albanians, Americans – each with a bunker underground... This time, it'll all be different... 'The sun, Jozo!' Sonia says. 'When it strikes them... The heat! The light! – highways lined with them, angels with bright swords, waiting for the word, the takeoff...'

'Angels!' shouts Jozo scornfully. 'Those swords must be of steel. Who heard of white metal armaments? No – our recent skirmish was a joke. New states are based on genocides – or else they don't convince. Genocide at once – or slipping down, a slender stream, like sand down through the clock, the *clessidra*, the guys casually creamed, expelled, or made to shovel crap...'

'Petar said that when a civilisation rises to the top, it stands on twenty dead ones – ones it's swallowed up, and defecated out,' I say – and Sonia and Jozo turn on me. 'The law persists!' shouts Sonia, 'It refines!' and Jozo says it's not the many stripes that make a tiger, it's the teeth.

'Petar loved those twenty dead ones,' I say. 'He made his money from them. It was the bull he couldn't come to terms with.' The others are silent – they don't remember what happened this way, either: I go on, 'He assimilated everything – his innocence, his guilt, the eagle flying away. Then it all passed to the bull.'

'Hey!' says Jozo, 'I never read the story. What eagle?'

'Forget the eagle, Jozo,' I say. 'Don't read the story.'

'The bull flew out the window,' Sonia says, laughing. 'Faster than Petar could grab! And those "politicals" all say they're innocent. That's because they appoint the judges.'

'Everyone says they're innocent,' says Jozo, 'because they're born that way.'

'When you're born, you're too weak to shake a stick,' says Sonia.

'Well,' I say, 'the war's over. The metals business seems confused.'

'Maurice did well to go into finance,' says Sonia. 'Copper's replaced in everything. It's tough for us – we pull out some steel – some guy makes stuff with glass or plastic. You can't stand still – you've gotta dig – sand, oil... always something!'

'Anyway,' says Jozo, 'we didn't sacrifice the bull! We're not idiots. We rescued it. We created it.'

'No one should sacrifice anything,' says Sonia. 'That doesn't come in at all. You have to be the driving force. Not standing still – that's all.'

Is that the meaning? Is that all? Do Sonia, Maurice, Jozo, have the key? Or – not a key – a summary, a nub?

'This clay villa you live in, Jozo,' I say. 'It's so mean, it looks as if you lost your war.'

'Oh well,' he says, 'Nina'll tell you – war is a question of the scale. The civil jostling sends her clients all the same – the twisted and the harassed. There's nothing new in that. No tears – all's taken care of. As for this clay – it's the dust, powders, clods that turn the world. If we get short – just scrape the wall – and there you are. But – we have had a serious thought. Producing a universal good – the steel: it doesn't satisfy our metaphysical part. We need a territory, a zone. Take Curtis now – the imperial urge, the macho rhythm. That's his anthem. But – it isn't dead elsewhere. No, not at all. Guys love the land, to have, to hold, to increment. They don't think to plant. It's the extent ... the people, settled, indifferent to how they live... And Sonia wants a courthouse, with a motto – and the wolf, the ram, her justice, tacked up on the tympanum, above the door that's always open...'

'More earths, and no back door,' says Kaja, when I tell her. 'And Curtis as the candidate, the empresses immobile, balancing their uneasy crowns...'

I feel I need to have things straightened out by Nina.

'Off you go,' says Kaja. 'Nothing you do, ever, can be considered adultery. Nor that I do.'

'Well then,' I say. 'All that, done or undone, or not – it's all of no interest. What matters is the earth and its hard, malleable core. Maurice and Jozo, Sonia's metaphysics.'

'Jozo and Maurice – they're the same,' says Kaja.

'Maurice is an artist,' I say, remembering the unyielding corpses in the gardens. 'Jozo puts real corpses in the bank, or in his shoe. Then he wants Sonia to tell him it's OK.'

'Jozo'll have to watch his diet,' Kaja says, not taking in distinctions. 'The bear fat and jute leaves! – his veins are tormented.'

'Criminals and judges have to get used to sitting down a lot,' I say. Maurice can roam the world. With more cash – he could rocket round the universe. Jozo's quite stationary – waiting for Sonia's sentence.

'As employers...' Kaja begins.

'And as statesmen too – they're not the best... Not the best informed,' I say.

'We must make do with them as friends,' she says. 'Although they hate each other. And maybe us. It's quite complicated.'

I find Nina lying on her couch. 'Oh shit,' she says, 'I knew I must be dead. Another gruesome patient up from hell to stick his finger in my lung.' She's wheezing, 'Oh, I'm a mucous mine,' she groans. 'Where does it come from, with no digging, just these evil guys inside, twirling it out like candy floss...' There's gouts of it, snot oxidising into black and brown. 'I'm drowning,' she says. 'I'm in a box of flesh, buried in what – oh no – seems like flesh...'

'I'm relieved, Nina,' I say. 'I thought you might be dead.'

I thrust two capsicums up her nose. 'With these,' I say, 'you'll liquefy. Then you'll be wrung out, reconstituted. Dried like a cod.'

'It's not the heating,' Nina says. 'Guys came with wads of bacteria – violated us, even the guys with metals for protection.'

I wring her out. She's still not well, she's moribund. 'The only suffering you're interested in,' she says. 'Is yours. From the rest of us – you just want company and chat.'

'Of course!' I say. 'How should it be otherwise?'

'It's all wedged in the minds of powerful guys, inscrutable,' she says. 'Maurice – no job was ever started, nor did he finish one. Perpetual his discontent, his search for something larger that he couldn't do. And – that hedonist, Jozo – morose, sat spooning pilchards with honey from the can, cogitating things inoperable. And Sonia – you'll have heard of justice, leaning on the arm of crime?'

'Not exactly, Nina,' I say.

'Punishing ... the desire's perverse. The order she announces never comes, the law is bigotry or slush, in the

Book or on the hoof – quite arbitrary in either case... Watch those two: their eyes are agates from another universe. Everything they do or plan's condoned because they make a war zone, built for two...'

'Your wisdom leaves no hope,' I say. 'But, Nina – you console. That signifies.'

'It signifies there is no hope,' she shouts. 'You think that bull encapsulates ... instead, it's botched and mute. I helped you pass from night to day. Well, now it's night again. My circle is complete.'

At last, she's silent. In her hut, there is no steel or copper wire. She's safe from evil thoughts. Her woollens dry and shrink into a shroud. Her circle is complete.

I go to tell Curtis: the tough guy outside says, 'It's "Lord" Curtis.'

I don't object. Civilisations grow like that – coral reefs layered on missed identities.

Here's Nina, bundled on her couch.

'There!' Curtis says. 'That lady sure don't move.'

'She can't be dead,' I say. 'Hers was just a walk-on part.'

'Here's a spade,' he says. We dig. He brings out from a shed a dusty set of tinny bones. He doesn't dust them off – white metal? Gold-and-silver?

'That'll be the trace,' he says. 'If they use detectors. They'll pick up on Maurice's ornaments.'

'Why should they try? Want to find her?' I ask. 'It's not us who's guilty.'

'After her, there's Maurice,' Curtis says. 'My patron, my chief. How I hate him!'

'Not everyone can be loved and win elections,' I say, thinking of Nina, consoling, and Curtis who resented it. 'It's mathematical. Nina's gone. There'll be others following. Even though she isn't dead – have her buried and unfindable.'

'Oh no!' shouts Curtis. 'We're all findable! I believe in the Resurrection and the Life Eternal! Don't you? You're supposed to. You're not to believe in paradise, like some guys here do – even on my staff. We're for the resurrection!'

'OK, Curtis,' I say. 'Rewind it. Dry Nina off. Tell it better next time. Stuff the ballot boxes.'

'That's for goddam sure,' says Curtis, spading clods on to Nina's cardigan. 'Stuff 'em.'

We cover her. Curtis crumbles earth, to check for ores. 'The Russians,' he says, 'they may come. To sort us out. I'm sceptical. There was a dancer – flamenco – from Suzdal. She came and entertained.'

'The Turks?' I ask, though I've quite lost my faith.

'Or the Syrians?' he says. 'They've a whole world there. All that beauty...'

'The Syrians won't come,' I say. 'We need a way to do the maps again. Where they used to live.'

'We'll have a proper class war then,' he says. 'That's an illusion too. Like maps.'

'Maybe we should mark her spot?' I say.

'No,' Curtis says. 'Maurice has done all that. His bones will rest on hers. She won't forget who's lying on her.'

'What's your next move?' I ask, although the answer's maybe an illusion too.

'Oh,' he says, 'I've learnt the play the game, to gain the love. That, and the cash. I'm quite electable.'

When I see Kaja, I tell her everything. 'Talk about me, not her!' she shouts. 'Nina's down in her hole, waiting to soothe more warriors. Me? I'm a cannibal. I eat me before you can. I try to entertain, I put on some personality. The new consumes the old. Nina – she's had her circle. I'm out there, beyond, somewhere in a space – its curve will bring me back, right where I started. Down I'll go – what will you say about me?

Will you sing? Dance? You can't do flamenco, that's for sure.'

'I'd no idea,' I say. 'I thought you'd found your destiny, advising hitmen. How they could be happy, working as they do...'

'Oh,' she says, 'they're happy. Happier than me.'

'I didn't realise,' I say. 'Something was lacking for you.'

Here comes the anger: mine... 'Look,' I say, taking out my claw, looking for something it can nip. 'The war is over. Maurice always wins, but Jozo's looking for another resource. Maurice has everything – the precious hand, the funeral rites, the bones. Thick culture, it is called. Jozo has nothing but his cunning, and an angry metaphysical by him on the divan.'

She doesn't take this in. 'Maurice says people like uniformity. Everything everywhere's made of the same batch of stuff. Gravity unites it all. Guys like wearing uniforms. They say they like a difference, but it's only when it's sex. They like their neighbours quite predictable. Your vilayets – they classify minorities, they layer up and down – the privileged, the rest. It's easier that way.'

I speculate along with her. 'I always said – the capitalism we have – it may not work, but it's how the species thinks... it's evolution. They like fascism too. They don't like guns and corpses: but the rest – it's the species having a good time. Parades. It's not how I'd intended...'

'But you don't count at all,' shouts Kaja, 'and you broke my screen. You never finish projects. You don't have a proper job... And did you make the bull?'

'I kept lookout,' I say. 'That's the most important part of all. As for the screen – a scat of rage, no more. Not personal – no class, no gender was involved...'

'Well, look again,' she says. 'When your scheming gives you time. Mourn Nina, you frigid bastard – not that I care what happens to her.'

My mind goes back to those parades and flags.

'Dirty work,' I say. 'I'm sure you will agree – had best be done by volunteers. It's only right. From what you do not want to do, to happen to you – you are exempt.'

'So,' she shouts, dismasted by my argument. 'No hand inside my bag! No thieving to buy food.'

'I have my project,' I assure her. 'People will invest...'

'Fuck the people, then,' she says. I feel my argument is won.

'So,' she says, calming, 'people came with viruses, infected guys, and Nina too?'

'I tried the antidote,' I say. 'It could even have made her worse. Her lungs were shredded – and the infecting guys, they wore strange clothes. They must wear them where they come from. Kill and cure – it's the paradox of any *pharmakon*. The cold there – it's a scourge. Nina didn't make peace: it was resignation that she traded in. Her mistake!... Though for her, peace or fatalism, it was all the same.'

*

'Something.' Maurice says. 'Not nothing. The brass, the steel – they're something. That's the modern world – at least, it's modernism. But it's all been done before. Something, where there's nothing. But it becomes banal. And so – reverse it all. Nothing. Here we come! Pull it out, all out. Withdraw the copper belt – watch the cosmic pants fall down. Take out the steel – those Soviet dentures! Holes, gaps, starvation: *minestrone* becomes our fate.'

'I always knew you were into art, Maurice,' I say. I don't believe it.

'Metal – it's universal form, and change. Best – brass: it's marriage from the earth. Copper – it thins, it greens, it ages –

more comely than a person...' And on he talks – we've all
seen old brass stuff.

'Maurice – you're interested in something else, for sure,' I
say.

'It's true,' he says. 'Capital, now – it changes form, it
disappears, it grows – it lifts you up, it casts you down, it
reams you out, it plumps you up. It comes from nothing, yet it
comes from everywhere – your arm, your brain, machines and
cannons, mines and bribes...'

'There's more than that,' I say.

'You know there is,' he says. 'There's peace in having it,
and being anywhere and everywhere.' We're silent.

'And,' he says, 'there's changing everything, and ruling it.
Then, while you look – it frizzles all away. You laugh,' he
says. He doesn't smile. He lays his glowing hand out, where I
can see its length. It's longer than a hand of flesh – a super
hand. 'A royal flush', he says, and now he laughs, delighted.

I tell Jozo everything. He pays me for it. 'Jozo,' I ask.
'Your connection's with Colombia – do you do coca too?'

'Fuels?' he asks. 'I'm not into that. Carburants – for
people? Shrubs? It's like the sunflowers they say can run your
motor. I'm not at all a metaphysical. Sonia even, won't
approve – she says it muddles up the crime. She's quite old-
fashioned when it comes to consciousness. No fuddle! I tell
her – it's all written down, not real – the fiction that she gets it
from, the Crime and Punishment, and the laws. That's not
where we operate, it's fantasy. I guess there's guys that do
that stuff, up the nose, straight to the imagination, the
accelerator – the mind that voyages, it comes in everywhere
and in everything – bottles, paper screws... You never would
find out who's involved. Maurice even less. I guess we're in
the traffic, all of us, it's there, beneath the crust. But – it's not
germane.'

We are wordless, looking at the interconnectedness of what we do, don't do. Jozo says, 'Whatever I do, the result's the same. Steel, no steel. It cancels out.'

When Kaja hears, she rushes to him. 'Look, Jozo. This *accidie* – you rose from greed to ambition, on to power and then – what next? No wonder you have stalled. Here's the perfect plan – the perfect crime. You or your guys – eliminate your lady, Sonia. The perfect crime, eliminating crime. And – with no punishment! The beauty of it! You don't like the sour old hag. She's stalled, like you. It's all trip-hammer, or a mousetrap, what she does – here's the rodent, BANG – goes the trapdoor, the body's dangling, palefaced through the ceiling in the judge's office. Automatic. Now – if she's gone, the scene will open up. No Crime – no one to punish.'

'Yes, Kaja,' Jozo says. 'She won't be there – but what if I've internalised it all – what if I feel remorse, or guilt?'

'You must discriminate,' says Kaja. 'Be selective. Some awful things – you're not aware of! Don't remember doing them. Let this be one of them. Take Maurice. He's morose – the things he did, and didn't do. You can regret the one, things that you did – but not the other.'

'Oh yes you can,' says Jozo. 'If you've a slippery tongue. What you don't do's as material and positive in its effect as what you did.'

We see he's interested. Shuffle the pack and hide the queen. The end of crime – the end of punishment.

Kaja's brought a bottle: Absolut, it says. A good name for a vodka. 'A good name for anything,' she says.

The argument is rocky, that she makes – but none of us likes Sonia and her prudish threats.

We drink the Absolut from cups. It's like a *pharmakon* – we lie, hogs in the sun, as if we've all been hit with spanners. It only takes a moment, wiping us all out. Maybe we'll forget the plan...

But no! Jozo has stuck to it. 'It liberates, exonerates,' we hear him say. 'I can move on to bigger exploits...'

*

'Ah yes,' says Maurice. 'She held our secrets, Nina did. Who has golden limbs, whose eyes are pearl, who has diamonds in his hair. Who took the prisoners, who let them go. There's always lots like her around, a chorus with floury faces. Lamenting, and making sense of horrors. You're sure she left no record? She's pinned under my skeleton?'

'Yes, Maurice,' I say.

What's his next move? He fears nothing, he's mobile as glass hairs. 'I got out of materials,' he says. 'They're risky now. I might try animals. A reserve, a park. People arrive in charabancs to watch – the animals die off. The space is never big enough, or settled. And beneath those padding paws and slithery bellies – there's always something rare. An emerald mine, let's say. We all move on. You see our tails, seeping into river mist...'

I'll be Sonia's avatar. Before she goes – she'll have my key to everything.

'I'm desperate,' says Kaja. 'Maybe if someone would do for me some terrible thing – the design would be clear. Where we all stand. What it is we stand in. What threatens. What's this on our shoes...'

'No one will console you,' I say. 'That was Nina's job. She's in abeyance.'

'Abeyance. That's a good place,' says Kaja. 'There's even a bey in there, sitting by the glassless window, the wind a breath of cinnamon, a frozen midday, the seals down on the rocks, like slugs. What is it beys do next?'

'Oh, I think they wait for someone to come through the door,' I say. I've no idea – I hate the theatre – it's always different from what it should be, a mishappening.

'I wish it wasn't to be Sonia,' Kaja says. 'She's so lumpish. On and on she lives, pretending it's difficult, that she reflects. It should be Jozo. He is second rate.'

'It was your choice, Kaja,' I remind her.

'Oh well,' she says. 'It's an approximate, always – you see the people fighting here and there, for causes hot and tepid, some deluded, threatened, dispersed, or poor, hopeful and hopeless. On they go. The thing is – to be there. That's what I want, even if they have to dig me up.'

'Just curiosity,' I say.

'Yes!' she says. 'What better is there? Beyond doubt and certainty. Seeing it all scroll out, rewind and scroll again. Me being cool, natural, poised.'

13

We can take Sonia to see the world – Paris, New York, Sao Paolo: we just need to switch on. Scenes on the magic lantern. Then, for her exit – back to the karst plain. There, an execution doesn't shake the dust. We hope she'll find a place where she can judge: the dead'll pass down, by her: she's a demon for precision. She does each one an estimate. It doesn't matter crucially, of course – they're the dead. But – so's not to live in vain, she'll be the guardian of the void...

She could be the Grand Inquisitor – so we don't go to Seville. Sonia thinks she treks the world with people that she doesn't like, so she can spend some cash. Seville would let her see what could become of her, her new position. Burn the heretics! That wouldn't do, not from a tycoon, as she is: a moralist!

'We must be kind to her,' says Kaja. 'When she's dead, we'll respect her judgement. Her moral tussles.'

Those, I've never seen. She will judge the dead, Maurice the living. Positive and negative – the result's the same. Out goes the metal – down something falls. Then – up it goes again, the building, taller, the plane – higher. Take out the wires – the energy's renewed, the sun's reflected, doubled. Storms of gas deployed, whipping up the ocean waves. I don't know how it's done, the technicality – I see Jozo, mouth latched open, some guys explain it on his phone. It's like those brooms and Mickey Mouse ... you try to stop them, but they multiply, on they tramp, miniaturised into soldier ants... Hotter and hotter, more natural, more abundant ... only the water's scarce, those bucketsful Mickey and his brooms have poured away – a Tantalus in reverse. Tantalus never reaching

water, Mickey never free of it. Tantalus, his punishment from
the gods, eternal. Mickey – freed by magic – and we don't
believe in magicians or the gods. It's still eternal, the
punishment. The crime – insubordination. Wanting to cheat
the order.

*

'My, it's hot. I need a drink,' shouts Sonia. We have showed
her everything. It's all familiar – the view from the divan.
Cities, performing animals, *acquaria*, the sticky rivers. Show
her everything, so's she's missed out nothing, nothing to
regret, no stone untrodden, tramcar not ridden in, funicular not
marvelled at, slum not abhorred, rare food not hunted down.

'There you go, mad Majnun,' says Sonia, dangling Jozo
from the Empire State. 'No salvation. This tower's all cement.
Chalk and sand and quicklime,' and she shakes him in play,
her plump arms without an elver of muscle.

'Well,' says Jozo, upside down, 'I may be mad – but if I
go – you follow.'

'We're embarrassed by the tiff. It's not even literature.

However, we're quite indulgent. If she lets Jozo slip – it's
her last, her condemned meal: slippery feelers on the lady
mantis. The people whose names we don't know, but follow
us on landmarks – they seem quite amused, pretend they're
shocked. Jozo does the same to Sonia – there's a glass floor in
the Eiffel Tower, that invites such plays. She's a weight –
down she nearly goes. It would resolve the end. Majnun and
Layli, whatever the local variants are – all end the same, the
madman and the night. Dead – the key to everything in
Sonia's hand. 'Is that all there is?' she asked. No wonder
Jozo's obsessed by night and persecution. It's what madmen
are. You'd need to be quite strange, to have the tungsten
market in your hand.

'No,' shouts Jozo, 'we're not brother and sister. That's a provocation! Let me go!'

'Drop you?' shouts Sonia back. I'm sure he doesn't mean to twist the story round like that. Although there is a variant...

Turn the sound up loud enough – anything seems menacing. But don't break off a lug of the world, killing a prominent character, a tycoon. Jozo or Sonia.

'When love dies,' Kaja says, trying to hold my hand, 'mayhem must follow.'

'Just for some boy or girl? It's even worse, if it doesn't die,' I say. 'If it's for God – or self, more awful still.'

'Don't list them all, the instances of love,' says Maurice. 'If Jozo and Sonia had been serious, this iron tower would have gone long long ago.'

'Of course,' says Kaja, 'these fabulous loves must end in death – both, if they're young, with no way out. Or one or other, when they've taken different paths – when they mature, Juliet takes over from the nurse, Romeo – a boss. It figures so.'

'Remember,' Maurice says, 'no one but us knows Sonia had pretensions, or had even read a book. She was a boss, and into metal futures. She made a pair with Jozo – that is all. No one knows she was a punisher.'

'Oh,' says Kaja. 'This is so old-fashioned! People must get wiped away, or else the same old tale would last for ever, all Methusalehs...'

We're all wired hot as peppers, wanting to see someone – at least someone we know! – sacrificed; over the edge, and you down after, and lying still beside them. Then getting up and running, shouting, having a good time. I don't care who goes over. Kaja says, 'The end of punishment. That's my aim, my humanism. Sonia has to go.'

I'd rather it was Maurice. He never did that job for me. and I owe him one big task that I don't want to do.

Maurice says, 'Everybody's reached the end. Inventing crazy things. Looking for the start point – where the string begins... Going into history, finding the good rule, the primal light, and nailing guys on trees. Eternal war, eternal peace – some for the one, some not: it all comes out the same. While you're looking for the start, to do it all again – you find you've reached the end. You've used your rations. Time for someone else. Me – I'm into things that have no substance and no life. I can't believe they'll last – but there's no way that they can end.'

'It's just money, Maurice. You think you own a stash of abstract, but you have to pay for booze with coin, or else they throw you out,' I say.

Throw you out, or over.

'That's fine,' he says. 'I'll take the throwing out. Me – I'll respect no dress code, pay no tax, catch your bullet in my teeth and spit it back at you.'

'Don't let Sonia hear,' I say.

'Oh, she's wondering where her love did go, and being a harpy with Jozo,' Kaja says.

The bull knows peace. It's all it's ever known, will ever know. Abundance, patience – it knows there'll always be others when it's gone. A paradise.

Naturally, I know what some of them, the animals, do to one another.

'You know, there's cities set up by big guys, that they don't know where they are,' says Jozo. 'Alexander – dropped cities all over, like they were empty bottles, and lots of them – they can't be found. Now, for a sum – you can go everywhere on earth, and see it all. You could even set up cities that have disappeared.'

'That won't make you a big guy, though,' says Sonia, who hears everything. 'It makes you rather small.'

Everything that's worth it, we have seen. 'Time to go home,' I say.

'That's not our home,' says Sonia. 'And I'll not go in those old DC3's – they always make my nose bleed.'

'Oh, we'll go in style,' says Kaja. 'There's horses still, and carts. No nosebleeds there.'

'It's not her nose,' says Jozo. 'She's afraid of holes in the plane floor, going through, then – impalement on a cross, a minaret. She wants to be the prisoners' eagle, flying off without a metal skin around. Or legirons.'

'And Petrović?' Kaja asks. 'She can't want to land on him. He's in for life still.'

'Oh,' says Jozo, 'I guess that was to be me, the womaniser, getting punished, inside for life. In Majnun's story, love's a torment, forbidden too. Best heed your parents and the priests – if there are some...'

'This carriage is like a tumbril,' Sonia complains.

'It's a hard ride,' I agree. 'These carts without springs – they used them in the Thirty Years War.'

That satisfies her. 'No black horses,' Kaja says. 'It gives the game away.'

We have two greys. Losers.

'These are all good people here,' says Maurice, lying back on a knobbly sack. 'You can't be good unless you've suffered.'

'Suffered, hated, wanted revenge, forgiven. Then got revenge. Then you can be good,' says Jozo. I wonder if he's good.

'The experts came here, and told them how to come to terms,' says Maurice. 'It's a good profession, not badly paid. Sitting around, hearing the same story, giving the same advice. Taking on the sins, and moving on. A diet of barium meals, in case you've caught the other people's sicknesses –

you expect to come up clean, although the edge is always there.'

We're an alliance, all of us, against Sonia. Each has some memory of injustice she's done to them, a curl of lip, a gift unacknowledged. We shan't miss her – though we may regret she's made us, each one, an assassin. But – that is life, is order, is keeping balances, and up to date, not sliding back into the medieval ages, or the dark...

We've not discussed how it's to be done. Who'll do the deed?

Maurice – is the warrior. People stay clear of him. He swaggers, and stays mum. Jozo's a murderer – no one knows, they chat with him.

It's important, when we've done for Sonia – to avoid discovery. Avoid the punishment. Annul the crime.

'That could be Nina's mound,' says Maurice. 'I thought it stirred.'

We watch it, thinking of a swift despatch for Sonia. We're stuck, for hours. Maybe it heaves, or maybe not.

We hear a gurgling – as if some fluid travelled round in Nina's skeleton.

Then, we see, bound to a corner post of our once sturdy cart – a figure. We count the company – it must be Kaja.

She's moribund. Then, she's restored. 'Someone tried garotting me,' she says. That's for sure, they did. Garotting is a compromise, between a hanging and decapitation. With Kaja too, it made a compromise – between her life, her death.

'Thank the wood. It's rotten, wouldn't hold the wire,' she says.

Kaja had her punishment before she could commit the crime. The crime she proposed, that then was done to her – turned out a failed execution. The crime for which she could be punished – didn't happen. A failure. Followed by another, on her neck! Who tried the garotting, and for what? Was it meant to fail? or was that accidental? And – what if it was Sonia, creeping up behind? Suppose she knew she was the victim designated – then, turning like a serpent, righting, as it were, the wrong? Revenge before the fact? Punishing Kaja with a crime? Paying wrong with wrong?

We're confused – we can't ask Sonia, evidently. She's maybe not involved. and if she is, she can't be judge, victim and executioner... Maybe she can.

'Maybe she can,' says Maurice. 'But no one's much hurt. there's no suspect. Or – everyone's a suspect...'

'There!' says Jozo. 'I'm sure there's movement under Nina's mound.'

'I can't judge small stirrings,' I say.

'That's where you fail,' says Maurice. 'Not judging. Me, Sonia, Jozo – we judge all the time. That's why we're where we are. You and Kaja don't know how. Judging is everything, not being comfortable and fitting in. Being nice.'

'Are we nice?' I ask. 'Then maybe it's us, is Majnun and Layli.'

'No,' says Jozo. 'You're not nice. And you should know – you're not those two. You're not worth being victims, even. With you – what happens is just casual.'

'Maybe food and water's a good bet for investing in,' says Kaja, her ambition flowing back, nourishing her veins. 'Metals is just rusting stuff. Food – a corner in it, big as France – that brings wealth, beneficence too.'

'Don't think of it,' says Maurice. 'You'd be for ever justifying profits from the eats, and heaping speculations into storage space. When I take out the copper – I'm resigned that guys will find alternatives. Jozo's quite a different beast. He's local. Traditional. When buildings fall – they make the new ones taller – but they're always there, stuck in the same spot.'

'See!' Kaja whispers to me. 'They're enemies, Jozo and Maurice. Each in his cloud. Abstract, when it comes to paying out, but a sideline in real things, materials.'

We gaze at them, Jozo, Maurice, Sonia. Maybe they're real, maybe we're just used to them.

New people muster, that we can't join. Not the old Turks, and not our sort at all, new organisers in the ways that hurt, offend. It is not for us. We can't join. Must we fight, then? We're terrified. It doesn't hurt us – not yet. Our sort, everywhere, is under threat, offended – the rest, everyone else – maybe they've been waiting, hoping. How many of them...? What are their faces? What's their beef? We all draw close – it's instinct...

'And how about that refuge, the bright house?' Maurice asks me. He laughs. He knows the refuge hasn't even been designed.

'Oh, the storm! It's just a bird, a dark bird, passing over,' Kaja says, shaking off her apprehension. 'Or else it's hunters. It'll all be sorted out. We'll dig for food, and drill for drink!' and she laughs too.

'These new things,' I say. 'We fear them anyway – and what if they're the old ones, dug up and pure? Not Nina, twisting underneath the weight, but revenants, bright and terrible, starting off along the bony path, forgetting it's all been lived before, shouting and chanting to dull out the pain?'

'We all need living space,' says Kaja. 'Five meals a day – like in the past. Everything fits in. It always does. What seems new and terrible – it's just for territory, and to have a following.'

'If you'd gone in the tub,' Maurice tells me, 'you wouldn't be afraid.'

14

We climb back in the cart. No one leans on the corner where the garotte was. We've marked Nina's spot – maybe we'll need it, later.

'You naughty boy,' Sonia says to me. 'You want to make your mark, I know. Wanting to eliminate the punishments. A murder plot against me. In its way, a noble hope. Pass it on, the inquisitor's burden – up the line, at least. Up to the bosses – who know nothing. Besides, they don't take responsibility. But – everyone gets punished. Dying young – you escape it... But you don't, you see! Escaping lands you in the hottest stew! Anyway, you did it for the best, I know,' and she embraces me. My! she's strong.

'Actually, it was Kaja,' I say.

'Thanks,' says Sonia, letting go. 'That's what I thought.'

*

'Lighten the load,' shouts Jazo, who is driving. They leave us, Kaja and me. The big guys truck on. So, the road's not as empty as it looks.

I say to Kaja, as I'm looking for diversions, 'Those ants. Little machines. If only we could replicate...' It's what Hop o' my Thumb said.

'Yes,' Kaja says, 'I see you miniature. Since you lost me my job. It's better that way.'

'Wasn't it Maurice? And I've always followed you,' I say.

'That doesn't matter. You never dissuaded me from my mistakes. You stole from me.'

'Let's start again,' I say.

'What?' she says. 'Falsify my memory? You know it's all we have. Without – we're speechless, running into one another, like the ants.'

'Not ants,' I say. 'We're supposed to love individuals, even if they can't be prised apart, stay in the clump – we're poor people, featured on some expensive vase. Waiting for some others, impoverished too, to make their move.'

'Well,' she says, 'I'm not poor. I had a desk, a screen – until some cretin nipped it. Authority too. A generation before that – you can't imagine how much worse it was.'

'Oh, I've a good imagination,' I say.

'My father was big in the Party,' she says, sniffing a little. 'It does no good.'

'Why should it?' I ask. 'I never thought of you with a father.'

'We had two cats. They slept upon his desk,' she says. 'Then we had nothing.'

'Sonia and Maurice can get to us whenever they want,' I say.

'They got to me,' she says. 'Though it was my fault. You were spared because of the bull. You were part of that.' You can see the red line on her neck. I remember 'Lord' Curtis, and his 'thin red line'. It all reverberates.

Kaja says, 'In the Thirty Years War – everyone got a ride on a cart.'

'You've had your ride,' I say. 'Then the Swedes were decisive for a while. Then there was Peace.'

'It's good to know a bit of history,' she says. 'It settles you.'

We must walk. We don't ask where to.

'Those bastards who abandoned us,' says Kaja. 'They have the cash to make the twist, be benefactors. Saints, even.

We can only make good deaths, and hope. I'd like to be known as good, in life.'

She stumbles silently along.

I have to carry her. She's tall and heavy, but that's what you must do with saints. 'I'm like a cross,' laughs Kaja, recovering her spirit. She splays out her arms.

'It's good to be up there, I bet,' I say. I'd like to dump her. But I might get caught.

Here's where the gypsies gathered, with their little carts, low as a cot, the ponies running like machines, guys lying comfortable, grinning out. There's no sign left here.

We can't go back to Stuttgart, even if the train goes there. We've learned a lot, though. How the world is run... the doubts and the vindictiveness of those we travelled with, our friends. Knowledge to use – even if we might get caught.

'Steal some food,' I tell Kaja. 'That's what we must do now. I'd love some *burek,* and gold and silver, if they're hoarding some. Circulate, circulate. Preserve nothing! Into the crucible!'

'And must we jump in, be gold and silver too?' asks Kaja – 'You were nervous last time.'

'Changing your mind – that's the nub of it,' I shout. 'Luther, Tsar Boris, Stalin, whoever you first think of – they all did it, and they're remembered! No PR crap for them, no ads in papers: all's in our heads, our consciences. We'd all be saints if we didn't change our minds – think what a mess that would make! All good, martyred, or both! Someone has to survive, dither, write the necrology. Guilt, grandeur, making up minds, unmaking them ... the hat is full of names – just pull them out, and read your fortune.'

We run through stands of pampas and bamboo, we are quite restored – it's like infancy, like spring. Maybe it's always springtime here, all year now, the new climate.

We steal some *burek* – in that house, there's no gold. No tub – that, I can live without.

'Someone could shoot me,' I say. 'Stealing food. That's pretty bad. Though as endings go, it's quite refined. More honest than waiting for the *coup de grace*, the *coup de dés*, someone's retribution.'

'It's not pretty, being shot,' says Kaja. 'And it's not greatly honest, thieving. It hurts, I'm sure, the wound; you'd not like that. Why not settle for a transgress? Resist. Enjoy the eternal spring. Wait till you see them coming for you. Then – be displaced, not martyred.'

We push on to a tram that's so full we can't be asked for money. Kaja's still talking. 'You don't know what's important. That puts you in a stall.'

'Oh Kaja!' I say. 'You need to be important before what's important matters. I've a string of principles – a parade of thoroughbreds.'

The passengers are all wearing paper hats: that's quite disturbing – some ceremony. Some community, belief – it's good not to be in it, bad to be out... I'm pressed against a beauty – maybe eighteen, and I think of Petar. My hand touches her arm. Is it involuntary? You could say it was. The flesh feels like still air, distilled, deep. Like nothing else. The sadness that – that's that: I may never be in such a crowd again. You could weep.

We climb down. The life of passion and devotion I shan't have clanks off down the tracks. There remains Petar's violent death that I should avoid. It all repeats, it never is the same. History is never still, it bubbles like a bog – preserving some, sucking other corpses down, twisting the bones into likenesses of roots... 'Displaced'? No place: a new place? – or like nomads, lots of places; people think of them as none.

'Kaja,' I say. 'There's nothing for it. To be credible, you need to be a boss.'

'Yes,' she says. 'Now's the time. There's room for that –
the will. Like Sonia and Jozo, or like Maurice and the tub. It's
the determination, to put your body in. We could do that, if
we wanted, and there's nothing else to want,' says Kaja. 'It's
not about being good, but it's not hiding either.'

'Personally, you don't need lay a hand on anyone,' I say.
'If you're a boss. In fact, it's all done for you, the setting-up.'

'When you're powerful, you can play around. But you, no
unemployed women,' Kaja says, holding my arm tight, setting
out my diet. 'No under-age, no fooling yourself. They've all
the day to betray you, wear exciting clothes, have a good
time.'

She should have lovers. Maybe she does. People think
they're transformed by love and passion – see them on the
train – they look the same as all the rest. Yet, there is a pattern
– not one you'd like clinging on your back... Persistent
shipwrecking of reason, then new heavier ships are fitted out
– the same mission: to finish on the rocks. The emptiness of
lives lived under the flag of reason – yet that's the game! The
aim is – reach the end without upset. Not to risk too much,
suffer little. That's the point.

The opposite is also true.

We've eaten all the *burek*. Now we're thirsty.

'You realise,' says Kaja, 'the refuge, your shiny palace, is
the only project that it's sensible to start.'

'Kaja,' I say, 'you don't know much about the
metalwork.' Nor about sequences, finding a narrative, like the
books they read on trains, thinking there's a project that runs
like golden thread through all the happenstance, believing
lives are rendered down into an hour or so of fat and gristle...
'The will, Kaja – it's a bog-light. It leads you to your death –
not like a torch, but like a stammer from the soil... It's a dance
of bees.'

'No!' she says. 'No shirking, no excuse!'

We gaze around. 'This river,' I say. 'Better than a cart, for travel. Better than some box on rails. It has a life. And yet – it isn't blue, it doesn't dance. You need something that is both of those.'

All the fighting here. It's a surprise there's someone left...

*

So, the cube, shelter, palace, tower – is cast. The die is tossed. The refuge – built.

It took intelligence, and skill, of course, and people obedient, modest, humble too. It casts a shadow, but as the sun strikes at its shine – it answers back, a glister duplicated, multiplied. I could have left the surface grainy, like porridge. I prefer it smooth, a brother to the sun. Of course, towers have been built before. But never cast, in metal, not dwindling as it rises up, but solid, squared off to its top. Nor will one alike be made again. Without an ornament, a sign, a flag. There just remains to fill it up inside, for living in – a structure, decor, maybe quite fantastical, relaxing – rococo, traces of the birds, the sea, and flowers with filmy heads.

'It's tight to everything – but once you're in, you can't get out,' says Kaja.

'You needn't wish to, Kaja. Anyway – you took the step that brought you in, the danger well perceived, or not. It's up to you to work it out – how you can leave, and maybe go back in,' I say.

'It's tight,' she says. 'But there's a flaw. It's indefensible. No sallies forth, no objects, fluids from the roof. If it's attacked, it stands until it falls.'

'Oh Kaja! Soldiers get bored and hungry quick,' I say. 'They go back to their mess. From the outside, it appears the refuge is just an abandoned shell. No loot, no prisoners, no ransoms, and no massacres. They'll go away. Or write on it. Their stuff will just bounce off.'

'Well,' she says, dismissively. 'To me it's just a metaphor. A folly. Triumph of technique, no more. What people call – a *hapax legomenon*. You didn't sign it – but it's you, all you. No room for me, who pushed you to it. Produce something more accessible, I said.'

There's nothing much to say. They make animals look into a glass, to see if they recognise their 'I': identity. If they do – they're promoted. They can be eaten. They have rights. For the rest – too bad. It's the same with casting. There's an author, a furnaceman, and the others do their job and stand around. I'm enlightened: 'to each according to his need,' I say, even if abilities are limited, and only one accomplishes...
 'It's done,' says Kaja. 'Now what do we do?'

'We should make peace,' I say. 'Just you and me. Because of genitals – they're different shapes – it doesn't mean between us there must be either love – or battle.'

'You broke my screen,' she said. 'And genitals don't come into that. But – there's a war, it's true, who knows when the thirty years is up? Or when we'll be on some list? With all our inner reservations ... we should make a truce.'

She hugs me, without interest. 'Of course,' she says, 'the fighting's not decisive – it's gone on for ever. It's running out of stuff that counts. No vodka in that house. No pots, no pans.'

'The trouble is nothing to do with that,' I say. 'It's that there's no one left to borrow from. Maurice and Jozo – they just ride the waves. They land upon no shore. It's the waves, the wind – they've died right down. Everyone but us – they all have debts, and that brings on the rest, the trembling and the fear. We two – we're the happy ones – not owing anything...'

'Courage!' says Kaja. 'On we go, and soon we'll find some guy who'll lend us cash.'

'The crime and punishment,' I say. 'That seems quite irrelevant, after what has happened. And if Sonia wants revenge...'

'Oh, that again,' says Kaja. 'The thing is, to keep going for the thirty years.'

'That train – goes to Bratislava,' I say.

'What, with us together?' she asks: I push her on. People push her off. They shout, 'There's nothing for you there, in Bratislava. How'd you fit in?'

'It's true,' she says, 'I'd always been so good at it, the fitting in. Now, I see these trains, packed, gliding off. The travellers – they won't come back. They stare at me, the heads shaven, like potatoes, the women with the glitters on their breasts, a dirty motto, proverb, perhaps, the children – a mouse, a shrew, their toys – in rags. Where do they go? To Bratislava? To work there?'

'There's a bar,' I say. 'They'll have vodka here. Maybe you could work, pay off the bill we'll raise... Don't take things so to heart. We'll talk, like we used – pinning the answer to most things. What if the answer to the whole is easy? In the end – "nothing". Solves it all, neat and simple.'

'I'm disappointed,' Kaja says. 'I thought Maurice or Jozo – was a lion. I see they all are foxes. Sonia – she's nothing. She's the gravel in your knee when you are dragged, have fallen off the cart. It's all by chance – the crime and being caught. You,' and she mimes to me the nipping claw. 'Except for those – the nip, the shelter – you've done nothing; you're a slug, innocent, yet you feel some guilt...'

'That's just psychology,' I say. 'It doesn't count, when you are adding up the bill.'

In the bar, we talk and drink, as we may have done before. 'You shouldn't see in crowded trains a mark that's sinister,' I tell her. 'They didn't like the look of you, is all. They're running, escaping, nothing more. There is no threat, except from poverty. They were good people, there is no crime about them, so no punishment. Those terms – don't stick.'

'We've never talked like this,' she says. 'And Sonia: you're sure she doesn't count?'

'Oh not at all.' I say: then, 'You might get work here, in this bar – just cleaning up. And so you'll get some tickets for somewhere else: new life! And pay for all our vodka too...'

'My bag,' says Kaja, digging down. 'It's been cleaned out, there's just my broken screen. Maybe I shan't drag this ... this sack along ...' She fluffs it out, she climbs inside, the bag becomes a sack... 'Oh no!' she shouts from deep within, 'Some bastard's stole my screen!'

'Don't be bourgeois,' I say. 'Your screen had lived its life. One day, they say, we human ones will live a thousand years. Years lived like lions, for sure. We'll long outlive appliances. Some guy now, a happy thief, will fix your screen, write a book on it...'

She's inconsolable: 'Fuck his book.' She weeps. 'It was my bond, memorial. Made me recall your scheming traitor's heart, each time I saw its vacant face.' She rounds on me, 'I'm the dependable one. I'm steady.'

'No, Kaja,' I say. 'You develop like an epic.'

'I wish all of you weren't here,' she shouts, waving her empty sack. 'An earthly paradise is what I need. A harmony. No humans. No celestial eye, no crime, and eating sensibly.'

'Where'd you be, Kaja?' I ask.

'Brisk up,' she says. 'There's lots of ways to spy and not be seen.'

'Like me,' I say. 'I'm cool. I'm the beginning, probably the end. I had you meet Sonia and the rest. I was into all the big stuff, the base metals.'

'You haven't the guts to make it to the end,' says Kaja. 'You'd be happy riding on my back, in this empty sack.'

'Oh no,' I say. 'I have a hunger for the crowd. Just think –
going among the clans, the families, the politics – like who
went to which *madrasa*, who to which school, who to Yale.
The complexity – the wondering how the mountain moves,
then seeing it go live and twisting with the wind...'

'Well, you may say,' says Kaja, not believing. 'But I
grant you – without you, there's no story. But – you don't
intervene. It's the cosmological eye we need – over and
again.'

The guys who ran the bar, here on the station platform –
maybe they rode the train. There's no one here to take the
money that we haven't got. We take some of their stock, put it
in Kaja's sack. We're both quite drunk.

'This is a fertile plain we're on,' I say. 'Though it maybe
doesn't look that way. A duke, a marshal, a Vojvoda – then up
a bit, there's the great Hungarian plain, that's called the
Puszta, something like...'

Kaja hears 'march' not 'marshal': we're both vague.
'Here, if it isn't marches, it's some marshes. How do you tell
the flat from flat?' she asks.

'Geography is settling, Kaja,' I say. 'Even more than
history. But – you, when you take the train – it's all quite
different, the aspect changes.'

'We must try hard,' she says. 'To put ourselves right,
while we can, when there's no tests or trials now, or anything
extreme. It's all taken place here: to hear, there's just the
sucking of the wave receding. We must set ourselves right,
before what's certain for us – going on to be with Jozo,
Maurice – wherever they are, in their splendid slippery places.
Assailed, it seems they are, by people, aggressive. Much more
determined even than they are – parading not with sticks and
such, but just the cut of chins, the stride. Must get right, while
we can, in this undemanding place.'

'Get right?' I ask. 'You mean get sober? And Petar – he was irritating. My! he was irritating! Smug, prejudiced, dogmatic...'

Petar's a warning, and a threat. The death that pinned him – could be pinned on us.

'That was trivial stuff,' she says. 'And anyway, I wasn't there.'

We don't seem to reach many conclusions, Kaja and me, though the environment is conducive – but at least, we don't fight.

*

'You're right,' says Maurice. 'I was in this for the long haul, the long term. The riches of the mine, its symphony. That thug Jozo – he was too, I guess. But it's the short-term guys – they give you hell. They bite your bum, while you're trying to philosophise. Ministers abound – not of religion, the other kind!'

'Kaja and I were taken by the Thirty Years War,' I say. 'Those Croatian soldiers. Full of jokes. And the Swedes! They needed the money then, of course.'

He ignores me. He holds his golden hand down low, as if its weight oppresses.

'Those countries without territory,' he says, asking, too. 'People without citizenship who trek the world and never move. What do you make of it? It seemed what I was looking for.'

'Everyone has heard of that,' says Kaja. 'We've all had one of those: appliances. Until they're broken. It's quite banal. Have you come to this, Maurice? Dementia?'

'Anyone who's living here, here in Ürümqi,' Maurice says, 'knows the answer is not "nothing".'

'It was hard getting here,' Kaja says, placating.

'It'll be harder still to leave,' he says. 'Anyway, where'd you think I'd be? Some steel town, like poor Jozo? And Sonia – her mission's done. What is the point of all this punishment? And – look at it another way – what is the point of all this crime? If everybody stole who's poor – would that even everything? If we all killed the guys we didn't like – would that be humanism? Would the sum be true, and space for all, and all good guys?'

We chew on this: when we came up, we paused, and had a drink below. *Cent'erbe*: nature in a glass. It makes you madder than a dog. The guy behind the bar has stacks of forged two dollar bills. 'How'll I get rid of these?' he asks. 'The ink runs to and fro – and stinks. The guy who's pictured on the face – he looks Korean. Few Koreans pass through here.'

We wonder – should we chase his boss, his printer? Remonstrate?

'Don't think of it,' says Maurice. 'Remember – there's a law against collective guilt. You're not supposed to punish everyone – although it's true, they all get punished anyway. You have to find them one by one, and finger them: and make a story of it.'

We look out of the window: Maurice is up so high, it seems you can't see anything. Or – you can see everything. It makes no sense.

'That fog – it isn't air, it's sand,' he says. 'You learn to tell the difference. Elements – they have the same effect, although it helps to tell them one from t'other.'

'My, how well you've settled in!' says Kaja. 'Without my help, without my screen.'

'How true,' says Maurice. 'I can buy peppers here, and other stuff. You often can't see anything at all. We all muck in. This is the centre of the world, you know, if that impresses – as it should.'

'You've gained in wisdom too,' I say. 'You've never done the work I ordered from you. Now – I've nothing left to ask. You've reached the bourne. If you were Alice, you'd need to start again, a crown of brass and lacy clothes. But as it is – you're just a boss. Higher – you cannot go. My compliments. A life well spent and satisfied.'

'It's true,' he says. 'Remember Nina? There she lies, beneath my skeleton, ready for my call. If I need consolation – she will rise and come to me. She won't explain, she'll hug me, and she'll smell – not of the grave, but of a thousand sheep. I'm climbing – there's the uplands, there the mountain top...'

Kaja interrupts, 'What for, Maurice, what's it for? Why don't you lie quiet, let her console?'

'Just tell me why I should, dear Kaja?' Maurice asks. 'One thing or another – what's the difference? I used to think a plan had to be for everything. Now, I think positive. Exclude – that's the secret.'

'What's in that closet?' Kaja asks: there's a pictogram on the doors – looks like a stack of bones.

'No,' says Maurice, 'it's not "skeletons": it could be "here", or it could be "destiny" , or both.'

More than a cabinet, a closet – it's a high room, shelves around, with metal piled. Is this the pale pale Central Asian gold, washed down from snowy heights? It's ingots, that's for sure. It's like Petar's room, the shelving nudged aside by tons of smelt.

'What'll you do with all this gold?' asks Kaja. It's clear, with this you buy some tanks and bullets, or maybe pictures... open a zoo, a mine...

She takes my crab-crackers, takes a nip: the bar yields little – but enough: she says, 'You dog! Maurice! It's brass!'

'So what?' he says. 'To me, it's worth far more than gold. Besides – this is reserves. It's never cashed. You put it on the balance sheet, is all. It's a memorial to Petar. It's like the amber room, the hall of mirrors. It's all the bull you'd ever want.'

Kaja hums the song, 'Bulls may safely graze...' and Maurice tunes in, says, 'Who ever saw a bull that grazed? Grass! Smokes it, maybe, lying back, to cool down, like the artists show the smoke out through its nose.'

'Maybe he drinks *Cent'erbe* – a hundred grasses, nature pure and raw,' I say. Maurice ignores me.

He's in good form. 'I'm on to something big,' he says: 'These Han – one by one, they best me – but in the mass, I'm more than a match for heaps of them. And – all the people here below,' and he waves down to the floors piled up beneath us – 'they're mine.'

'We didn't see them,' Kaja says.

'They're not there to be seen. That's their treasure,' Maurice says, taking an ingot from a shelf. 'Here, take this. My man downstairs will change it for some notes.'

15

Jozo and Sonia – in New York, of course. 'Not in some crummy rusting place,' he says. They live high up, like Maurice – in a cage. I guess it's steel. There's hundreds, dangling way up high. You see the guys and gals come home from work, they eat, they screw, they dream – all in full view. It's dull.

'It's like it's from Petronius,' says Kaja. 'The hundred days.'

'Oh no,' says Sonia. 'My, it's chic! This way they know our secrets – and here we eat, we dream, we screw, like all the rest – no pictures on the walls, no china ducks ... we're free as eagles, all around there's air...'

'It's intimate, because we share our intimacy with everyone. That way, it disappears,' says Jozo. 'Like we were penguins.'

We're much impressed. No doubt like Maurice they've devised a plan, and keep their bullion out of sight.

'Here, in our steel,' says Sonia. 'We cogitate. There's talk of our extinction – up high, it makes some sense, when you can see the colony extended, its fear, and its resource. Extinction – there's no crime. No guilt. And, so it seems, no punishment. We, species, signed up to no plan. We aren't so pretty, and we eat whatever comes to hand. We're omnivores, and so – if we aren't here, no one aspect suffers. And most gain.'

'Your mission, Sonia, is done: accomplished,' Kaja says. She's much impressed. 'The dialectic is negated. There is nothing. Not something. No synthesis – a blank, a gap. And – you might say there's earthly paradise. The modest beasts are left – they have no destiny, except that they survive. Or maybe not. But if they do or don't – there's no one there to take the blame. And that is paradise, my dear.' She embraces Sonia. 'That means the Thirty Years is up,' she says, though Sonia doesn't understand.

'Hold it,' says Jozo. 'Modest beasts? We made the bull to show the opposite: the truth. Those creatures – they are bold and indestructible. Make no mistake.'

Kaja whispers to me, 'Maybe Sonia remembers how we tried to kill her. I could wait for her, hide, jump out – there's so many street corners here...'

'No,' I say. 'You've gotten so aggressive! And – those aren't birds up there, it's artificial crap comes down. They're special agents. They'll swoop down on you, and peck.'

'It's true,' she says. 'There's guys all round that's dangerous – big hats and guns. Here, bulls won't safely graze, I'll bet.'

'Oh no,' I say, 'it's cows that count for them. But – big hat and gun – only if you're a stranger, rode in from out of town.'

'Well, I am all of that,' she says. 'But – these stereotypes – they wouldn't work at all, back in Ürümqi. Tight hats – that is the rule out there.'

'We've tried some new religions out,' Sonia breaks in. 'You could try some too – but watch those birds up high. Their eyes are wired to spy on heresies; and chiliasm, prophecy, the holyrollers – don't try all that.'

'Sonia,' says Kaja. 'I know I'm quite direct. But really – cages? Spirits? It was fun to see you smuggle, petting on the floor... You've gone quite solemn now, and Jozo too.'

'It's true,' says Sonia. 'We've aged. Our veins stick out, some have collapsed. Our teeth flap to and fro as if they're hinged. But always – there's a plan. There's rivalry, and settling scores, and general doing down. The question is, to raise our game. A global challenge, while we simulate our innocence, long-suffering...'

'You're finished, Sonia,' Kaja says. 'Your destiny's been reached. Fortune – it's like bed, a screw. The first one you remember. The next hundred, though – a whiteout. Oblivion.'

*

'Do you remember me, Kaja?' I ask.

'Oh yes,' says Kaja. 'Like an amputation. You can't have those more than once.'

'That makes me feel quite good,' I say.

'That choice is yours,' she says.

'Hey,' I say to Sonia, 'this seems a town where you can ask most things. Your cage – doesn't it get cold?'

'Hey yourself,' she says, 'there's some smart guy behind you, asking sharp questions?' She pretends to look for the distant storyteller at my back: 'The bars are heated. We go up against, like cats. Or tigers. It's a feature not in zoos or jails. And when it snows, we wear big hats.'

'You guys are inscrutable,' I say. 'I guess I don't understand living in a town. Maybe it's a defect – like autism. Seeing the detail, the snail's eye... Like going through your life, your penis shorter than the other guys', blaming all incomprehensions on this one unalterable quirk. Lots of things I never grasp. People! Then the flash: of course! The heated bars.'

'Autism – that's a new one!' Kaja says. 'The rest is on the record.'

'The Turks – they'll never come and organise this place,' I say.

'Oh, you're Majnun,' says Sonia. 'You haven't had to run or go to war. Your story wanders on and peters out...'

'The bodies in the bushes,' Jozo says. 'You wouldn't notice them. Anyway, those Turks are tough. They wouldn't waste their time with you.'

We wander through a square, Kaja and me: she jostles the people passing, wandering. Some shout. She too shouts, and leaps about:

'They think it's the rage
To live in a cage...
I'm in rags on my cart
No bread in my sack.
No horse in the shafts,
No whip to crack...' she sings.

'No one will notice you, Kaja,' I say. 'They don't care about you, your humanism, your broken screen. They're all refugees, that's why they're aggressive, just like you.'

She quietens down. Her hair sticks out like serpents. It's the rage.

'Sonia and Jozo – they plot. They have houses, mansions, palaces for sure,' I tell her. 'The cage is just for sunning in...'

'Movement! Colour! Away with the greys!' she shouts. That's right!

I join her – 'The Sun... while it glows and warms still – the Sun!' I shout. 'Suffuse us with colours – like leaves, like plums...'

We're almost a sect.

We shout, we sing, we embrace. It doesn't make her Layla.

We can do anything we want, more or less. No one – more or less – prevents us. It's not Ürümqi.

'Oh, how I wish I was back there,' says Kaja, exhausted. 'A city built on sand and mud. Maurice has class. He's a rock. He's his own flag, nothing to add, nothing that you can subtract.'

'I wouldn't say...' I start to say.

'No envy,' Kaja says. 'You've done your big deeds. That's you parcelled up. Maurice – he hasn't yet begun.'

'Kaja,' I say. 'Don't tip your hand...'

Our hair is wild, up it ramps – they stare at our bast shoes, our eyes are hot as tarmac pits, our mouths work – two drowning fish...

'Kaja,' I say, 'there's what people want – that's sacrosanct, of course. Then there is what endures, that isn't satisfied, that feels no hunger, only pain... The rocks, the elements – the ores, they go into the crucible, they fry, they roast, they boil and bubble – out they're poured, weak simulacra of our dreams ... then back they go, into the furnace, turned around, shafted in some concrete hull, to rust, crumbling unseen... Beyond our wretchedness, indifferent, they burn, they freeze...'

'Yes,' Kaja says. 'Maurice was a soldier, did what soldiers do. But Jozo – did for Petar. Petar was a spar of light, dancing in red and green – and down he went. There's no excuse. And Sonia knows ... there's no redress, no punishment, nothing restores. It's like the brass – a marriage of convenience, metals indissoluble, joined in the fire with hammers...'

'I'm not so sure Maurice didn't have a hand...' I say.

'You were there,' shouts Kaja. 'Maybe you did too. You squalid people, confessions made to Nina, who absorbed it all – now squirming underneath her mound, your thoughtless acts tormenting.'

We make a space around us. People scurry far away.

I say, 'Kaja – you know, it suffers, but does not endure. Not even capital. Green flowers, pinholes, corrosion – the metal thins and creases, cracks, the patina turns black and flakes. Nothing holds, dear Kaja. The prisoners are freed – they die. The eagle flies – a crossbolt does for it. Some prisoners remain – they die. They are the ones who expiate, who pay for crimes, and die in chains, washed clean. The crime, the punishment – it's all the same...' She weeps. I weep.

There's no one near.

We run some more. Kaja says, 'You know, stopping to think – what you say – it makes no sense.'

'In the context, yes it does,' I say. 'It's not all flat surfaces, Kaja – think round the corners too. Must we prefer to go with Maurice against Jozo? What is the plan?'

'There's the refuge,' Kaja says. 'We could wait things out in there.'

'That's for the end,' I say. 'I may have reached a conclusion, Kaja, but there's the middle, and the beginning to be found as well – probably, they're more important.'

She's the only person I know well, and the most extreme, shrieking and raging. What good does it do, to know her – from the park, the heads on spikes, to her vendettas?

'Maurice is hard to fathom,' I say, enticing her with the banal.

'It's all about the tub, the hand,' she says. 'He's a gold person, just a touch alloyed.' She likes the game – 'Jozo, now...'

*

'Kneel!'

We kneel. Some guy, a cop, has told us to – explanations always come, like the bird of wisdom, when the action's done. We're innocent, but probably that is not the point. We're guilty – not of what you'd know.

We're tiny, kneeling. Tall as *homo habilis*, our ancestor. 'Knee-high'. Can't walk, can't reach a fruit. *Homo-phobia* – watch out! you animals! – *ecce homo*'s getting born. Here we come! Dig and chip, flake and smelt.

'Put your hands on your head...' Yes, we're simple simons, but you're not supposed to say – 'Stupid'. This is the beginning – we're on the road, in a million years, this way or that. Iron, bronze, gold and steel – here we come! If only we could stand. Knap a flint. Swing those arms. Whittle that long stick. Stick something with it...

'Hi guys,' says Kaja. 'I guess you're curious about Jozo.'

'This is the beginning, Kaja,' I say. She's not impressed – maybe she's seen the movie – how the humans start.

It's easy, talking out of this one. We're innocent, and we have speech. There just remains the middle, the development. Some millions of those years – you don't need wait long before you're aged, out in the rain, and fossilised. Those fires, the snow, the drought. The first few times – once in your lifetime – the world dies and is recast – then we're born. The poem, the burial, the first Majnun – how does that fit? Cast out, Layla running after, probably with kids, quite unavailing. The movie's already on the fire...

'Kneeling this way, hands on head – you can't get up,' I say. It's evident.

'Jozo can,' says Kaja. 'That's why they're interested in him.'

'That's a myth,' I say. 'No one can. And Jozo has other peculiarities.'

'Those agents learned something about evolution,' says Kaja. 'That lockdown position. But Jozo knew a bit more.'

This takes us to the middle of the journey. 'I love lions,' says Kaja. 'But I love steaks. I'm glad we fought and won the battle for the meat.'

Next day, we climb back to Sonia's cage: 'We have a friend in trouble,' Jozo says. 'They want to execute him. But we've asked that he get the thousand cuts. That should give him quite a chance.'

'They don't know how to do it,' Sonia says. 'And they won't learn. You need practice – so he's safe!'

'That's just a fantastic thing!' says Kaja, admiringly. 'It's the kind of trick you'd hope your friends would do for you.'

'If we fail,' says Jozo, drinking coolly from a bottle, 'the result is just the same. On death row, you live longer than if you were in real life.'

'All that is not my doing,' Sonia says. 'Alas, we women – don't get to wield the axe. We follow on, playing the ethical role. We're the courageous idiots,' and she cuddles Kaja, who's without words. 'So, I've decided. Me and Jozo – we'll have a sex change.'

'Both of you?' I ask. 'Then what's the point?'

'Oh, point there is,' says Sonia. 'That misogynist! He's worse than Maurice, in and out the tub...'

'So,' says Jozo, stashing the bottle, 'I get to play the blind lady?'

'Oh no,' says Sonia, 'forget that. There's no justice in the scheme I'm laden with. Only in jail will they tattoo you thus – "crime" on one fist, "punishment" on the other. Like in the movie, "love" and "hate". A left, a right, a combo – punches from both sides. That is how it works, dear Jozo. There is nothing in between – remorse, repentance, forgiveness – forget all that: and justice too.'

'Well, it's all OK by me,' says Jozo. 'But – no knife. Each will abstain or practise sex in their own way, like before.'

'I guess it's in the head,' says Kaja, sometimes impressed, and sometimes not. 'The body, though...'

'Doesn't come into the equation,' Jozo says. 'As for the politics – the truth is – it's all done by Iranians. Those Arabs, they're so dumb, they couldn't pile a brick on brick. The Turks – they're idle. Slavers too – too smart to fight, their pots are made by the Armenians. No, it's Iranians. They have a splashy religion too – parades and shouting. That's the stuff!'

Sonia explains – 'He thinks that Maurice has some plan to redesign the maps. We deal in substance, earthly stuff – but since he was in capital, he gets ideas – to intervene in who rules what, to set the figures dancing round the clock in counterclockwise mode...'

All this is news to us: Kaja says, 'I'd like a drink, dear Jozo,' and he turns on her. 'Kaja, your problem is, you're tall enough for two, but with proportions classical. If you go underneath the knife, they cut your bones to size – you're ruined. Disproportionate. And as for drink – tycoons don't share. This stuff is made by heretics from Daghestan, in the next cage...'

'Don't listen to his lies,' laughs Sonia. 'He's an idiot! The still smells ripe. I'm sure the cops have old police dogs, left from prohibition, who will sniff them out!'

'Well,' Kaja says, 'That would explain why the cops are interested. Not just because you are tycoons, but for dear Jozo's liquor...'

'When I'm a man,' says Sonia. 'And Jozo's in the brig, I'll run the show, and buy my booze like all the rest, from guys downstairs.'

We can't stand them. They're not company. They set your head to go around. As we go out, we see the doorman. 'Frogs all down his coat,' Sonia shouts down. 'That's my design. That's class.' The coat is long, like a Moscow coachman's.

'When Jozo's changed his sex,' says Kaja, when we are alone, 'he'll be like Petar. Picking up chicksters in the liquor stores.'

Here comes the snow. We don't have big hats. We're not persecuted, as they did Layla, and her man. Worse, we're ignored. 'If you have a hidden love who's far away,' says Kaja, 'it means you'd rather be alone. That's why I love

Maurice. He's alone. Doesn't obsess with absent loves. He loves himself, and doesn't cry about it.'

Kaja's hidden love! It's a moment clinging to the inside of your head – a pearl you'll always fish for. Electric itch. Take it out at night, see if it's grown and what it's worth. That's the core of it, the story, my fancy. Of course! – Layla falls in love with someone else; and with Majnun – it was just a fad.

'What's more,' says Kaja, 'that tattoo. No one, not a prisoner even, can fit "crime", or "punishment", on a four-finger space. Find the language – four letters each, or pictograms – and you'll find the interest, the goal, that Jozo and Sonia have.'

There's logic! 'I thought Jozo was a bigot, nothing more,' I say, 'without a scheme.'

'Oh, bigotry's his strength,' she says. 'Decisive. And they have in mind – inked on those fingers – pictograms, for sure. That is the clue.'

It's not, of course: the words can stand – quite small, on just one finger on each hand, each fist, done vertically – any length of word you like.

'Now, they don't bother to take out substances,' I say. 'The girders, or the wiring. It's not the state that withers away – it's the economy. The state goes after someone else's cash. We can't do anything with Jozo, or with Maurice. So – what is it that we do?'

'Well, we can spy on them,' says Kaja. 'Trade information true and false.'

'Is it availing, Kaja?' I say. 'It's not noble either.'

She looks hard at me. What can she be taking in? 'Towers, tall women, bulls ... is that a miniature of you?' Kaja asks. 'Your hopes and fears, at least.'

'Meddling when they draw the maps: it's worse when they're redrawn,' I say. 'You run a risk. Think of Napoleon –

those poor horses... Don't do psychology, Kaja – maybe we'll end as heads on spikes, outside your office, in the park.'

'We'll outsmart them all,' says Kaja, pointing here and there at the motors; the people swarming up from underground.

'Look at the chimps,' I say. It's a theme I wonder if she should hear from me. 'The fewer resources, the more aggressive you become. Stuff gets short, you fight over it. But Maurice and Jozo knew – that if you limit the resources, control them – stop and start – the effect's the same as if they don't exist. Whatever your motives... No girders? Cut down the trees instead. Then, there's no fruit, no shade, no fires. Whatever you do, things are scarce, and getting scarcer, whether you think hiding them tricks the market, or you think it's virtuous. No, Kaja, it's the digging... The steel, the gold, the going underground. We – we two at least – belong up high. In the trees, maybe. Somewhere near the birds.'

'Birds – they're selfish,' Kaja says. 'I like underground. And gold and silver, just like Maurice does. You're crazy. You're a primitive, and not one of the good sort. Only other shamans think like you.'

'Well, there you are, Kaja. Now you know, and I'm sorry I told you. I don't believe in telling,' I say.

'You've seen too many movies,' Kaja says. 'The good guys fighting lords of everything. It's not like that at all.'

'Look at the sky,' I say. 'Those stars... The science guys have this fantasy – they stick a flag and claim the rocks. There's no one there. That's what they hope. Maybe there's savages, or worms. But underneath the grey – there's caverns – diamonds and rubies, big as heads. Treasure – all you can carry back, and some for relatives as well. Eldorado without massacres, they think. It's not like that. The twinkles that you see, up there – they're towers of refuge, just like mine. Each star is crowded out with frightened people, waiting for some

guy with pistols, a big hat – to land and want to start to dig.
What will it be, for him or she? How'll they be rid of him or
her? A guillotine? A pelting? Hanging from a crane? Don't
think our lookalikes don't think of that. The only light that
comes for anybody – is from their metal shelter – the one-off
bolthole, made from the forbidden ores, a totem and taboo.
Each shelter striking the silver beam from the next bright
beacon, passing it on...'

'You're sure of this?' asks Kaja, though it all adds up.

'I'm convinced of it,' I say. 'Every fact fits in. Like you
were good with people, Kaja, fitting them in, so I'm good
with fitting sparkling rocks and metal cubes. Yes, the heavens
– they're all filled with people just like us – exactly so. The
calendar's the same in every place. The seasons and the birds,
the rains, the storms. That's why the laws are all the same, in
every place. In the beginning – not the Word – the law. Not
discourse – but space cops, enforcing laws of gravity, and
measuring off with bits of string.'

Kaja is silent. There's nothing left to say.

'Those multitudes up there,' I carry on. 'Maybe they've
dug it out, the gold and silver. If we shoot up – not some guy
who thinks that he's stout Cortes, a conquistador – but useful
people: a poet, prostitute, a sociologist – we'd have their trust.
They might not have the minerals to pay us with. Precious
things at least they'd have. Those poor afflicted people,
imagine their fear, their dwindling powers...'

'I'm not so sure,' says Kaja. 'I'm off to talk to Jozo in
their cage. I must keep my feet in friendly air. And – you
surely don't believe those poor people in the universe are all
our dead? Or we are theirs, their dead?'

'Of course not,' I reassure her. 'For now, we're all alive.
That's where the problem lies.'

I've told her what it's all about. Lords of the earth – what
vanity! Jozo and Sonia – they have cash, and so the space to

think things through that we don't have. The law's the same
for everywhere, but every vilayet is on its own. Rule just one
– there's millions more outside: mining and smelting, pouring
and casting: digging out, through to the other side...

'What a sadness,' Kaja says. 'In every universe, people
like us, people straining to be heteros, dragging along with
their ragged bundles, their Jungian "others", man or woman.
Company! The war, the camp, collapsing in the street, losing
the file, risking jail, celebrating... It's a joke, a horror...'

'People find it reassuring,' I say, 'to think everything that
exists is an eternal hall of mirrors. But then – we're all
matrioshkas too: soldiers, beggars, laundresses, tycoons,
thieves...'

'I'm terrified by matrioshkas,' Kaja says. 'Being hollow
is a fact – but being tiny and solid, with all your shells
discarded, stripped – is that your soul? What's become of the
"you", what you strip and clean and fondle every day? All
that's left – the irreducible wrinkled kernel, the fossil walnut.
The petrified heart.'

'Your misery, Kaja,' I say, astonished. 'You've distilled
it, poured it all around.'

*

'Oh, in the cage, there I feel free,' she says. 'The air –
blowing everything away – it's lifting on invisible seas, the
gulls like fleets of flying fish... What's there to do next, Jozo?
More laws to write, more dividends to bank? And – Sonia –
there's no crime you haven't seen, no punishment so deeply
seared into imagination that we should all be good for ever,
walking on the other side, eyes closed? Time to give it up, my
dear, the search for balance, order of some kind, redress? Let
it all happen, hohum, cut down the trees, it's coffins for the

lucky few. For me – some guy has dug a ditch beside the road...'

I hear her wheeling off, sticky in her North German mud. Another hopeless wanderer.

'They've flown!' she says, bursting back. 'The nest! The eagles went. I was in there alone... Such peace! The traffic – a hum of termites sorting leaves... The snowflakes – die, as they see the tall buildings. It's terrible!'

'Jozo and Sonia – they'll be in their mansion, skating on the swimming pool,' I say. 'Or maybe Sonia thought your murder bid was unforgivable.'

'She had her own quite back,' says Kaja, rubbing her throat.

'That's not forgiveness, Kaja,' I say. In silence, we know it's not.

16

High up, there's empty cages. Down here, I see some steps, down to an emporium. A tiny sign says – 'Everymetal', and even tinier, 'Grownupfun'. My legs a-tremble – the ultimate taboo. I think of miners in the caverns, blasting out the rockwalls, scenes of animals – the primitive, the hairy elephants, the ochre and the lampblack, old watercourses dried – someone scratching out a deer come down to drink ... at nothing. The smelter, final as the voice of God, a hell high on the hill, the slag trains pouring down the red and smoking loads, into the blue and green, the pools of sulphur ... I pull the bellrope, and a madam comes. Inside – there's all the metals of the universe. Zinc baths, and oh – the copper! spirals, retorts, alembics – and the brass. There's sets of knockers – a set of Greek empiricists, bald as door knobs – here's the knobs, shaped to your fist, the nickel-plated pistols on a rack – and metals ever heavier, and rarer, scent of gunny sacks, and here you slip into a space suit – underneath you feel your nakedness pinged with the radiation and explored ... now you glow with cobalt, iridium, paladium, viridium, valadium – selenium and iron, there's tungsten, rough lumps of ores you'd like to heft and smelt... Here's a long hall, pink lit, of cannons – brass and billon, soft dark inviting mouths, some big enough to crawl inside, the culverins, long Megs, big Berthas – here's the heaps of balls beside and ready for the fight...

'I'll take them all!' I say. 'It's scandalous – you've torn them out of every landscape, poisoned every well... How can you – I – live with all this plunder, exploitation of our

patrimony, excess, availability of what should be a treat ... a
ritual tidbit?...'

'Aha!' she says. 'I see you're avid for the rare!' and off
we go – and here's the silver, then through hangings of bright
tin – here's the electrum – further on, the gold – in thrones
and armour, plates and knives, bidets and pillows – gold pale
and red, in sheets like onion-skin and blocks that weigh six
tons... Here, squares of lead, awaiting alchemy...

This is the dream, from which I'd hope I'd never wake. It
is a nightmare too, a cleansing one – incubi and succubi – you
wish your hands had memory, so you could touch and fondle,
bear the surfaces away and have them always at your
fingertips.

'Say,' I say, my voice is thick and soupy – 'Madam! I'd
an old friend who used to loiter in the bookstores seeking
some sex – now the books, and he, have gone. Is there a
chance of picking up...?'

'What?' she asks. 'Leftovers? The filings, tailings,
discards, miscasts – not a chance! The merchants come from
everywhere, and how they steal! Those magnets underneath
the burnous! But only you're aware, it seems – this is
forbidden stuff ... so precious, it can drive you mad...'

'No, no,' I say: 'Forget the metals. Do women come in
here, maybe to browse, or make acquaintance? Susceptible,
maybe, to cultured talk? To some guy who's worked with
metals base and not?'

Beware, I think: for Petar, this all led to Sonia, then to
Jozo, and the bull. Finally – full stop for him.

'There's me,' the lady madam says. 'Don't fool around –
those cannons, loaded for their bang, the perilous chrome, the
nickel – treacherous, magnesium that creeps inside your
shorts. Be very, very careful... If my face won't fit – I'll wear
a veil – of mail, of course, the finest steel. It is our game. I'll
set a tinsmith tapping out my socks. This stuff,' and she

waves over the glistening, sullen mass, 'is nearly all extinct. This is my zoo. Here, nothing breeds – it's all been cooked, castrated by the fire. Museum specimens, at their last breath. But me – I live, I yearn, I throb...'

'It's all been processed? All these ores and flakes?' I ask. 'It's not a sample here – it's the whole lump?'

'The guys keep digging on, they blast – there's almost nothing left,' she says: 'And you – your casting days are done. You've known the craftsmen and the profiteers...'

Yes, I think – there's Maurice, then there's Jozo... But – there was Petar too, his murder unavenged, and unrecorded too... My casting days are done, the hammer rests...

'Have no fear,' the lady says. 'I can be what you want. Some days – aluminium. At the weekend – platinum, of course...' and on she talks, her knowledge deep and wide, the titillation tinkles like a distant bell... I think of Kaja. Oh, the guilt! It's worse, that there's no sexual bond between us, Kaja and myself – now, total fusion with this woman – that's the promise. Was it for this, all the philosophy, the lives I might have lived? It seems a dreary end, the bleary mornings and the early nights... Is this the ending of the quest? Apotheosis?

'Just sex, and sometimes love?' I ask. 'Is that the best, the all, you have to give?'

*

I can't tell anyone about her – Edda. Too dangerous.

'Edda?' Jozo asks. 'Not Layla? A zoo of earths and ores? You must be very very prudent.'

'It's not at all what I was looking for,' I say. 'I shan't go back. But if I don't, I'll regret the loss for all my life.'

'Ah yes,' says Jozo. 'Regret. You'll have a gold plate full of that, whatever course you take.'

'It excites,' I say. 'The end of mystery, of things extended underground. Abundance hidden under us, just like they said – "Easter eggs, concealed in an overgrown garden, waiting for discovery". The hidden – how it excites – and when it disappears – we're greedy for it. Edda – has a vein of all we have experienced – and yet it's worked: each surface cooked, and chased and tooled.'

'How I sympathise, my dear,' says Jozo. 'Arousal and revulsion – that's your destiny. Passion and hangover. Disaster. Me? I'm into changing to a woman. That way, I'll have experienced it all, from both sides, the other shore...'

'Don't bet on that,' I say. 'You're always with your Sonia, retribution personified. And – your brain remains the same – the details change, and that is all.'

'And that's enough,' he says. 'Why should I ask for more?'

'It's too bad, Jozo. You and Sonia decide to live and spend your money. It's so empty. Your cage... The fashion! Maurice, now...'

'Maurice has some little dried-out countries,' Jozo says, 'with nothing underneath, no prospectors, and no drills. Guys like Curtis, taking the cash and torturing some other guys. Is that a project, or a plan?'

'Well, there's Nina, troubled in her mound,' I say. I'm not convinced she's anything.

'Edda. That's a Nazi name,' says Kaja, when Jozo's told her of my games.

'They get their names a while before they even think of party cards,' I say. She tacks around:

'You like confusion, not complicity. I wish you pleasant times, of course – but what becomes of me?'

'We're giving up,' I say, 'Jozo and Sonia too. They – their cash. Me – the whole that they call love.'

'Love means you have to hang around,' she says. 'Maurice is loyal to the ancient hopes. His candidates; the flim-flam. Planting seeds and frightening birds away.'

I feel guilt. Poor Kaja. Sonia says that means there is a crime. Edda plays all night, but makes me graft all day.

'Find dwarves that make the heroes' rings,' she says. 'We need some hundreds. Brass will do.'

Mercury, asbestos – on special. I ladle out the mercury from casks, asbestos comes in bags. I'm unsure about asbestos, but it's quite extinct. We fire the furnaces with gas – it sings to me of Russia, whistles of bears and wolves that scratch their backs against the pipes, the nomads cursing as the tundra turns to mud.

'Higher, higher, burns the flame,' shouts Edda. We make new alloys, with new properties – stuff that flies, that floats, that moulds like plasticine. Gold you can eat.

I'm bored, bored with it all, the work, the play.

'When you tire, I'll not take Edda on my cart,' says Kaja.

'We've bronze chariots, bronze horses too, to go,' I say. 'Edda is rich. I have a leather apron, that comes to my ankles. She says, "Many who've your task – it comes down to their knees."'

'Edda doesn't run a zoo,' says Kaja. 'It's an emporium. She sells. You bow the neck.'

'Then it'll be over. There'll be something else,' I say.

'You're macabre. You, Jozo, Maurice. And the dead. Nina, the sedative. There's new people, on the move. Or stuck, dammed up. You – you're Belgians dancing. You're full of lead. Forget that it's all ending. New peoples! I know them...'

'Are you sure they're not the old ones, jumbled up?' I ask. 'Displaced by armies? Chauvinists? Bigots? Essentialists?'

She doesn't respond.

'... Just nomads, clinging on, being shunted. Their animals dissolved in acid clouds,' I say. 'Guys with many languages, passports for dead countries – or a long trip with no papers?'

'Of course,' she says. 'How else would they appear? They have a past, and they forget. The past is always there, but smaller. It's a revelation: not the old stuff but – new peoples, without a name, without an alphabet. Enormous numbers, no protection, improvising. Don't worry about your skin... Nothing's coming that is unforeseen – heads on spikes is an ancient tradition over here. There's nothing fresh, no unknown royal in the deck. New Huns, new Yuezhi – like Albanians, Bulgars: there they are! Where'd they come from? Who are they? Why? All colours. Everything you don't know, they know. That's them, the uninteresting novelty! They're here already, they're white noise. They don't see you, your cities, suburbs, stretch limos. They're from Africa, from Babylon, the wrong kind of poverty, the wrong kind of religion, there's millions of them, Chinese pissed off, Filipinos tired of living in a midden – giving up all that, growing bright wings and fluttering to new ground. Exiles from no place... No *Heimatland*, workers with no country. No religions – not traditionalists. And for sure, your Turks won't come – not as Turks at least, they won't.'

'I know all this,' I say. 'You may want to join the flux...'

'I may,' she says. 'I may have.'

'It's that big, Kaja?' I ask.

'Oh, bigger than railroads, bigger than techno. It has no form,' she says.

'It has form,' I say. 'It's that you can't describe it,' and we leave it there.

She says, 'See that ring of former Bosniaks? Over there – that's what I mean.'

'Don't insist,' I say. 'They'll become Americans.'

'You're wrong,' she says. 'You haven't understood. Not even about you and me.'

'That part's trivial,' I say.

'Go back and sell your buckets,' she shouts. 'Crawl inside your iron maiden.'

She's right about that.

I quit. It's emotional, I guess.

'Give back the apron,' Edda says.

That's easy.

*

I make a long and crowded journey – what else can I do? It seems that everyone is moving here.

Maurice says, 'I was wrong about Ürümqi. It's Kashgar. That's the centre of the world. That's where I'm moving to. All the money's gone in there. The wise ones transfer from the sea – that fog they have out Eastwards – it's the oceans going putrid.'

He waves his golden hand, like it can attract more cash, and this time printed by some real big boss. 'Poor Jozo,' Maurice says. 'There's too much violence in him. He should have let it out in war. And Kaja too, her spat with Sonia sets them both apart. They do forget – things cancel out: but they are far from us, they're in a basket of their own. The would-be murderers amongst us...' He shakes his head. Does not shed a tear.

'Kaja's idea,' he says, pouring me weak tea – 'That there's a movement, atop – or underneath – the others that we see around, made up of guys removed and disenchanted ... is not so wrong. She's an essentialist, of course. The disenchantment's an effect, and not a cause. Those guys are on the move because there's nothing they can do, nor anything to drink while they're not doing it,' and he laughs.

'No water, and no work. What pays off,' he says, 'is confidence. Know what you want, and go and get it. That's what people here have got. If you or Kaja want to sell a yak, you'll wonder how, and where, how much ... and so and so. Guys here – they sell them all the time, in threes and fours. They know the score, they deal, they sell. That's what you need. The metals – that's all gone. No one will dig for ore – it's gold or nothing, in the rivers ... here, there are mountains, made of gold. It washes down. You put your hands in water – and you see!' He waves his hand.

I seem to have another story, how it came, the hand. He must be right, though. It's confidence and sacrifice that does it all. Faith – that's there's rewards, no punishments.

'Maybe you'd like a pipe of something blue and cloudy – or a pill to boost that tea?' he asks.

'You never did that job for me,' I say.

'No one has seen your refuge,' Maurice says, his eyes pale jade, 'but that's the point of it, I guess. But you'll have set your sails on Nina's breasts, I'll bet, gone to the edge, and over, where nothing matters much.'

'The bull,' I remind him. 'A joint creation. Inedible, eternal, skill and wisdom incarnate.'

'A very early work,' says Maurice, smug, relaxing on his beanbag. 'Amateur stuff. Now, I'm valued here. I know the secret – how to turn gold into paper; paper into nothing. An account – on a screen, but not a narrative. A statement. Potent and ephemeral. How they love that! Simplicity. No sound, no smell. No –' and he winds himself up, 'bullshit.'

He never used to laugh like this.

'It pains me,' Maurice says, 'that here, there's guys look for the origins, back to the start, some pure belief. These parts were where there was a traffic, and a confluence. All faiths climbed on their dromedaries, camels too, they travelled, they cross-fertilised. All was mixed up. You took the best – you didn't think you had a truth, a card that trumped the rest. The gods, the demons, exiled sages, epicurists – they all went into pictures in the caves, to figurines, to poems jotted down on bark. To art, not bigotry...'

'Maurice!' I say, 'you've changed! Being right – that was your specialty. Now – it's all consolation ... brushstrokes, lampblack. The figures in the caves...'

'Think what you like,' he says. 'It isn't me that's wrong – it's everybody else that ought to stay in plastic arts, not certainty...'

He's smaller, so the hand gets larger. 'Of course,' he says, 'I tell lies. The Iranians do it – it's polite, for them. Not being direct. Of course, my lies are not material – it's that I like it, being on both sides.' He leers a little. I remember the tub, the smiths a-frolic.

'I always tell the truth, Maurice,' I say. 'A bad habit.'

'When next you see me,' Maurice says, screwing his Tajik cap down to his eyebrows, 'I'll be in Kashgar.' He stresses its first syllable. 'Without Nina, without Curtis – this is how I survive, and prosper. The world is perilous, remember. Even aluminium, cooked right, can give a nasty bang. I love it there: the space, the buildings – all unlikely, made of gold and platinum. I'm better off here than poor Genghiz Khan – those rowdy sons! Wealth is nothing – the trick is, to make the nothing settle, encysted in your being. Swallow nothingness like air. Waddle. That's the style they most appreciate.'

'Maurice –' I'd like to say, 'you're a thin shitstick; in you there's no air, no light, your face – a mask of sandy skin, that plum cap, plum velvet shoes, a dandy off the comic book – the hand aloft and uncontrollable, a lobster claw that gropes for living flesh...' but I don't say anything.

He says, 'Nina's grave – was most unquiet. They had to dig her up. She was quite dead, of course, but wriggling.

She's in a tomb – they shuttled her between a church, another church, a mosque, and finally they roped her down, and made a special case for her. There's pilgrims, wandering and spending cash...' He waves me away. 'You don't need consolation, my old friend,' he says. 'You've a good way of getting rid of folk yourself.'

At the door of his block, he says, 'Poor Jozo: those veins, those hernias! There must be some inside, holding it all together. The plumbing – red and blue: electrics yellow – all hanging out. Is there a structure, a centre, behind it all? Sex and violence: his specialities. Those are "being", that's for sure. I fear Sonia's into "nothing", with crime and punishment. Labels and consequences – those don't count for much. The sex, though – requires presence, agency. The violence – well, that's fairly much the same – speaking as philosopher, of course.' He laughs. A few guys walk past, dressed like chorus men from operetta, wandered on a set for Valkyrie.

'This is not the best place,' Maurice says. He's made up by maybe half, of nothing. Philosophically, you couldn't have a better self.

'Oh!' he says, 'I forgot to tell. There's no work for you, not in Kashgar. It's all been done: metal, with wolfram, I'm afraid. You could go to Nina's mausoleum, though. You don't need her – but I have comrades, comrades in arms, her arms, perhaps, longing for miracles. Let me know how she vibrates.' This is not his interest. 'If Jozo makes a move,' he says. 'Of course, I need to know.' *That* is his interest.

'Big countries,' he shouts, as I leave. 'Not shale, not flakes: big, well-centred ones, whirligigging, like a potter's wheel.'

Maurice, I reflect, has no bodyguard, no tiara, no ambassadors, no army. No doctrine, no plan. No gas, no miracle. So much power – no one could think to take it; so precious his person, no one could take his place. Jozo – the same. Coarser, perhaps. But he has Sonia. Sonia has him. She's become his punishment, he – the crime upon the divan, drinking his Absolut. She has no interest in war, revenge, in justice, in the right, the wrong. Crime. And punishment. There is an infinite chain. She'll be a link in it, so she can't act as judge. She's a suspect, like the rest. Victim and executioner. Punishment precedes the crime, and on and on, one thing meanders, into another – a roundabout, a figure like the copper coil in stills. Maurice's copper, coming and going. An inexhaustible supply of crimes and consequences, of consequences, crimes. That must be punished: everything. And are, somehow, maybe. The simplicity amazes.

Crimes invented – and their punishments, quite disproportionate. There's a snag! And Jozo's associates – punished. Maybe they were criminals. Are they collaterals? Or crimes of necessity. And if you're born that way – it's all necessity. Or in a place where everyone is destitute? In my life, it's all necessity. I must read that Russian book one day. Those Russians look so innocent... Sacrifice, confidence – and hope: gives you that look that past is past ... buried, a bad seed ... that will fruit pineapples, with pepper vodka.

Here's Nina's monument, a cenotaph, another mausoleum. 'She died of plague' a notice says – 'a sacrifice. She died of being good. A warning to us all.'

A crowd stands round. Maybe the mummy moves. So what? Her face is wrapped, the body flat, a beetle's shell sucked out. 'What do you want of her?' I ask a guy.

'What we all want,' he says. 'Being told that what we've done is right, and if it's not – then it's forgiven.'

'You're easy satisfied,' I say. 'But you could have spared yourself the fare and stayed at home and read a book.'

The corpse is wriggling – maybe it hears my voice. Her arms are pinioned, but she's no wings to spread, the breasts shucked flat – potato skins.

Maurice wants his money's worth from me – 'A sign!' he says. 'Of anything.'

He's given me a brick of dollar bills – his printer's upped from twos to tens. I can't disappoint.

A portent? Above poor Nina – there are birds ... they'll net them, crossing into Africa. 'After death, there's flatulence, and sometimes fermentation,' I'll say.

Will it satisfy him?

Here's the stalls, the cooks. Out back, corroded tubes, chipped baths. A pile of Maurice's skeletons.

The guy who wanted miracles is hanging round. 'I'm Greek,' he says. 'Forget those Indians – in Peru, and Mexico. They don't think twice: sex-and-violence. You don't need study that. No – it's us, we, the ancients. Miracles and punishments: those were kissing cousins: imagine, a female, turned into a bush, for safety. Those gods – walked near the line. A laurel bush, maybe it sings as you go by, if in doubt – stick it on your head! It could have been an elderberry, or *anice*. Whatever came to mind. Want to do some dirty deed – a swan, a shower of golden rain... Who'd ever notice that? Scot-free. That was no example for us. A human sacrifice, abducted brides – wars for thirty years... The puzzle has been endless since. Those categories quite confused...'

'You're right,' I say. 'It muddles it all up. Europa and the bull.' I pull out a coin. 'There it is! In circulation. What's the lesson there?'

'Bulls may safely graze,' says the Greek. 'But not near our women. That's the warning.'

'Bulls and bears? A continent impregnated – with dodgy dollars?' I say, lightening it all up. 'I knew the saint,' I say. 'Nina. We were bosom pals.'

'It was the war,' the guy says. 'She took it on herself. There's no point in that. You go on, till you can't, not looking back. If you do, you lose your wife. and then you lose your head.'

'There's nothing you can do,' I say, anxious to be away.

'Those are crimes,' he insists. 'Mostly against women. "Crimes of the Olympian era". No statistics, no politics, no plans – crimes without justification: sex, violence, and self-regard.'

I want to get away. Not see Kaja, spy on Jozo.

Kaja is waiting. 'You broke my screen,' she insists. 'Took my job. Would be neither lover, nor my friend.'

'Somewhere in there, you have the reason,' I say.

'No,' she says. 'Not the reason. An answer. Like you with Edda. There's no reason you can't sell her stuff.'

'It's back to the start,' I say. 'I'll be a mediator. Where there's been war, violence – I'll give my services.'

'Sex too,' shouts Kaja. 'It was fine with Edda, I imagine. But everywhere there's violence, there is sex as well. Have you considered that?'

'I could go back where there's Slavs,' I press on. 'I was getting on well there, the war and after. Travelling East, maybe I'll find the answer to the mystery – crime, punishment ... the book.'

'Nonsense!' Kaja shouts. 'No mystery! That's it: crime, punishment. Is that so hard to understand? You don't need travel to grasp two words.'

'I must have colour, where I go,' I say. 'It's like food for me. Metals is dead, for sure, but think of feldspar, blue john, moonstones... Then, while there's time – I'll try again to pass it on. Anarcho-syndicalism. That's what Petar wanted. Of course, no one will pay to have you teach it – some academy, the Belle Arti – too dangerous. Theory and practice –

medicine of the ligaments plus leaping. No one would let you do that...'

'Everybody does that,' Kaja says. 'It's that you don't understand the terms. Anarchy. Syndicalism. You've the naive thought, that these are contradictory. But that's you! You don't want fitting in – that's anarchy. The guys go down the mine, without an order. That's syndicalism. You want the result, but not the process. The result's your gratification. The process is guys working for you out of love. It won't happen.'

She's so assured: I say, 'If it's a gold mine – I know how guys work. They'll stuff the gold in every orifice: eat it, smell it, hear it, shit it, piss it – and we'll all be happy. Life will be fun.'

'No,' she says. 'You—' she shakes me, 'you work, or else you seek some crime that's not full time.'

I don't tell her about the spying, and the dollar bills.

'Jozo has given up philanthropy,' I say. 'It's spend and spend. Then there is nothing. Maurice – save, save – accumulate, build up a capital – there's nothing! It's a figure, virtual. Nothing you can see or spread on toast...'

'You temporise,' she says. 'Nothing comes from nothing. Remember how Petar ended. Anarchic talk. Everybody does it now – paid, in offices.'

'Listen, Kaja,' I say. 'I don't want fitting in. I don't want thirty years upon your cart. Without a horse – it's absolute monotony.' She opens her mouth – there's too much speech backed up, to make a sound.

She manages at last – 'You're exasperating. You and your "guys", your males, dug it all out, and now there's nothing left. The more there's nothing for us all – the more you fight, and sign us women up, and wring your hands, and mediate, and flex your legs and leap... And now I'm into it...' She weeps: it is frustration, not true rage.

Maybe I should take a trip to Edda's store, see how she's doing, and propose a game... Sex, like the sea, for ever starts again. The street's still there – the store has gone. She must have sold the stock. There's nothing left. Edda – I reflect – was not a person you should lightly give up on, lacking, as you do, the commercial bent.

She makes you ask – does life fill you up, or does it empty you? She understood exactly what she wanted to; not like Kaja, who wants it all to fit, even by forcing, pruning it. Of course, if you had a place to stay in, with the passport corresponding – in time, the place makes sense of you. Take you out your skin and into history. But even then – things don't fit in: think of the fantasy – the DDR, USSR. Fantastic! Ending your country, cancelling... 'no, it won't do, we can't continue...' Now, that shows imagination, shows there was something special going on...

Jozo's around – it doesn't seem he changed his sex. 'Jozo,' I say. 'Maurice has the secret of – well, not the universe. Economy. Big bang it started – so it ends.'

'Boy friends,' says Jozo. 'That is Maurice, start to end – in big bang, if you like.'

He laughs. Well! Jozo is coarse, I knew.

'You're wrong,' I say. 'He lives only in his head. Live in a flat land – you track the sun each day. Where does it hide, where does it rest, to rise so vigorous, and set in coronation mode?'

He has no answer. I say, 'I've given up on Turks. Another of my bad ideas.'

'Well,' he says, 'you never act on any of them. Makes you feel part of the sway, I guess. Sonia's going to those parts. Though what she hoped to find... Just crime and punishment – but that we knew.'

'Maybe you should both read that Russian book,' I say. 'Give a sense of where you're going.'

'Oh,' he says. 'I know. I'm back into those metals. There's a woman keen on wholesale – used to contraband. Has the commercial bent – an apron too, though I'll not get into that.'

'Edda!'

'You know my moves!' says Jozo, admiring. 'Sonia's away. My time for play. And you've not understood. What Sonia does: it's not about a book, philosophy, or what. Sonia takes note. She doesn't judge. The earth is made of rocks and clods. There is no crime in what we do. We transform, we cook. We take the useless, and make it shine. There's punishment for sure...' He waves a knotty leg. 'For everyone. It comes down from the sky, quite indiscriminate. That's mine – the leg. But – we work the ores and speculate ... just like the old hymn goes, "we plough the waste and harrow..." The wolf, the ram – where do they come from, where do they go? No one knows, no one cries for them. Or for you. Or me. Sonia watches – but she sets no traps, carries no axe.'

'There is an end. A finality for sure, a purpose – but also an exhaustion: when there's "nothing left",' I say.

'Yes,' he says, his face red and splendid. 'We'll be the last. It's glorious, heroic. "Something", one "thing", one by one – we'll dig out, and consume. Things by themselves – we confection into – things for themselves. It is a destiny. Quite liberal, in fact. Waste not... *Es ist genug.* After that – nothing. Try something else – perhaps those wooden towers, founded on straw,' and he laughs. 'We follow our path right to the end. Do you think it would make a difference, leaving those clods where they are now? Things have been put so's they can be finished off, digested, not abandoned on the plate...'

'That's it, then, Jozo, the plan? Finish it off? Refine? Use it all up?' I ask.

'That's it,' he says.

'And Sonia? She's the blind lady, but without the scales?'
I say.

'Maurice needs the scales to weigh his substances,' Jozo
says and laughs. 'He knows – "nothing" is better than
something you don't like. Or who doesn't like you. Like you
say, he's consigned everything to his brain – sensations,
lovers too. He had hopes of you – that's why he never did
your job. He was mistook.'

'I know,' I say. 'I don't like anybody much. Enough, that
is.'

'Edda's quite the same as you,' he says, 'That's why you
didn't make it.'

'Oh, we did, Jozo, we did make it,' I say. He's uneasy.

Edda's his plan too.

I can tell all this to Maurice. Will I have Maurice's plan to
tell to Jozo? That's surely not my life.

'Petar Petrović,' says Jozo. 'That bull was his freedom –
since he wasn't there himself to enjoy it.'

He's quite drunk. Petar was free enough, until Jozo came,
with Sonia.

These guys – they're so powerful, they don't need other
guys to vote for them. Maybe no one would.

'I'm never sad,' Jozo says. 'If I am, I go up in the sky.
Sonia's day has come – open the cage! – she's flying off!'

His house has many rooms – though he can't be in more
than one: Maurice can, but Maurice has no cage, no company.

'You don't want to see around,' Jozo says. 'You're not
that stupid.'

'What was it Sonia went to do?' I ask.

'You so soon forgot?' he asks. 'Those Nazis said it all
already – if you're setting out to punish, you must go in for
crime. We know it – it's a universal rule. Sonia's slow. She
needs to see it in the flesh – someone else's.'

'I went to Nina's shrine,' I say. 'It's quite a draw. The tourists, waiting for a sign – those movies, where no one survives... It's gone in deep.'

'Of course there's movement after death,' says Jozo. 'All those that hadn't run away, were bulldozed – they made quite a mound, there's unquiet chemistry still working there. It squirms. And Nina went on top.'

17

We're all at the ceremony, standing round. Some watching others, some to show their innocence.

Curtis is to make a speech... Nina's a lady who does move, but only slightly. Here, they fought, but not for scarce things. Things were scarce before, and scarcer after – it was excess that did it, solidarity.

Here's Kaja, following me like a fury. 'Why do you persist?' she asks me. 'You're just a toy for them. They don't tell you what they have in mind. They're everything you're not. Jozo's free – that cage is security, not a prison. Maurice is one who follows conflict – there is no complicity. So you – why are you here?'

'I guess it is the fear,' I say. 'My life is founded on it.'

'Well,' she says, 'it does no good, if that is what you hoped. Don't mention Ottomans, my friend.'

I say, 'That's past and buried, Kaja. That too.'

Curtis reads each sentence of his speech with equal force. We want to get away. He says, 'Our benefactor...'

Maurice says, 'My skeletons are buried under here. That's all the tale.'

I say to Kaja, 'It's a mystery. Curtis compounds it. And there's so few of us.'

'Significant people,' she says. 'Need to control their past. Maurice, Jozo – they aren't here to remember them, the dead – they didn't know them. Not then, less now. Those two want to flatten down whatever they had done, their part in everything. Find a bandage, in the right colours. The bereaved hurt every day. The present's theirs, it stops them thinking.

Jozo and Maurice – they come so they can be benefactors. Fiddling the future.'

'That's neat,' I say. 'Kaja, you fit things in! It means you're not original, though.'

'It's an important day,' she says. 'You feel the tension.'

'I always do,' I say. 'But I'm not significant.'

'You're sensible,' she says. 'Underneath. You've nothing, and you don't pretend.'

'Edda's here,' I say.

'Business,' Kaja says. 'And Sonia enjoys a scene.'

'She can't be reached,' says Jozo. 'She's off gawping – crowds of people!'

*

We eat our chickens from paper cones. 'Jozo's the best type we have,' Edda says. 'And as for copper – Maurice is right to be careful with it. It comes clean – but it starts off dirt.'

'You look for profit, and find philosophy,' Kaja says. Maybe she approves.

'Curtis buys his clothes off his computer,' Edda says. 'Those poacher's pockets! A giveaway.'

'These fowls – they taste of fish. That must be what they eat,' says Maurice. 'There's not many people here. They can't eat well. They should move on.'

'No carts for us,' says Edda. 'We've got motors.'

'We must trust them, Jozo and Maurice, even if one murders the other,' Kaja says. 'There's no one else they can trust. That's the same for us.'

'That chair factory,' Maurice says. 'They could make wooden legs instead. Except there are no trees. Not my fault at all.'

'Burying all sorts together,' Edda say. 'It's an advance. Those old epics gave rights to your land to someone else.'

'Don't broadcast this,' Jozo whispers to me. 'Sonia's been taken. Some sort of hostage. Or a ransom. We can't act, of course. Do nothing – that's the theme.'

'Maybe she's fed up with Jozo,' Kaja says to me. 'Seeking attention. No crime's been done, after all...'

'She could be raising money for her side,' I say.

'These butchers,' says Maurice, pretending not to hear, 'are my old mates – pipe-fitters. These chickens come in pieces, dismantled ready. Who knows how they'd fit the bits together, if they had the job! Dodos, that's for sure!'

'We could have a whip round for Sonia,' Kaja says, pretending not to hear. 'Or maybe we all left our cash at home.' She feels her neck – Sonia's job, the thin red line. Kaja'd look fine, without that gawky body underneath.

'It used to be so innocent,' Jozo says. 'The boundaries were sound. You believed there were things to believe in, firmly, always. Then Maurice cornered copper – the lights went out, the trains stalled on their tracks. Real things disappeared.'

'It's the uncertainty,' Edda says. 'People love to think of going back.'

'Everybody thinks they think like that,' Kaja says, quite brusque. 'It's crap – a paid ad slogan. Some things are certain, and we don't say what.'

Here's a heap of tubing. Long bones – and funnels – just the sort for me! These would have warmed the hut, just stuck in the earth, the heat that makes you think of cicadas, strumming on the pines. Maurice could have done that job – changing everything, history never baking out the same, each time a curlicue, a lick of dough, that's different.

'Curtis dresses English,' Edda says. 'Americans say what they want – it's what you don't. The English – tell you what you want to hear. Then do what they want.'

'Oh, Edda,' Kaja shouts. 'Clothes again? Take them off – what have you got?'

We don't know. People are always buried wearing them.

'Respect the dead,' Jozo shouts, 'if you can't respect the living.'

I say to Kaja, 'Sonia's right in the middle of our fear. The primal one – being enclosed, then born into our world. What are called the secondary ones: being trapped, imprisoned. The next adventure – not birth, but death. No crime, just punishment. People on you, convinced, using all the power they have left, or always had: – it feels the same. Will they soften? Will your company drive up and smash their heads? Will the forked tongues interlace and do a deal? Maybe you don't still exist. If it's history grinding – there's no hope. Something, though, will go on. That doesn't console at all.'

'Yes,' Kaja says. 'Sonia's redeemed. Being horrible – it's all wiped out. Maybe she wasn't horrible, but terrible. A rich person, jumping in the fire – it's quite anomalous. It's the poor, some with cockades and some in rags – they slog it out. The battle. Not Sonia, milady crime and punishment. And in the end, maybe it'll end in smoke: to each a religion, according to their residence. Is it for that? Stop looking for a person in her – she's epic now, Majnun and Layla wrapped in one, their story like a falling stone.'

'It's pass the parcel, Kaja. Jozo and Edda – they're the lovers now – Sonia's the shut-in,' I whisper to her – not remembering who knows what, or, if it is charades, time to shout an answer.

'She asked for it,' says Jozo, cuddling close to Edda. 'She's tumbled into her speciality. There's a lesson – separate yourself from your beliefs, or end up as the cook who falls into her stew.'

They prepare their motors. Kaja and me, we're to be left behind. Edda turns to me, 'It's not Jozo that repels,' she says.

'I can scrub off, after we have done. It's the louche guys that come for orders, before breakfast. Me – it's business that's the passion. All the rest is – well, heat loss.'

'I didn't expect as much, Edda,' I say. 'An explanation is exceptional.'

Wasn't it me that dumped her? – one does forget...

'Humans don't save,' she says. 'The animals that save, think of next year – go in for lethargy and sleep. Hope, if they wake, it's spring again. We're monkeys that gobble everything at once, or tigers that browse in carrion. We flare up – we're phosphorus – and we're gone. The best thing is – there are no tears, no one regrets.'

'Maurice is more reflective, Edda – it goes with having capital,' I say. 'He'd leave you to unfurl your sales. Jozo insists, he's always there.'

'Maurice is magic,' Edda says. 'And that's no good. He's natural. He knows – sex with your own kind's convenient, without a consequence. See – I'm a consequence – as you'll find out.'

She climbs in beside her Jozo. 'The law,' she says, as they move off. 'Is made by guys like Jozo. It's a hatching – lines crossing lines, a grid full of electricity. Jozo flies in and out, around – he loves near squeaks and squawks. Guys like Maurice – don't involve themselves. Unless the wires are copper. The rest, the human kind – they live as outlaws; now and then – a foot will touch a line. A spark, a flare: alert! Then you're inside, locked in, shut up, a cage within the cage. But Maurice: he has golden feet – he never feels a shock, the current shoots up through his head, and passing – brings him inspiration...'

'And do you think of Sonia, Edda dear?' I ask.

'In those straits, the thing that serves you most,' she shouts, as they all disappear. 'Is underwear. You need to have it fresh...'

'Now what?' asks Kaja. 'And do we walk to it?'

We're all alone – that's a relief.

She peers at me. 'There's something lacks in you,' she says. 'All the soft stuff, the reflection, the tears – that all comes after. People came here to fight – they didn't think they'd end up in the mound, Nina on top. The guys already here – they had their rifles in the roof – they knew they'd want to use them. Have to use them. It's only you – sees the soft side, the consequences, the pain of starting up again, pretending it's forgiveness time.'

'No, Kaja, no,' I say. 'War or peace – they come, they go. There's nothing to be done. The nurse, the mutilated warrior, the general on the hill – the parts, the roles, remain; the shouting too.'

Here's the original tub, a scurf of metal round. Electrum. An old invention – what I want is some new metal, looking for a purpose – between mercury, gold leaf and tin, that sticks itself, viscous like a tongue, into your mouth, your eyes, takes over every pipe and tube inside, and makes you something else. Metal that flies and pours, solid and flux – that eats you, like a jigger with no soul, a tiger, a cobra – quite heartless that eats your heart and purrs.

'These little buildings – they've been knocked down, rebuilt so many times – fortified monasteries, you'd think the people had a stake in quietness, the spiritual,' she says.

'You're way off, Kaja,' I tell her, but I don't insist.

'You'll be a prospector,' Kaja says. 'That leaves for me – an earthly paradise. Make a few beasts so comfortable, they believe in providence until they die.'

Bratislava or paradise. That's the choice before us.

She says, 'You can be Adam, if it amuses you. Adam delved, and he's forgotten. Everyone remembers Eve, though there was no passion between them. That's what you get if you wish for a present – you get a woman and lots of murderous kids. Passion – that's Majnun and Layla – or Sonia and Jozo, if Jozo raises the cash to free her.'

'I shan't dig, Kaja,' I say. 'I don't want a precious metal, that Maurice bathes in and turns to his credit. I want something, perhaps it'll look like potin – that they have to invent uses for...'

'You're right not to dig,' says Kaja. 'Wait till a nomad brings a gunny sack, with something to identify. Me – I've no intention of shovelling either. Real animals – all too human! Full of shit. And you have to kill to feed their appetites. Not for me!'

There's a temptation – not biblical at all – to strike up again with Edda.

'After these civil wars, you are diminished. A state you can forgive. But – you never forgive your neighbours,' Kaja says. 'You never make new contacts. And if you survive, you can't bear to meet old friends.'

Edda never took a side. I think: she's just full of metals – iron, copper – everything that stars are made of. And – she's green! It's the chrome-plating, gives her a vernal tinge.

I leave Kaja still walking. With Edda again, I fantasise:

'You missed your chance,' she says, her green and yellow face turning plantlike to the sun. 'The world is heavy with its scrap. You could melt it down, and make a moon, another earth. We, the surplus – we could live on it, hammer and forge. And sell. They'd have to send us food, of course – but the conveniences ... all ours!'

'I dreamt of you, Edda. We listened to music – *veni creator mundi*, come – creator of the world. And when I woke, I'd been crying.'

'You've got the words wrong,' Edda says, flattered. 'Yes, in a way I'm God – or at least I've much in common. I love making things, concocting huge projects and making them in bronze. I don't much care how they turn out.'

'Well, Edda,' I say, 'we're all supposed to have something in common with that guy: the spirit... It's just that Jozo...'

'He creates,' says Edda, 'though he's not appetising. And Sonia – where might she be?'

'Avenging and being victim – it's a thin line to tread,' I say. 'Nina – dead. She's a consoler – being dead's no consolation. Sonia – the punisher – up for ransom. Quite anomalous!' I talk on. How the gods must hate religion – many of them never even wrote a book, a memoir. I ingratiate.

'You could say, you know, you want more sex with me,' says Edda.

'Sonia never mentioned suffering,' I say. 'It's in crime, and without it, punishment would not exist. Maybe she doesn't suffer, where she is now.'

'I avoid all that,' says Edda. 'It's not money I want. It's coin. Big bags of it – each one different – the coins...'

'Each maybe a different metal,' I say, enthused. 'You know, I'm looking for a new, a special ore, but for sure along the way I'll find thousands of unknowns.'

'You think Jozo expiates the beating up of Petar,' says Edda. 'And that's why he lives in a cage. That's wrong. Each cage is the scene, the unit, of a bande dessinée, a cartooned tale: it's the fashion, it's a story, all those rich guys living in the clouds, hung up.'

'Are you saying I can't have sex with you, Edda?' I ask. 'Loyalty, even love for Jozo?'

'Wrong words again,' she says. 'I pity him, his success. How proud he is. Up there in his cage – the story – quite surreal. You're not one of those, I guess? Surreals?'

'I could try,' I say.

'You'd try anything for sex,' she says. 'But you know it isn't worth it.'

'In a refusal,' I say. 'There is always something quite profound. Nothing more you need to know. Person, people. The totality.'

'Knowing people. Sex – you really are prewar,' she says.

A woman shouts at Edda, 'Why were you so *bad* to me?'

'Oh, just an economic thing,' says Edda, to both of us. 'Underpaid in notes. Coins are the answer. They go round and round. You can't tell when they'll wear out. They do – but not so quick as notes... Then – into the crucible they go – they end, and yet the show goes on...'

'I know, Edda,' I say. 'In general, ends are good. You go to movies, knowing you can leave, get out. Up it comes – *Fin, Fine, End, Ende.* Then there's the exit, the judgment, and maybe you'll want to do it all again. It sets the shape, let's you stick a meaning on what you've been through, seen... Or maybe not. It doesn't matter. Ends – they're what matter. Jozo and Maurice – they'd in mind a choice of ends – a sudden one, or one more deliberate, more refined. Use everything at once, or take it slow...'

'That's total crap,' shouts Edda. 'They're not like that at all. You know them! They don't write the end, or make alternatives. The end is always there, you hope it's like the shapely one that Petar got. And now there's Nina, wriggling in her crystal casket, and Sonia, tethered like a goat. Punishment and consolation, worship and ransom... It's all ends, you cretin...' and she shakes me to and fro. 'That's what sex is all about. Making the ending good! And that is what you want?'

'Edda,' I say, 'I know all this. It's all been written many times. Forget the sex. We cling, we think that others like to cling. Forget it. It's the rock we're on, that melts like toffee in a mouth...'

'Circulate,' she says. 'Wear out. Restrike, and redesign. The planchet – stick it in the die – and strike – the new! The shiny! Remember the song – "We are the hammers, we're striking out the new world..." And it *is* new. New head, new treasury, new confines. Turn the handle – that old hurdy-gurdy magic. Majnun and Layla – the quest, union and death. Then – here they come again – still more enclosed and impotent, here's Romeo, his teddy-bear... But – every day is new, all the same.'

'Some decisive move,' I say. 'Jozo, Maurice, both or separate. Saving nothing, changing everything.'

'Yes,' says Edda. 'Yet you'd settle for some time in bed!'

'No one is completely dead,' I say. 'Not Nina, not Sonia. And, we metalsmiths – we still coin it out...'

'Yes,' says Edda. 'If you sleep with me – who knows? You might find there's a child. Or some disease from Jozo. And imagine – maybe Jozo has an army, one of those that struts about – quick conversion, steal your telephone, make an ad. An army he doesn't even know about. That way – embarrassment for both of you – a secret neither wants to handle. The thing important, always: get rid of people you don't like. That suits for everyone. One person, could be you: or thousands. Those that are left – together, into the tub. All friends, though not the sort that talk. Precious, the new limbs. Cumbersome, and prominent.'

'Edda,' I say, 'you know everything, but say it much too fast.'

'No doubt it's self-defence,' she says. 'Sometimes, even not believing anything exposes you as bad as a believing dangerous: that's what Petar – Petar Karamazov, or something like? – that's what he found out.'

'What happened to old Petar – he didn't exactly find it out,' I say. 'It happened, it was his big fact. And – he didn't hold with brothers, not at all. Nor jealousy. He was an innocent, they let him escape. With an Inquisition, you get to confess your guilt. He had no say, no guilt.'

'Yes,' Edda says, 'it's better to have guilt.'

*

I tell Maurice, 'There's a story round – that Jozo's money's bought an army. One that struts about.'

'If you've got cash,' says Maurice, 'you never know what it's got up to. Sometimes your guys are keen to fight, sometimes they're not and others are. Sometimes the guys regret what they have done, and sometimes not.'

'That can't be your statement, Maurice,' I say.

He's in the same high room. I don't remember what there was inside. Perhaps he planned it so, nothing to hang a memory on. From the window – there is no view.

'I don't know what you might expect,' he says. 'But I'm sure it's all quite different. Never mind. Neither of us is Inquisitor. We dare to ask, to judge, to know – but that's not all we want. I guess you want your bankroll now?'

'Those lovely silver coins with dragons on,' I say.

'No, no,' he says. 'That can be a noisy job, striking them out.'

I make a joke. 'One day, the bucks could be quite real.'

'Oh,' he says, 'the guys round here used notes for centuries.'

18

The camels walking round – they calm your mind.

I tell Kaja almost everything. 'The armies. How it complicates poor Sonia! And Jozo, discovering beliefs, having ragged guys to fight for them...!'

'Everyone knows that,' Kaja says: 'Jozo's always had some soldiers. Everybody has beliefs, I guess, though what they all amount to... Thinking of death – that is the surest theme. Believe in death, you can't go wrong.'

'Yes, Kaja,' I say, 'but there's fitting in as well...'

'We should have a bird,' she says. 'The rest will follow, that's for sure. There's cages in the Chinese stores. A cat. They can live anywhere.'

'I'll have one in the Refuge, Kaja,' I say. 'Sonia now – she's the prisoner, like in the tale. The innocent, who's waiting for some benevolent – some tsar – admitting his mistake. Freeing her, so off she flies – not like poor Petar Petrović, who'd faith in nothing but himself, ends lying battered on the floor...'

'Maybe, but Sonia isn't innocent,' says Kaja. 'And who knows what she had in mind...'

'Perhaps you're right,' I say. 'And that's the key. Keep them guessing – they get bored, and let you go.'

'The prisoners,' says Kaja. 'They'd be more use if they were tied to science. And – don't tell me it's been done. I know. It's that if you're locked up – you should get some credit too: catch some disease...'

'They'll send the soldiers, looking for poor Sonia,' I say. 'Now, there's a different twist. Those soldiers – they know how to punish!'

'Oh, you're a cynic,' Kaja says. 'There's rules. Those are the light.'

'I need some quantity,' I say. 'Some weight, some substance. Like Maurice's skeletons. There's always room for more of those. The Refuge – that is quality. You must stick at one of those. It's like the bull. One bull, and only one. If everybody had a refuge, no one would be safe.'

'What you need,' says Kaja, 'is hopeless passion. A singer, or a pianist. They give you hell, and so you write some songs that curdle people's ears.'

'There's devastation, over where poor Sonia is. Just marching to and fro, until the truce. You, in your cart – you'd be too obvious. A target, or a prize...'

'But still you chisel, you engrave, you write your music, and you dance – although you mustn't...' Kaja says.

'Even to transgress, you need some talent, Kaja. I'm unsure. It's true, I tried my hand at metalwork. And Maurice – never did that job for me.'

'We must resolve all this,' says Kaja. 'We must be up and off.'

'If only, Kaja, you were the one,' I say. 'The Layla. A miserable trek, yours, yes – but consistent, to the wretched end.'

'No one has a story now,' she says. 'Stories – they're all broken. You must join the pieces – some of me, then Edda, even Sonia. Don't go to the sages – Petar was the last who trusted sex, and he lost his wallpaper. Odysseus had a ship, his structure. You don't. My cart – it doesn't float. It'll end as metaphor – turned into barter for a slab of *burek.*'

'If I had the flame,' I say, 'I could burn you guys together. Turn you into something like.'

'No, my beautiful friend,' she says, and laughs. 'Broken stories. Everyone. Containers, tented camps – or scurrying through the bush, the taiga, or the *maquis*. And sand, lots of it.'

'Your animals, Kaja,' I ask. 'How will they work for you?'

'It's a zoo of metaphors, that way is cheap on food, and clean,' she says. 'The animals have all the qualities we humans like to see in us – aggressiveness, cupidity and lust. Curiosity and greed, sloth too. One thing they lack is parsimony – but in life, there's always something lacks. What do you think?'

'It's whimsical, Kaja, that's for sure,' I say. I may think 'fey' – but do not say. 'How will you live on metaphor?'

'I'll charge, of course,' she says. 'Metaphor requires more work than capturing. I'll have an entrance fee that makes you think while you trudge round.'

'Their family life,' I ask. 'Will there be lessons too?'

'Some do, some don't, of course,' she says. 'And some have kings and queens, and some just tumble in a heap. They do what suits. And you – your unknown metal in an unseen mine...?'

'Kaja, you laugh,' I say. 'The strange thing is, that guys will pay enormously to have me search. I'll go to Jozo now! They all want something they don't know, how much there is of it, and what it does and if it's toxic. Money – no problem – all go wild for the unknown.'

*

Jozo says, 'Those aren't metaphors. If you can walk around, it's probably conceptual. She's left out fear. Animals have lots of that. I bet just now that Sonia does – more important than the punishment. But if you're in a cage...' He hesitates wisely. 'There's nothing to be frightened of. Now, cash – of course, there's all you want. Some substance we don't know if it's valuable or not – that's always worth a lot.'

'I don't know grammar, Jozo,' I say. 'Or what concepts are. I'm here – that's all the grammar that I need. But as for mining – I thought "strip" first. That way you pay off the important guys at once.'

'Of course,' says Jozo, flapping thoughts in and out with his fat hands. 'When you're setting up your earthly paradise, everyone must keep in line with their own nature. Or else there'd be no point.'

'I guess,' I say. 'I hadn't thought.'

But – some would need to change, some restrain themselves, much more than others. No harm in that? Yet – if they're dead, as paradise would indicate – they wouldn't eat, still less each other. If they're concepts, where's the appetite?

'And where would Sonia be?' I ask.

'Oh,' Jozo says. 'If she's alive, she's fine. Her value falls to nought if she is dead.'

'This squabbling,' I say, 'to make a buck, from some resource. It led to massacres. Now, we're down to individuals...'

'Well,' Jozo says. 'I'm one of those. I'm worth a lot. Maybe they're right about individuals. Everyone can identify with themselves – it's not like facing foreign tongues and oddball priests...'

Edda comes in. 'If only everything was cash,' she says. 'It's symbols – those go on and on. Cash – you have it, or you don't. In seconds, you resolve the lot.'

'Listen!' Jozo says. 'I had a dream! There was this woman, younger than me, I guess. She wore a knitted suit, one-piece, all black. Her face was pale, like summer clouds. I felt a sympathy at once. We kissed, and then I felt her, all of her – my! she was a bowl of flames... Her breasts – just like I always dreamed. More than a fantasy, it was a sign, a route that you can follow.'

He goes vacant.

'Edda,' I say. 'How about it? It's like the song says, '*Emmenez-moi au bout de la terre.*' This metal unexplored – there's everywhere that we might search, just you and me. Prospectors need their partner. Kaja's sedentary now, in her menagerie...'

Jozo hears us. 'No, Edda. My sexy visitor: it wasn't you. And don't go with that guy – over and over, he's been hunting something inexistent! All his life. And lives of many more, I'm sure.'

He thinks Edda won't leave him, not for a scoop of ore.

Edda says, 'Jozo, your spectre in the knitted outfit, black from head to boots ... you spliced so friendly into her... You know – she's Death. And you so keen on it, on her.'

'Oh,' Jozo says, 'I'm not concerned. She was my type. Besides, there's Sonia. Death could be meant for her.'

Edda says, 'I'm happy here, with my ironmongery. watching Jozo suck on the breast of Death. The rest – is plating. You, and all the rest that blow along. Plated.'

I say, 'Edda – it becomes so easy. Fall. Let yourself fall – it's like an endless shaft. It passes by – the slabs of porphyry, the pyrite eyes that wink as you flash past, the lapis lazuli, chalcedony, blue john... Rubies and tin, albino rats, confounding everything, the colours, the crushing and the panning out...'

'Yes,' Edda says, laughing. 'And when you hit? what then?'

'You never hit,' I say. 'No one can tell you what it's like. No one comes back.'

'That's all you do?' she asks. 'Falling?'

'It's like sex, Edda,' I say. 'Only longer and faster. But I'm into other things – curiosity. I want to know everything, before...'

'I might come with you,' she says. 'New metals have some use for me. And I could check how you're spending Jozo's cash. Spend lots and lots – that way he won't waste it on the guys who say they're holding Sonia.'

'When you go digging deep,' I say. 'You need cash: a mountain, even bigger than the hole. I'll get a sub from Maurice. That way, everyone competes, and I can hold the bag.'

Down through time, down to the soft sea. Edda; sort everything out – the truth about people, and materials. A maturity, a scope, freedom. Freedom from the fetishes. Once more we'd belong to an enlightenment. Just drop, fall – let yourself go. I tell it all to Edda.

'I wish you hadn't said all this,' she says. 'It takes out all the fun, the sting. You blunder on...'

'No,' I say. 'It's all sacrifice on my part: courage and conscience. No one recognises, because I don't shout it out.'

'Then you should,' says Edda. 'If you haven't learned that, you've wasted all your time. If you don't shout, you're not here.'

Everything done – it's done for principles. Nina, Curtis – they're part of my principles as well. Governance and consolation. But – enough of that! Faces in the clay, as you drop down, and see the sky – shrink to a wormhole.

'Everyone has too much sky,' I say. 'The universe is made of it. Useless. Then there are clots of dust and mud, spiralling around. And in the mud – the metal. Muscle, energy.'

'That's right!' says Edda. 'Let's go get the power! And get the cash from Maurice too. That way, it won't go on bangs and guns. That bull of yours – a feeble start, a tiny blink of power. Nothing to what we'll find!'

'But still a start,' I say.

Jupiter too, he was a wanderer.

19

Maurice, among the sand. 'A forger in the cellar, and a sniper on the roof,' he say. 'That's what you need. The guys here are hard. We say "unscrupulous". We mean they're crooks. It won't last, naturally. You think of coming out on top – forget to dig and hammer. I'm a warlord now, you see. It's in the tradition. A stash of arms: and legs to carry them around.' I'm amazed: I say,

'It sounds incautious, Maurice.'

He stares at Edda: 'She's the middle ground,' he says. 'A case of "is" or "want". I can't see what she is – I can guess what she wants.'

He means sex: I say, 'She wants new metals.'

'The edge waits to be the centre,' Maurice says. 'Here we are, stuck on the periphery. When those iron plates hit – impossibly deep beneath us here – they throw up alps. That's us. That's where we are, up high, like those big eagles, seeing every detail, every flaw. We'll start things off again. A new centre. I'll make the order.'

He holds up his electrum fist, and twists it into the thin light.

'When it all comes down,' he says, 'and falls into its old pieces, I'll be there, ready. Not for myself: in the service. It's what you don't find in War and Peace. There's no contradiction: "service before everything". That's me. War and peace – always simultaneous. Metalwork, the skeletons – and for the next time, I'm ready. We always need skeletons, and rads. I'll be there. At the beginning, not at the end with Nina and Curtis. They were the sweepers. They tidied when it was done. Next time – I'll be more active.'

Up high? Or on the sandy plain? His options are all open.

'Maurice,' I say. 'We need kitbags full of cash.'

'Then leave me Edda,' he says, much taken with her. 'I'll sort her out. In the tub, there's things you can't hide.'

It's true, she has an androgynous cast. She sings from the window, in her androgynous voice ... about looking for the golden light. 'It's who you are,' she sings... 'I'll always belong in the sky,' she chants.

'Come on, Edda,' Maurice says, holding her from falling out... 'You have to be somewhere when the music stops.'

'Keep buying stars, Maurice, like the song says,' and Edda strokes his precious hand. 'But you should know – the stars all the same, and all the same as us. The stardust – identical, all over. Here too, every earth, it's all made identical. No contemplation, no spirit – just dig. You find everything, and it's all the same. Dig anywhere – and you shall find ... the same. No great brain created difference – it's all a scattershot. The magic bean burst out – and made a ton of twinkly chick-peas. Twinkle, twinkle, Maurice. Like your hand...' and on she talks, reducing him, ensnaring him.

'Maurice,' she says, 'you should be punished before you commit more crimes. To stop you... Oh, I don't know. I'm a simple girl. I forget who's done what. Kaja – she's innocent, that's for sure. And Sonia – she's a judge, so she decides, and that should let her off. Yes, Maurice, you get punished – but not by Jozo ... Not by this guy here,' and she pushes me back against the wall – everything here is lined with black metallic stuff, the doors of pebble glass that shrinks you when you knock... 'You're not really worthy, not equipped, to say who's innocent. It's not the same as ignorance, which you specialise in...'

Maurice is amused. 'Oh,' he says, 'I'm just in readiness. The situation calls, demands – and there I am.'

'Maurice,' I say, 'you never did that job for me.'

'That's wrong,' he says. 'You work for me. I pay you off.'

'Experience,' I say. 'That's what I've accumulated. Not the starry heavens – now, you can go anywhere in them. They're all the same, just stuff's distributed a little differently. Space – it's a waste. Someone with no idea how to fill things up... I work the hard stuff, and observe. No fights for me. I come – after the fact: the Balkans, Africa...'

'Yes,' Maurice says, 'you're a jackal. You tidy up the fields. Experience, you pile it up – but where's the growth, the education?'

'You dig,' I say. 'That's what you learn. Not fly.'

'I find the opposite,' says Maurice. 'You prepare, your eyes are like a fly's... Look at your Jozo now – a violent type. Lives in a cage because it's smart! His trouble started with Colombians. Behind them, there's the Yanks. And then the kidnap. Crime and punishment – those guys don't recognise things like that. You win with the last card – last trump! Without that, you are lost.'

'Jozo is spoiled,' I say. 'He wants to find a new material. To cover up. To come out clean.'

'Wrong!' says Maurice. 'He wants you and Edda to find something new that he can contraband.'

'Come on, Maurice,' Edda says. 'Give us real bucks. Don't be mean. Melt you down – the world will see you're precious.'

'How do you know? How do you know?' asks Maurice. 'If what I'll do is good or bad? For sure – *I'll* never know.'

'We all hope that, Maurice – that we'll never know,' I say.

'Jozo needs conflict – his business rests on that,' says Maurice. 'Me? I hear the creaking. Holes in the sand. After, after the banging, the shouts – into the tub, those that are left.'

'You don't seem to like them much,' I say. 'Those that survive.'

'I'll give you cash,' says Maurice. 'Maybe you'll leave Edda, as security?'

'No, no,' she says, 'I'm not secure. I smelt, but I don't weld.'

Whatever his idea about her, Maurice abandons it. Edda's a puzzle to us all.

'I'll share your stake with Jozo,' Maurice says. 'Here's a fine Gladstone, full of bucks.' And there it is... 'The weight's some platinum slabs to hold it down,' he says. It needs the three of us to carry it.

'My babies,' he says, 'take care of them. If I don't come through – make them into new hands and feet.'

*

'With all this cash,' says Edda, 'we needn't take a plane. We've enough for dromedaries.'

'It irks,' I say, 'to think we'll spend this cash, then give something – pyrites, a grey lump, novel, unexplored – to those two. Then have them fight to see who'll have the rights...'

'We could trip together,' Edda says, grinning maliciously.

'The trouble is,' I say, 'you're greedy. Kaja – she's dull. I broke her screen – that handicaps us both...'

'There's nothing wrong with being greedy,' Edda says. 'The fact that I am Jozo's... well, we're all someone's. No one's, that is. It's just a figure.'

'Like Kaja's woolly metaphors. Her muddy cart. Her persistence, her slowness,' I say. 'A charcoal figure in the cannon smoke.'

'We made love once,' says Edda, 'only once, but it went on for ages. Then we were friends. Now what? What comes next?'

'A long time?' I say. 'Time's always the same length. It's always long. Or short – but mostly long. Like thirty years. Then it's short, and here we are again, our boots, the cockade, the ammunition pouch with its one bullet. Goethe unread in the backpack.'

'I'm not like Kaja,' Edda says, 'but that doesn't make me need to travel with you.'

'There's variety with her,' I say: 'Often, you get stuck in the mud. It takes an age to dig out. That soon takes up your thirty years.'

We've both had the idea – to steal the money... I have a pamphlet – 'Stealing no theft', written in Gothic script, perhaps for Goths.

'Kaja's cart!' says Edda. 'We can't carry this platinum by ourselves.'

And if we steal the cart – and then Kaja resists ... a fight... Maybe she could join with Nina, wriggle in the crystal box, cure schizophrenia like the other saints – who knows?

'Perhaps the cart's a metaphor,' I say. I know it's not.

'Most of the universe is desert,' I go on. 'We're lucky to have mud. Only those religious freaks – their rockets and their Michelin men, they can't believe their big god only managed to do it once, made a bunch of men and stranded them. Our ancestors knew better – be afraid of what you've got.'

'I know all that,' says Edda. 'But what do you find in me? Search for my personality. What's my quiddity? And – where do we hide, if Maurice and Jozo come after us? Or there's a kidnap scare?'

'There is the Refuge, Edda,' I say. 'And knowing about one another – that's quite against the trend. It's tolerance and empathy – not character – that count.'

If we stash the platinum in the Refuge – we can't use it for anything. And if they know about the Refuge – it isn't safe.

'If we steal their money, we don't need analyse Jozo and Maurice. They'll be after us, to show,' she says.

'It's true,' I say. 'Why analyse them? Everyone looks peculiar. Still, the new material we find – it's free. The money we've been given – it is already ours.'

'Are you sure the metal's not a powder?' Edda asks. 'It might make pans, but it might make you wise or happy too.'

'So, we can't steal anything, as everything is free. Is that the deal?' I say. It's what the pamphlet says.

'Horses are free,' says Edda, 'so you never stole those?'

'Transport was Sonia's affair,' I say.

'And Sonia – she's free too. So the kidnap's pointless,' says Edda.

'We all think that,' I say, trying to leave the argument. 'She's into crime, not me.'

'At least we treated those dromedaries well,' says Edda. 'A while ago, we'd not have bothered.'

'Way back, the problems were all solvable. Some we hadn't even thought of. Lots of people – they felt driven,' I say. I read all that, about the past – I wasn't yet alive.

'Oh,' Edda says, 'I like fancy causes. You need to keep your eye on them, though, constantly. Concentrate.'

'Kaja says there's good in everyone,' I say. 'If you know how to look.'

'It's better looking for the evil in everyone,' Edda says. 'That gives you some result.'

She doesn't say what it is, that result.

'Everything is free now,' I say, 'but we keep our platinum. It makes us wealthy, but there's nothing that we want to buy. Or sell.'

'You could buy an army,' Edda says. 'Those are useful.'

'We'll go back to the plain. We'll see if Nina's moved,' I say. 'It's what interested Curtis. Those ladies that didn't move – others that did.'

'That kind of talk,' says Edda, harvesting resentment. 'Makes me want to go with Kaja. Not with you. With the platinum. Lenin and Confucius, they both said – "Hang on to the metal. It's useful, like the soldiers it can buy."'

'I never heard that, Edda,' I say. I want to go back, start over, where those guys had had their war. Maybe the tub... Maybe a golden limb – it shows you've suffered, and that you pack a punch. Then, there's prospecting. I've been everywhere, watched the spoils, the tailings... There's nothing new and useful. There's a combination – copper, zinc, titanium. That could make the strongest trumpet ever known. Make music, or make war – the fanfares are the same. The bull – and then the trumpet...

'These musings,' Edda says, 'they're useless. You must choose your side. There's no nice guys – even to vegans, you're just meat. Don't believe there's mediation, being nice, or sitting at your screen. Decide.'

We stand, as if we're waiting for a bus. The road is paved with rocks. Someone will come along, for sure.

*

Edda hoists the bag – the bucks, the platinum, – on to Kaja's cart. Kaja is silent, and they move away – their heads growing smaller, closer together, like two balls of rags. A grey mule, or maybe it's a human mule – tugs the cart away.

Here's Curtis. 'I bet,' he says, 'if you had to betray a friend...'

'No, really, I've no time for that,' I say. 'What's done's invisible. I need some metal, something that looks like it's a novelty...'

Copper I can get from Maurice: the workshops here are full of zinc... Brass for the instrument.

Curtis points to a memorial. It drips with names. I wonder if they chose a side. Maybe there are Petrovićes. There's metal letters dangling from the plinth: '"Like water, dropping from stone on to stone..."' he says. 'That's how the song goes. The water's worn away the stone – just the brass, the names, are left.'

I prise out some letters: p-e-t-a-r. I don't miss him. I don't want him in my trump. I stick the letters back. I pull out a random handful. I can use these to make the trumpet. I can draw the tubes. For pistons, valves, you might use titanium. That comes from Titan, though, and the ship that carries it won't dock for centuries. I'll make a long straight horn, a trump like angels have. A flowerlike bell, convulvulus – not spun but twisted out.

Curtis hangs around: 'I'm clean,' he says. 'You can trust me. Me? – I wasn't in the tub. I have no metal parts. I'm washed in blood. I chose my time. The guys stopped fighting – they wanted loot, not to be subject to some law they'd made themselves. There was disillusion, theft – that's where I came in. We thought you'd be the big man – choosing the tepid moment. But it was me! I cleaned it all, and most of all, myself.'

'Thinking doesn't make you big,' I say. Surely, Curtis ... he was in the tub? Chosen and abandoned – certainly, by Maurice? I forget...

'No,' Curtis says, 'thinking's not about the being big: it lets you tell the story. Now, look! Sonia – we'll never see again. Edda – she's not into crime. She's into trade. The perfect partner for old Jozo. Kaja – she'd fit in with Maurice. Sexless marriage – they're the best. A punishment, but mild, for all the ladies. And an end to those concerns.'

'It leaves things as they are,' I say. 'The past, the future – crawling up from holes like crabs...'

'Don't be fooled,' says Curtis. 'Those are scorpions, not crabs.'

My trump... there's no mouthpiece. It can't sound. Maybe the new metal, if I find it – light and resonant, maybe that's its destiny, making the trumpet sound...

Curtis says, 'Those workshops – they were cursed. No custom. The chicken huts, however – people came to see poor Nina stir... All kinds of guy, all faiths and none – all those that haven't gone to fight again, they wear the piecrust hat, they eat, they live... Jozo and Maurice – they're our wealth, of course..' and on he talks. Far off, I see the cart, the platinum pulling it deeper into ruts, the metaphors, the earthly paradise, as light as snow, the metal, unusable, untradeable, heavy as allegory, grey as a walrus... Kaja and Edda pushing from behind...

'You could make me coins,' says Curtis. 'Copper coins. My head – and the saint. For local use.'

Edda could strike up some platinum – like the Russians did.

'You've been cut off,' says Curtis, and he laughs. 'By everyone. I'm the big man here, and you've done with circulating. No one ever did the job for you...I wonder if you did a job for anyone...'

Suppose, I think, the trump woke everybody up? A terrible thought. Rising into sun- and moonbeams, those newly fleshed-out hosts. Leaving the underground, maybe with a quip, an exhortation, a "told you so", or "who'd have thought". Quite indiscriminate, and so no lesson, and no triumph. A bureaucratic promotion of each and all: death – where is thy sting? Gone, gone like truth and justice, crime and what follows...

'Look, Curtis,' I say. 'I'm armoured against insults. It's evolution I'm against. What it leaves behind ... and its remedies ... war and peace. Neither works. I want a new beginning – no past, and so no blurry future, covered with age spots and wrinkles deep as cart-ruts.'

'No one has talked to me like this,' he says. 'You seem to be a gentleman...'

His face – the colour, texture, of a chamois leather when he sweats, like some not-too-tasty cheese.

'Doesn't it occur, oppress – how ancient everything here is?' I ask. 'Old, not just like you'll get, and Jozo is, but unimaginably old. Years laden with zeroes. A lake of stars: pods of mute whales, on for ever, dodging those rock harpoons, and then ... ploff! Oblivion. A flash of sulphur, saltpetre, like the souls in hell, their sentences expired – so then, nothing. It's all decrepit, lingering. Everything's been here for ever! – the metals, lying underground and then ground up, and rusting, brittling ... where shall we stack the relics? Underground of course – and start it off again...'

'Yes,' he says, brightly. 'Distance too. Look where the Ottomans were, and on to where the fighting is – some sandy cities here and there, no great reason, no purpose for where they are. Fortresses for refugees. And huge distances, of straggly fields of yellow beans...'

'That's not it at all,' I say. 'It's not agrarian empires, on those threads of river – it's senility: that, and extinction. We're set up not to respond to certain menaces – our nature, nature all round – we boldly go to extinction. Ah well, we say, we did our best... It's poison, Curtis, poison. Extinction.'

Curtis starts his speech. 'Afterwards, there's consoling, what Nina did. I do it better. I call it "reconciliation". Nina never spoke to two at once. It was always one ... one ... one. Of course, lots of guys moved away. There were casualties, all kinds. Nina brings them in now, to her tomb. They watch her, one by one, one on one. Waiting for the next move, the wriggle. I do the politics, the commerce. With me, after the end, there's more, on and on it goes. And Nina – sometimes she moves. But – there's never any pleasure. When she moves, it's to hurry things along. You know, she never loved, she never liked, anyone at all. It was her work.'

'Liking didn't come in,' I say. 'It wasn't what guys wanted.'

'She wasn't Layla,' Curtis says. 'That's for sure. And we weren't Majnun. At least now – we're not waiting for something. What isn't here – we've given up on it. Like Jozo. He and Sonia had a pact – if one was kidnapped – that was to be the end. No cash. They'd taken all the risks, the guilt if that there was – so, don't give cash away, not uselessly. Besides – if you're not Majnun and Layla, looking for each other, you're always on your own, wolf in the forest.'

'Is that why you take money from all sides?' I ask Curtis.

'That's what reconciliation means,' he says. 'Representation. Favours all round. And – if you want, those coins... My head, of course, your bull on the reverse. It was always tiny – now it can be engraved, encapsulated.'

'Not mine, the bull,' I say. 'It wasn't mine. It was Jozo's. Maurice's. There was talk of crime...'

'Of course, there's responsibilities,' says Curtis. 'That's why we honour Jozo, when he comes. He's a benefactor, and responsible.'

'There's so many people, no longer here,' I say.

'Jozo's used to that. Settling scores, finding – they call them "new avenues". He's excellent at that, not like Chinese or Turks...' says Curtis. 'Paths lined with disposable trees. Boxes carpentered, of juniper, cherry – never seen before.'

'So many people,' I repeat.

'You must get used to that,' says Curtis. 'Look! Here's Kaja and Edda.'

They've red ribbons in their hair. They'll have buried the wealth, laid one of Maurice's skeletons on top. It will beep for them.

It looks like Anatolia here, or Xinjiang.

'We're not refugees,' says Kaja. 'We're investors. We dug a hole – we can't be accused of anything.'

'Let's forgive one another – for everything,' I say.

'I've done nothing,' Edda says. 'And I don't forgive.'

'Some I do, some not, and mostly – I don't know about,' says Kaja. 'As for myself, I may feel bad – but don't seek punishment from you. Still less that viper, Sonia...'

'Forget all that,' says Curtis. 'Jozo and Maurice – they'll come here to see what's new. What you have found, or built, or made others dig for you...'

'Everything's been tried,' says Kaja. 'Each time something goes down, I feel I have betrayed. I guess I shouldn't take things personally.'

'They're not personal things,' says Curtis. 'So, no, you shouldn't.'

20

Jozo arrives. Curtis has told him we have something new.

'Sonia?' he says. 'It's her obsession with the Russians. Why not "crime and justice", "crime and the law"? No – it had to be the punishment. That's what she's getting now. Or maybe giving it. She could be on a ship... We all die of what we believe in. Mostly it's cash.'

'If you don't believe in anything, like me,' I say. 'You should be eternal?'

'Yes, you should,' says Jozo. 'But remember what the song says – "a throw of the dice can't eliminate luck". Or bad luck.'

That ends all conversation.

Jozo starts up, 'Curtis says you've found new music. That could be interesting. A song and dance, a tickle of the ears that turns out profitable. That bull, instead – turned out infertile.'

'Music's a way you can wash your cash,' I say. 'It struck me – how old everything is, how slow. Millennia to play electric guitars, and longer still to beat on drums. The earlier things are – the longer it takes to get to us. Discoveries – it's all been there, right from the start, like presents for a festival. And when you've found them all – there is an end. Faster and faster find the parcels – bodes no good...'

'Exactly so,' says Jozo. 'Things speeding up – then over the edge! Maurice and I – we tried to slow it down, removing girders, wires and such. It didn't work. We got more cash, that we can't spend.'

Here's Maurice.

'I hear you've a new brass fetish made,' he says.

'I have a little trouble with the flare,' I say.

It's just a tube. I could link it to the gas. Winter should come. 'It's novelty – just like the metal that we didn't find. It isn't lost. It's there. We can't lay hands on it, not this generation...'

'Well, hurry up,' says Maurice. 'Us – we're quite infertile.' We laugh. Good old Maurice.

He and Jozo – both have little armies. Cash and faith – make armoured knights. Both of them know how to use their power. Metals don't rule the world – although they almost do. Maurice says,

'Try running current down a straw! My copper's still the best. The buildings now – use wood and glass. Let's see those plywood tanks, glass 'planes. Or knitted cannons, wicker silos...' and he and Jozo laugh.

'This place,' says Jozo, 'it's unstrategic. We come here because the war left no one who can fight. Their fathers, and their grandfathers – they fiddled harmonics on the horrors, every one. Now, it's the safest place. Here, we can take stock.'

'Yes,' Kaja says. 'Let's talk strategy. She whispers to me. 'Of course, Edda and me, we're always on your side. It's just … the trouble we have with you...' Then she says, 'Edda with Maurice. Running the store. Me with Jozo – his front. Then we thought – those guys ... could end up under the knife, the axe – why take the chance? Together we could be an agency, Edda and me. Introduce the supplicants to Jozo. Failing him, to Maurice. Vice versa.'

'The capital?' I ask.

'Oh,' she says, 'if you've a trump that wakes the dead – that's quite unusual. That would do – be the return.'

I make no claims,' I say, modestly. 'So far, there is just the shape, the structure. The demand, of course, is always there, to recover everyone, have them all back – though making room for all those guys, fresh from the soil, slow runners, resentful, the vendettas... maybe it's best just to give a hint of presence, turn in your sleep like Nina...'

'Oh, heavy talk!' says Curtis, listening in. Then, 'Do we really want them? All those dead? When we ourselves – we see extinction marching near? And Nina – if she wakes – all the chicken butchers ... all those paper buckets, pathetic scene, all cast aside. Kaja has her earthly paradise, it's true – but those are metaphors: they're folded up and sleep all night, silent and dreamless ... in their envelope.'

*

'I hadn't thought of this,' I say. 'None of it. I'm a long way off invention, what you believe I might create ... this empty tube...'

'Maybe just one more,' says Curtis, whispering. 'Up from the dead. *Još jedan*, as they used to say. My old commander, my brigadier...'

'No, no, Curtis,' I say. 'This is science, not art, and not religion. It happens or it won't.'

'We wouldn't want all those defunct,' says Maurice. 'Kill the invention. Keep the cash. My skeletons are quite profitable as they are. Just leave it be.'

'It's all a guess,' I say. 'I've problems with the taper. It's a trumpet, nothing more. The bull was silent too, it had no orifice where you could put your lips...'

'Why not the martyrs?' Jozo asks. 'Anyone who I could be responsible for – their deaths. Resurrection would spare me discomfort, and the lawyers' fees... Just a selected few, I'd not even know their names.'

'Jozo,' I say. 'Live with your guilt. There's nothing to be done. Maybe we could just recover Sonia, if we only knew...'

'That's not my game,' he says, and sulks. 'She's gone beyond. Maybe it's right she suffers. There's nothing in the book that says you ought to like your punishment. Some say it's just, but in a while – they squawk, quite like the rest who say they're innocent.'

Kaja pulls me away from them. 'It's all a joke,' she says. 'They know you fall for any fun. The dead – we weep for them, but better that they stay down there. After the ending – up the credits scroll. Your ticket – that expires. You only watch the movie once.'

'But what they say illuminates,' I say. 'Jozo and Maurice – they're the future. The trumpeting – is all about the past.'

'I know about these things,' says Edda. 'Your tube – it should be conical.'

'Too late,' I say – but the idea has lit a fire with Jozo.

'Yes!' he says. 'Bring up the '70s, when the revolution became a band, and then committed suicide. Just resurrect musicians.'

'That was nearly everyone,' says Maurice. 'And if you bring them back – there's disco too.'

'Whatever's that?' asks Kaja, and Edda says they'd need their bosses, to show them what to do.

'An audience!' says Jozo. 'They'll want all that. And those old guys. What a bore! Can't even draft them, not for the good fight...'

'You broke my screen,' shouts Kaja, turning on me, hitting with her fists. 'So's I can't see what this talk is all about.'

'Then,' says Jozo, settling into the mode. 'When the music stopped, it was bizarre wars and storms.'

'You find the tallest wave,' says Edda. 'Stand up and hold on. It's normal. And when you fall – you can't cry for yourself. Be strong!'

'Oh, we are, we are,' says Maurice. 'Iron men, we are.'

The chicken comes in paper pails. 'Zinc is better,' Jozo says, 'but the flesh is not altered.'

'These chickens could be geese,' says Edda, 'from the length of neck.'

'Jozo and Maurice,' Kaja says, throwing her bird and pail, 'have lost the struggle. We could toss them down. We won't. We have to live off the ephemeral. They knew what must be done. They tried a little, then gave up.'

'Just like you,' says Maurice. 'It's exactly so. You dogs, you parasites!'

'We thought,' says Edda, 'at first, that our intelligence was oversize, compared to our destinies. But no: we're soldiers. You don't ask the generals if you're going to win, you march along, until you can't.'

'Jozo and I – we're wearing suits,' says Maurice. 'Not uniforms. We're clean. We have no territory. Our limos – they will come and pick us up – we *pay* the guys who drive. We *are* our side – no one would want us trying to join theirs.'

It's cold. The snow begins to fall – goose feathers grey and white.

*

'You make a war, you wake up memories,' says Curtis. 'You say they're just a sticky film, the bottom of the barrel, those beaten people should enlighten up, calm down and modernise ... you've learned, you know what's good, and profitable... It isn't so. Others see it quite the other way around. They blame you. They're sore losers. You are not loved, admired...'

'We want to stay away from that,' says Kaja. 'The past. The trouble is, Curtis, you have no mission.'

'True,' Curtis says, 'but I have values. Almost every one of them. I respect them all. But – I myself, I'm not respected.'

'That can't at all be helped,' says Edda.

We hear Maurice whispering to Jozo, 'This karst. Doesn't it look to you like aluminium flock? and those sea-green flowers – like the flowers you get on brass? Could it be – here's all a metal? Something to quarrel over?'

They walk away. 'Wait,' Edda shouts. 'Jozo! I'm with you!'

'I've always been with Maurice,' Kaja says. She hugs and kisses me, goes, holds on to his suit.

They go their ways. My search is done. The new metal's here, been here all the time...

'Those geese,' says Curtis to me, pointing up. 'One by one – they fall. But – the force that drives them, forces above Jozo's head, and maybe Maurice's as well, they're too enormous to be seen... The birds fly to the fire, they gather over Israel, falling as shrapnel from the heights...'

Curtis talks on. Maybe he's right – we're not perched on a rock, but on a ball of iron, spinning along, heating up, the skeins of geese like puffs of fluff, circling over what they call a holy place.

I say, 'Curtis, your dingy prophecies ... will be the death of us.' We laugh.

'Surely not the final battle, Curtis,' I say, and laugh again.

'Oh no,' he says. 'None of that nonsense. The first, of the big ones. The great migration, then the battle.'

'They're only geese, Curtis,' I say. 'If all this plain's aluminium, those chicken parts will end in shiny pails.'

'No, no,' he shouts. 'They fly too high. We, the survivors, we, the armed, we must prepare, and follow them.'

'How'd you know which side to be prepared for, Curtis?' I ask, humouring.

'It's quite irrelevant,' he says. 'Living or dead – that is the point. Suffering, retribution – that's what survivors expect,' he says. 'Look at us here. Destroy the people – there's no end

– dry wells, the animals stressed out and sad. You know! You broke her screen – your claw... The cold...'

'It's true,' I say. 'Maurice never did that job for me.'

'You cretin!' Curtis shouts. 'Expunge the past? You can't forget, there is no consolation. What if Nina moves? A miracle? So what. From you – there'll be no wriggle. Nor from me.'

'It all connects, Curtis,' I say.

'Of course it does,' he says. 'I didn't make it so. It's physics. It holds it all together. If it snaps – it'll all fall apart, like grannie's workbox.'

Sometimes the winners go on trial, the losers scatter, fight another fight. The survivors – are quite moribund.

Into the tub – acquire your precious member. 'My penis – is of solid gold,' says Curtis, holding my arm quite tight. 'The ladies don't appreciate...'

'The troubles never end,' I say: it seems inadequate. Though – it's the truth. Maybe I've found my metal. We're standing on it. It's splays out all round. If it only makes tin cans – it wouldn't be worth the hard life, the prospecting. Too bad – Kaja, Edda, into the maelstrom gone, singing, dancing...

'Everything of me is precious,' Curtis says. 'But not to me.'

'I should have stayed with Kaja,' I say. 'She's given up her war, her cart. Off she goes, fitting in once more. The treasure – useless. Nothing to spend on here. My Refuge – big enough for only one...'

'Don't whine,' says Curtis sharply. 'You have bucks – those you can spend. There's always peace, just like there's always war. Kaja's done her thirty years: now, she'll be placing skeletons for Maurice. Edda's back into her ironmongery. They have their plenty. They are satisfied. Your turn will come, perhaps.'

'How can it, Curtis?' I ask. 'My epic's complicated – there's no Layla. I've no mission. My quest – has found a metal sordid and banal. The earthly paradise is one-dimensional: it fits into this envelope...'

'I've understood the story,' Curtis says. 'The tolerant and peaceful Europa – skewered on the pizzle of the bull...'

'That's not it at all,' I say. 'You haven't understood. And – don't blame it on my bull, tiny and infertile ... not divine, by any count. No, no – that's not the right scenario. It doesn't work like that. The children – peaceful and tolerant – but on the rampage, aggressive, too.'

Curtis doesn't press his case.

He wavers like a candle flame. 'I've discovered geopolitics,' he says. 'That could be my thing.'

'You're unbelievable, Curtis,' I say. 'Any map – you could redraw it.'

'Look at those trucks,' he says. They're all over the plain. 'Like enormous toys,' he says. The wheels are taller than a truck might be. They're scooping up the karst.

'You were right,' says Curtis. 'In principle. Officially, Jozo discovered it, and Maurice – he confirmed.'

'If it's a kind of aluminium,' I say, 'it'll be explosive. The Americans – they say the new wars can go on for thirty years. They'll need some armaments that's cheap...'

The karst is trucked off, into hoppers. We see some bright skeletons around, laid open.

'You never suffered,' Curtis says. 'It's a deficiency.'

'That is the aim,' I say. 'They found someone else to dig the White Sea canal.'

It's all fantasy, of course. You never discover anything. If you did, they wouldn't pay you. I say,

'Is this resurrection, Curtis? The trumpet isn't ready.'

'No,' he says. 'Much better. It's riches. Nina – she'll be moved. They've bulldozed your hut, your old, first refuge.' He's satisfied.

'Me?' he says, rhetorically. 'What'll I do? With this wealth beneath our feet? I'll run for offices, bigger, better appointed. You? What can you do? I'll be the little father of my people. You could try assassinations, sordid and banal. Some new idea? The brain is finite, like all the rest.'

'I know, Curtis,' I say. 'I can't get free. I'm buried to the neck in shards. If I'd gone in the tub, I'd have a golden limb I'd use to force a way...'

'What way?' asks Curtis, laughing. 'Free? That's not your usual speech. And no one has fettered you. Hammer out your gewgaws.'

'Everything must be full of everything that is...' I say.

'That's always so, and that you know,' says Curtis. 'No suffering. So, no desire. A cart stuck on the plain. You're good, a better person I have never seen. Your crime – passing false notes? I despise! What a joke!'

Kaja tried a garrotte. Not a global crime. Edda – tired of measuring out her fiddly screws in paper cones – drinking some good wine, chasing it with Absolut, breaking off the flute and – sclatt! Into Jozo's eye, and interrupts the current in his head – fugitive and flickering...

'The stem of a glass,' I say. 'A nail from a horseshoe. It's enough.'

'They'll take off the surface,' Curtis says. 'It's no loss.'

'I must sort out my cash,' I say.

First, I go to Jozo's. There he is, on his back, the flute stem in his eye. Edda's sober. 'Glass is material I've no experience with,' she says. 'There's fuss about the heat you need, but when it falls, it breaks. Things transparent – what's the good? You look right through them. Poor Jozo – so many crimes, anyone could bring in the punishment.'

'I bet there's something you want from me,' I say. 'Like dealing with the corpse.'

'Of course,' says Edda. 'We could try selling it, piece by piece. Or making it a trophy, whole and lively, like poor Nina.'

'A lead sarcophagus,' I say. 'That has some class. Or firing up the furnace, maybe make a blade that we could damascene? Floating up the river to Colombia? A wake, for all his team, his friends...'

'You cretin!' Edda shouts. 'You think it was me, did him in!' I make 'no' with my hand, and say,

'A thought that passed – like Jozo's last, that died like his... Maybe – it was Sonia? Irritated that she was abandoned? Or someone from her kidnappers, irritated that he hadn't paid?'

Of course, dear trustworthy Edda ... the penalty is thirty years.

'If you admired me,' Edda says, 'you'd take the rap.'

'It might have been a justice done,' I say.

'Justice? Who by?' she asks. 'Surely you think it matters? Could be some fascist, or an alco... See, the glass is empty.'

'This is trivial, Edda,' I say. 'Our minds should fix on broader themes.'

'Like running,' Edda says. She's in control, but not of Jozo's corpse.

'I'd make a call to Maurice, Edda,' I say. 'But...' I pause, 'Maybe he's involved. Or next to go.'

'Jozo's a big man now. The metal, old and new... Makes him a magnate,' Edda says.

He and Maurice – together, they are magnetised, I think.

I smile, quite hidden.

'Perhaps he'd some cash awaiting me?' I say.

'Now, you have rights, not cash,' she says. 'Though who's to pay you...'

The killing – maybe it's political. Even – geopolitics. 'Curtis might know...' I start.

'Knowing and boasting – those are not the point,' she says. 'Jozo had a little army. Quite acceptable – though was he proud of that, of anything? He struck me as a slob, though generous, up to a point.'

There's lots of glasses here, quite scattered round, most empty. In a stinkwood frame – a picture of guys, pushing through tall grass, bundles of tungsten on their heads. You shake the frame – it's marvellous, they plod along, the bundles, faces, and the guns – it moves! 'Everyone has one,' Edda says. 'A moving picture. This is when the ship's been carted up, over the mountain. On the next river – it takes days.'

'I don't see it,' I say. 'Every story has a moral. And these bearers – is it about rights? You said I'd be paid because I had them...'

'Oh yes,' she says. 'Those are mining rights. I think you need a deal for those.'

'For sure,' I say. 'Jozo wasn't one of those who dealt in rights. He never tried. He might have done quite well. It had no appeal. He paid his workers, though.'

'Help me!' Edda says. 'If you think I need it.'

'Look, Edda,' I say. 'Just leave him be. This mansion – it has many rooms where Jozo can be left. Remember – "the man with a blue flower in his left eye"? Leave Jozo be. What can he become? He's done his crime, he's had his punishment – or whatever tale you make of him. He's the best kind of father – the founding father without children. As for me – I prefer potential. I'm all potential, like a capital, waiting to be turned to something else. But everything it turns to – rusts. I'm very, very careful, Edda, not to do too much. Or anything at all – that turns to rust.'

'Those are wise words,' she says, hugging me. 'We'll package up poor Jozo. He never left a word that said he wanted otherwise. Nor that foresaw his death – so beautiful and strange. So enviable.'

'Better see that Syrian glass,' I say. 'In eternity – a touch of class. One eye, so firmly fixed on it, the other, firmly in it. Find a worthy room, Edda, and lock him up.'

'It's all about him,' Edda says, and sulks. 'My childhood, my depressions, my playing with seals along the beach... That's much more interesting.'

'I understand you very well,' I say to Edda. 'You're my opposite. I don't want approval. Judgment – it means nothing to me. It's always external. I judge, and I approve. No others have the right.'

'Yes,' Edda says, 'talking of rights. Maybe you discovered nothing – all that flocculence – it was always there, beneath our feet. Rights – you're born with them, or else you write them in. That explosive stuff – you won't make that turn a buck.'

We stack Jozo in a tiny room, and lock the door. 'Leave the key in the lock,' I say to Edda.

She rhapsodises: 'The shells, the rocks, the painters bottling coloured sand...'

'Edda – that glass keeps all its heat. And Jozo too – he ran hot – the pressure...'

The glass expands, and Jozo too. They burst out. First the door is down, then the corridors are filled – it looks like bread – integral – or a sea cement, with horses-heads and starfish, trumpet-fish, and puffy poisonous ones – the salt burns indigo until the chimneys are filled up... 'Out, out,' I shout. 'The heat, the instability – don't wait till it explodes...' We scamper out. It stabilises – every crack and empty bottle in the mansion's filled solid with cooling stodge.

'Those materials,' shouts Edda, cavorting underneath the fountain's jets. 'Always marvellous. The sand! I told you! I fed Jozo with it – where he comes from, there's no sea, and so no tales of everlast, overbegun, and creatures from the waves with tails...'

We run. Jozo's a legend, swollen exorbitant. 'There'll be no autopsy, for sure,' I say, and

'Oh no! the animals,' says Edda, starting to cry.

'No, no,' I say. 'In that hard dough, they'll fossilise, become a curiosity. It's evolution – distances and times so vast – they're only metaphors.' I've really no idea, but Edda's comforted.

'You'd expect in death – Jozo would turn to steel,' I say. 'Absorbing all that tungsten. It's true – sometimes when you tap for steel – out comes bread pudding.'

'If, instead, it is cement,' says Edda. 'Made from the sea – that salt corrodes the steel, and down the structure comes.'

'Salt water used when you create bread pudding – it has the same effect,' I say. We laugh. It's evident there was something wrong with Jozo, that his biographers will never guess. 'It was the heat,' I say. 'It turned to the most convenient thing – the body. A man with Syrian glass, stuck in his eye, like tapping steel... It makes a story too.'

Maurice too – was tested in the tub, electrum melting into flesh. The heat...

'Oh no,' says Edda. 'That heat – it twists you till you can't sweat any more. I can use the hammer – not the furnace.' Then she realises: 'My stock! In the basement. Silted. The docs! His will! No triumph there! All in the flood, the flux, the magma!'

I say, 'Justice and mercy are brothers. They say that.'

'It doesn't seem relevant here,' says Edda. 'Neither one. Nor the whole family.'

There's things you comment, when there's a peculiar death. I say,

'You hope there's something that distinguishes your side from theirs. The bad things they may have done – certainly they've all been done. Or, think not to be on sides at all. But that's no answer either, Edda dear.'

'We're down to answers, now?' asks Edda. 'I don't think Maurice asks the questions, if that's where you're going next. There's nothing big that matters here – except my loss, of course. The pudding – the puddling, that is, of course – has gone already stale. This death business – you always want to link one up to many more. Don't. It'll paralyse you, crawling into history.'

*

Maurice has moved back to the plain, where first we met. His flirt – some dancer, maybe a Thai – has left him grim. 'You watch the fingers, not the rest,' he said. His flirt with China – much more serious, has left him exiled, grimmer still. He oversees the stripping of the soil. The karst ... into the crucible. Nina, expectant in her catafalque – is moved. No gesture there. Kaja – dumb as a flower.

*

Travel with Edda's tough. She gets her way, but with that screaming therapy they recommend, and crying too! 'My fittings,' Edda sobs. 'My screws. My nails. Oh, what disasters.' On and on she weeps, then, tears all done, her face is swept clean like the sun.

When Maurice hears about Jozo's death, he waves his shining hand – a quiet farewell. 'You guys,' he says, 'exaggerate ... iron, glass – stale bread, the symbolism's clear. From rigid molecules to living goo – and then the stasis. It stales, it all stales. A tragic life, full of success, topped with indifference to everything except his living – all exemplary.'

'No, no,' says Edda, 'nothing abstract. No truck with symbols there. The mansion's full of stuff, solid as terracotta, every keyhole plugged, the copper pipes filled with this brownish mucoid plug, like yellow peppers bronzed and stuffed and roast...'

'Enough!' says Maurice, shivering. 'We all change as the colours change...' Indeed, his hand is glowing coppery, the paleness of the metals now suffused with blood, becoming flesh, pulsing in irregular time ... he sees us staring. 'Yes,' he says, 'Our ends will be spectacular, those who survived the war, went in the tub...'

'Jozo never did,' I say, 'nor Sonia. Yet they both made exits extraordinary. Sonia – disappeared, melted in air, now Jozo, letting all the lymph run wild...'

'Well, anyway,' says Maurice, 'I'm not here to talk about humanity, its curtain calls, the greasepaint scumbled, wigs once bouffant, now laid flat. The Chinese – naturally, wanted assurances that I couldn't give. Supply. A price. As you know, I hedge my bets, and then I hedge my hedge. Being a warlord – didn't help. They felt I was a risk. I knew I was. All of us – we are a risk, quite terrible and unrecoverable...'

All three, and Kaja too – we contemplate. The silence could go on for centuries. Then Edda says, 'You were friends. Or enemies. You must be pleased, or sad, for Jozo.'

'That's so,' says Maurice. 'We had our armies. Peace is a good, of course, but it's not goodness. War is a good too, you have your thirty years, then all's resolved. The crime is punished. That is not the point. That's just banal. What is crime? And punishment?'

'Sentimental, Maurice, sentimental,' Edda says. 'That has no weight at all.'

'I know, I know,' says Maurice. 'You squeeze and squeeze, and all that's left is essences. A fragrance for your hankie. Kaja is mute. See – she's so thin. Those concepts give no nourishment. The animals – they're absentminded. Maybe they have no minds. The metal you discovered,' and he turns angrily to me, 'won't make a tin of biscuits!'

'I'm deserted,' Kaja says, speaking with difficulty. 'I see the camels, following the desert roads. They don't need think at all.'

'Courage, Kaja,' Edda says, shaking her. 'You don't need a Majnun to be a Layla. Essences have let you down. Look at me! Customers. That's what makes you live.'

'Not essences,' says Kaja, weeping a little, 'just metaphors. First my screen, its delights. Then, poor substitute – my earthly paradise. Scraps and spectres.'

'That's even thinner,' Edda says. 'No one does life like that now.'

'About my money, Maurice,' I say...

'You need do more than just discover what's already there,' he says. 'I can't do much to help. You never did a job for me.'

'You're doing right,' says Edda, turning me away from Maurice. 'I told you – find the wave and stand on it. You're nothing to these people here...' and she waves at the villages, the empty fields. 'They all died here in the war. You never joined in anything. You did quite right.'

'If you finish up your trump,' says Maurice, laughing, 'waking Jozo's your great challenge. You're a loser, my dear: your Refuge – it sank down. You have to enter now on hands and knees. Like a pilgrim, or a hetero. Then, you're not alone in there – if you can find the door.'

'I've no intention, Maurice,' I say. 'Of waking anyone. Jozo was always oversize. I live in the real world. Saints don't move. You never see a bull eat grass...'

'Well, then,' Maurice says, 'that's where your money is, in the real world. Go seek it there. That's where Kaja's cart has ended up – the axle pins broken, the wheel spokes splayed. She didn't know her luck – free transport.'

'This invention, Maurice,' Edda says, 'the latest metal. Could be explosive, or you could write letters on it. It's what we've been waiting for, I guess.'

'I'm here for profit, Edda,' Maurice says. 'You wonder how I'll spend it all. Well, if it's just dross, we'll dig a hole and bury it. Then – dance. To me, it's fundamental. My expressiveness is limited, of course,' and he waves his blood-red solid hand to show. 'There's people too. Thugs, innocents and warriors, of course – wanting to break away. I give them all a hand. I don't discriminate.'

'When you were here,' says Kaja, 'which were you? Not an innocent for sure. Too late to be a warrior. Maybe you were on the side of thugs.'

'Oh well,' says Maurice, 'that's the only risk you need to take.'

'Dance for us, Maurice,' Edda urges him. 'You're our benefactor now. Jozo's gone, and Sonia too – you take over everything.'

'No,' he says, 'I won't dance. The dance excludes intelligence.' But he does some steps – his heavy hand he holds aloft, *à la russe,* as if it's anchored to a cloud. It's rather crass, but it holds all his memory of expressive moves, and so it ties in to ours – mostly our wasted time. We weep, for him, for us, for what he hopes to bring.

What will he bring? I've heard – 'Joy to Islam': 'repose, for the toilers of the world'...

'We're halfway through act three,' says Maurice, at rest again. 'The plot, the style, the characters – they've been long fixed. How does it end? Tragedy or hohum, with a laugh? You see – I know that guy has made his move. He's at the switchboard. Up go the house lights in a glare, and then... "all off".'

'Maurice,' I say, 'we've been through everything together. We have aged. Some dead, some not yet, quite. What's the lesson? Edda – she's lost that fine erotic charge. Curtis – has grown responsible. Jozo and Sonia – gone, and with them, crime and punishment. Kaja – no more stripping off. What's left for you? A small army, some good cause? Too small to be visible from space, but big enough to cut a deal? Well equipped, for sure. In no particular place...'

'Oh,' he says, '"army" – that's a heavy word. Small groups. You have to have them, or else it's fantasy, me doing everything.'

'Back to Petar, then? Inexorable talk?' I ask. 'The big idea that circulates. And then the threat. The threat's a promise too. You take your side...'

'I know,' he says. 'It's glib. Water, air. You need those too, I guess.'

Peace, brought with swords. Anarchy and union. Then – is it peace, and – oh, some transcendent state, contradictions all resolved, where there may be room for you, 'For me?' I ask.

'You've talent,' he says, 'but quite unreliable.'

Edda pulls me away from Maurice. 'Enough!' she says. 'Come away with us. We're too wise for that Layla stuff. Unfinished quests, jobs never done, or only half... We're the good guys. We get rid of bad guys. Maurice – hmmm – mostly bad, though it's true – he did hand out the bucks. But – that's not for you. Maurice wants you to perform. Try out his schemes – and now, you'll see, the karst will all be ploughed in, it's back to chicken nuggets, Nina's twitch... We ask nothing, nothing at all from you. At most – a trumpet tune. Forget the bull. Forget Maurice...'

'You can't forget what's there,' I say. 'Maurice – is a presence.' I'm tempted though... Maybe the thirty years is up.

In the distance – maybe forty horses, maybe more. Uighurs? Tatars? Pushed westwards. Or tourists, driven too.

'Of course, I'd go with you,' I say. 'Kaja, Edda – I've lived my life with you. It's fun. And – you have it all sewn up, the trading, the initiatives.'

There's bulldozers raking off the topsoil, and diggers digging a deep hole. 'Bury it far down,' says Maurice. 'If we ever want it – it's harder to exploit. It's the industrial process, makes it more valuable.'

There's guys, mostly standing round – I see no electrum limbs. 'I don't want to comment on real people,' Maurice says, 'and what has happened to them.' That seems fair. He goes on, 'There's something of a Faust about me, don't you think? This engineering, my faith – and hope it all ends well, without some soul that's wanting to be saved.'

'I don't see you in a fiction, Maurice,' I say. 'And in a story, women are a delicate branch. I don't know why.'

'I don't need like people,' Maurice says, staring at me, at my thoughts, inconclusive. 'Because I'm rich. You're a different matter.'

Kaja and Edda move away. 'I hope there's trains that go elsewhere,' says Kaja. 'You get tired of Bratislava.'

They walk off the site, sometimes they look back, make a gesture to me, like you call a cat, a dog.

Maurice says to me, 'Well. I think you know where things have led. No crime – only just causes. The best cause would be to have it last, go on for ever, even just like this. Even go back? Bring back the fallen? All beginning over? Maybe that's a bad idea – you'd need write in some other ends. You'd need another story altogether,' and he laughs. 'You know, you'd be with me till the end. I keep myself a wee bit distant, but of course – I'm with you, though I've other things to try, I'm sure.'

I wait for more, some instructions, consultation, who knows what.

'Don't give up the trumpet,' he says, clapping me on the shoulder. Good old Maurice!

He moves away, salutes me, raising his special hand – is that an open palm? A blessing, with some fingers? A clenched fist?

About the author

John Fraser has lived in Rome since 1980. Previously, he worked in England and Canada.